Catchfire

Graham Dunstan Martin was born in Leeds but is half Cornish and half Scottish and considers himself as a Celt. As an avid young reader he was strongly influenced by poetry, mythology and the works of Tolkien. This is reflected in his considerable output as a writer for adults and children.

Both GIFTWISH (also a Swallow) and CATCHFIRE reflect his love of fantasy and story-telling.

'Fantasy is essential to the child's imagination, for it reflects and expands the mind. Those who have not imagined the impossible cannot begin to understand the real, or even to perceive it as it is.'

GRAHAM DUNSTAN MARTIN

Catchfire

Richard Drew Publishing
Glasgow

First published 1981 by George Allen & Unwin

This edition first published 1989 by
Richard Drew Publishing Ltd
6 Clairmont Gardens, Glasgow G3 7LW
Scotland

British Library Cataloguing in Publication Data

Martin, Graham Dunstan, *1932*-
    Catchfire.
    I. Title
    823′.914[F]

ISBN 0-86267-260-0

Printed and bound in Great Britain by
Cox & Wyman Ltd, Reading

To my mother in remembrance

Prelude: Sun and Shadow

The plains of Feydom spread north and south, east and west, in a smooth high tide of yellow corn. Abruptly, out of their midst, like a great ship becalmed among the motionless billows of the fields, there rears a single mountain of stone, round and white as a giant's skull. For the legends of that country relate that it is indeed the skull of the giant Oskelan whom Varos the first King of Feydom slew – and on whose fallen head he afterwards raised the citadel. A fifty-foot wall rings the mountain, and within it, clambering perilously up the steep slopes of the rock, the narrow winding lanes of the city of Midknow climb to the King's palace. As Midknow stands at the centre of Feydom, so the King's palace is set at the summit and centre of the capital. Golden-white in the sunshine, it towers above the city like a jagged crown upon the giant's head. And at the very pinnacle of the palace a tapering tower stabs skywards, aimed at the heart of the summer sun. Starhigh, the tower is named. It is here that the Royal Wizards of Feydom live and work their magic, gazing out upon every quarter of the compass from its topmost chamber. Apart from the wizard's servants, no one may enter here except the King himself, and then only by invitation.

For if the peace of the kingdom depends upon its king, its prosperity depends upon its wizard. And he must never be interrupted in the middle of a spell, lest the kingdom be visited by earthquake, plague or famine.

It was an evening in early summer. The sun was poised above the western plain and over the narrow line of sea scored between land and sky like the glittering edge of a knife. For there lay Eventide, the Western Ocean. The Royal Wizard, Hoodwill, sat in the topmost room of Starhigh, frowning and muttering over his books. There was not a cloud in the sky outside, and the sun's golden light flooded the room, gazing straight upon its further wall like a face stooping to look in at the window.

Hoodwill sighed, put down his book, and raised his eyes to the long mirror on the eastern wall. Then he rose to his feet, smoothing his white and silver robes around him, settling his conical wizard's hat more firmly on his head. He advanced towards the mirror till he was reflected in it from head to toe. He gazed blankly at his own reflection, barely seeing it, his lips moving as if he were still struggling to get some spell by heart.

'What is wrong with my mirror?' he muttered to himself. 'It used to reflect the whole wide world for me. But now . . . ' He fell silent, his lips still twitching silently, as if in doubt or fear. For indeed his first spell on coming to the tower some forty years ago, when he had succeeded his grandfather as Royal Wizard, had been to turn the tall man-size looking-glass into a window – but not a window which looked out merely on the east of Feydom, on its fields and orchards, its woods and streams, but a magical window on the world. He would point his staff to the south, and the long oblong eye of the mirror would swivel its gaze towards the ocean of Moltenbrim, and he would see the tall ships of Feydom riding back from their trade into the southern ports. Or he would turn it to the east, and it would hang like a window in the tall sky, far above the mountains of Kendark, and gaze down like an eagle into the den of the Necromancer himself. He would see the little castle of Midnight set at the foot of mighty Eversnow, with its tiny wizard's eyrie and its narrow circling battlements; he would observe the comings and goings at the Necromancer's gate: the captives brought to his dungeons; the riders setting out at a gallop with messages of fear and pain for the sorcerer's subjects. Or he would turn his staff to the north, and watch (with some contempt) old Caperstaff, wizard of Witshift, busy planting herbs in his garden, or set the mirror to peer through his window so he could glimpse the old man, plump as a capon, entertaining guests in his dining-room, quaffing the wine of Hemdark and boasting of the excellence of his table. What annoyed Hoodwill was that Caperstaff's table was indeed excellent, the best in the Two Kingdoms, it was said – though, to be sure, he did not care for such pleasures himself.

Oh yes, his looking-glass! It was so much better a peephole on the world than other wizards' crystal balls, where you have to draw the shutters or wait for night to fall, and you strain your eyes gazing into the depths, and can call yourself lucky if you catch a glimpse of Old Mother Cackle in her chicken-run. No, *his* mirror gave a proper view of things, things as they really were, the evil goings-on in Kendark, the hardly less nasty behaviour of the kings of Kennaught, and the loyalty – the exemplary loyalty – of the mayor of Cheatfair. Truth – that was the virtue of his mirror.

And the close, far focus. Why, on one occasion had he not been able to peer over the Necromancer's own shoulder! And see the book he was reading, the very words he was gazing at. *Mena Keruna Trismiasa gwivam iois didasti* (None but the Crown of Unity will give them life again). But then the vision had faded; and Hoodwill had only been able to wonder who 'they' were. The people of Feydom? They need no one's spells but mine! The folk of Kendark? May the Sun forbid it! He shuddered. For the folk of Kendark were the ancient enemies of Feydom, his own land. If they ever got free of the Necromancer . . .

What was the matter with his mirror? For a long time he had seen so clearly in it! But for some years now there had been something like a shadow across its face, and when he followed the movements of the Necromancer he had seen this shadow moving too, and had found it hard to tell which was which. Then lately he had seen that the shadow was his own shadow, his own reflected image in the glass as he watched. And he had cursed at himself when he realised that he was following his enemy's movements with gestures of his own. As the Necromancer raised his staff, so did he . . . Hoodwill had forced himself to sit still and watch. No movement.

But that did not do, either. If he did not follow the motions of those he watched, he found that he could not see them clearly. He could not tell any more just what they were doing. Their actions had become like an unknown language, meaningless, senseless. It was only if he hung across the mirror himself, miming their gestures, smiling when they smiled. But then he could no longer tell if it was they whom he was watching or himself.

But it had been worse recently. These last few months. Why, he had hardly been able to see anything at all – apart from his own image in the glass. Not an obedient image, either. His white cloak was there, yes. His tall hat and his wizard's staff. But the face! Sometimes it grinned at him wickedly out of the glass, when not a muscle of his own face had moved. And the hand had sometimes beckoned, so that it was all he could do to prevent himself stepping forwards towards the mirror in reply.

But how was that? The images of those he had spied on had danced only to his own movements. But now his own reflection disobeyed him, acted despite him. What did the Book call the magic of mirrors, the magic that had served him so well for forty years? *Sve-widya* (a seeing of the self). Well, that was not what he wanted to see.

'A new spell. Cast out the shadow,' he murmured. 'Cleanse the mirror, renew the charm.'

Fixing his eyes narrowly and suspiciously upon his own image in the glass – for if it did something *he* was not doing . . . ! – he raised his staff in the air with deliberate care. And began to intone:

> *Donum dona*
> *Vere visum,*
> *Verum speculum . . .*
> (Give a gift
> Truly seen,
> True mirror . . .)

His voice stammered over the word *speculum*, and sank to silence. For he had had the distinct impression that his words had sounded, not from his own lips, but out of the mirror. And now . . . they were continuing without him:

> *Imaginem capta mundi*
> *In mente captam*
> *Puram purissima . . .*
> (Catch a pure image of the world,
> Captured in the purest mind . . .)

Involuntarily he stepped back from the echoing glass. And dropped his staff. 'Nightshade!' he cursed. Muttering, he went down on all fours on the floor, clutching for his staff as though his life depended on it. But as he did so a chill wash of fear went through him. No, he should not have done this: such mistakes could nullify a spell, or even turn it into its own malign opposite.

Still, the voice from the mirror had stopped as he fell. The spell was incomplete. Perhaps no great harm had been done. Had his image in the mirror moved with him? With his hand checked in the air four inches from the carpet, poised to grasp his staff, he looked up.

The window behind him filled the whole space between floor and ceiling. The sun's beams were exactly horizontal; and the wizard was now crouching directly between the window and the looking-glass. Thus, when he raised his eyes, still cowering on all fours like a dog, he could see himself fully reflected in the glass. And around his image the sun had cast the larger, darker, more misty outline of his shadow. Hoodwill gazed at his own reflection like a man frozen to the spot.

It was hard to make out. The image was dimmed and obscured by his own shadow, and by the contrasting brilliance of the sun's light around it. But – strange! – the whiteness had been drained out of his robe. It now looked a fusty black. His hands, outstretched to grasp his staff, were frozen in a clutching gesture as if they were the shovel-like paws of a mole. The conical hat upon his head reared upwards like the long narrow snout of some animal raising its head to sniff the air.

Hoodwill crouched there, gripped with irrational fear. Rapidly he passed one hand across his breast in the sign against evil. The reflection shifted.

It was like some huge fish submerging soundlessly into a still pool of water. Faint ripples washed in across its outline and covered his image with a smooth glassiness that reflected nothing but the bright sky behind him. The image had been swallowed up like a dark metal behind a thin layer of molten silver.

The wizard, trembling, stretched out one hand to touch the surface of the glass. It was as suave and silken to the touch as ever. Only it no longer reflected him. The window behind him, the wall of books – yes. But *he* had vanished. It was as if he were no longer in the room.

Hoodwill looked down at himself, feeling his hands and arms as if to test their solidity. Yes, yes, he was still there, he was as real and physical as ever.

But he no longer had a reflection. No shadow, either. The reflections of window and wall, of books and blue sky, glowed as clearly out of the mirror's depths as if there had been no one in the room. But his own shadow, his own reflection, had both been washed away into the limpid smoothness of the glass.

5

Hoodwill's fear was followed by a sudden rush of hope. Well, then . . . he had succeeded after all! He had not even cast the spell properly. He had been interrupted. But somehow – the spell must be abnormally powerful – he had done it! He had cast out the evil image of himself!

Pure. White. He looked down again at his robes. He turned towards the sun and away again. Yes, they were as white on one side as on the other. The sun's light seemed to make no difference to them. You could not even see the folds, because there was no nuance in their uniform brightness. And he cast no shadow. There was no darkness on the red carpet: it glowed like blood even where he stood between it and the sunset.

Purity, light, all the shadows gone. What his power would be from now on! The boon was unexpected, but there! What do you suppose, with magic? You can't foresee every possibility! Now surely, clad in perfect whiteness, walking the world without a shadow, he would never miscalculate again. Smiling like a knife, Hoodwill turned to the bell upon his desk, and rang for his apprentice.

Who came running, paused at the door and bowed. Then raised his eyes and gazed at his master, standing there white as a cloud. And signed himself for fear.

CHAPTER ONE

Fourstrong

And now we move swiftly away through time and space. Late winter. Nearly two years on. Six hundred miles to the east. How shall we travel? Perhaps one of those black bat-winged dragons they used to draw upon the old maps of Feydom – perhaps one of them will carry us. Yes, let's fly!

But, as we go, look down at the strange countries spread out beneath. The land of Feydom, shaped like the mouth of a roaring lion, its jaws open as if to swallow the bright sea itself. A vast plain full of farms, little walled towns and winding rivers, laid out flat as a map below us. Save for the narrow green fringes along the river banks, the grass is as brown as sand. For it has not rained in Feydom for a year now; and the great river at the eastern edge of the plain, the River Hale that runs from Midriver in the north to the Forest of Rooftree in the south, is empty, only a snaking stony groove in the frostbound earth. Nothing grows. There is famine stalking the land.

Soon we must rise higher into the clouds as we fly east and the rocky barrier of the Forbidden Mountains looms up ahead of us on the other side of the River Hale. This is Kendark, a land full of rugged mountain chains, clad in dark forests, cut through with barren glens, traversed by swift-flowing rivers. And, at this season just before spring, covered with snow and ice that glitters in the intervals of winter sun. The men of Feydom call this land the Forbidden Kingdom, for they fear it as a country of witches, sorcerers and demons.

Six hundred miles, then. Deep into Kendark. The mountains slip away beneath us like wave-crests on a sea of milk – a motionless surf, frozen in the act of breaking. The black clouds chase the light across their slope, trying to hunt it down, seeking to destroy it. And now, do you see there, five thousand feet below, the little black flashing furrow of a river? That is the River Bane, where we are going. Here and there along its course there are tiny clusters of wooden roofs, villages huddled against the shelter of the mountain-slopes. At the centre of each village stands its castle. For this is a wild land, and the villagers need protection against their neighbours. Or used to not so long ago, before Ewan reigned in Kendark.

We hover now over the empty landscape half-way between two castles: to the south, a slender round tower ringed with battlements, tucked away below the cliffs and screes of Eversnow; to the north a square stone fortress with a tower at each corner and a tall keep rearing from its centre, roofed with painted red and green tiles. Fourstrong, the King's own capital.

There is movement on the white desert of snow beneath us. From the north three riders, mud-splattered, weary, their horses kicking up a foam of snow, urge south along the road to Fourstrong. Over their heads there waves a bedraggled pennant: the flag of Feydom, a pale Y of blue and a white fleece pinned across it. They are going too fast for this weather, but there! They have an urgent message to deliver, and when the King of Feydom commands, or rather when Hoodwill threatens . . . Come! Onwards! There are still ten miles to Ewan's castle. An hour's journey at least, with the roads in such a state!

And to the south of the fortress, a more leisurely party, now already close upon the gates of Fourstrong. A little line of black dots winding along the edge of the river: seven figures on horse-back approaching the ragged outline of the little town.

Let us drop through the cold silver air and take a closer look.

Six of the riders are helmeted in fur-lined bronze, and muffled in black bearskin against the snow. They carry longbows and quivers slung across their shoulders, and the boots in their stirrups are lined with black fur too, and rise to the knee. As for the leader, she is all in white fox furs, with a red woollen cap on her head. A girl of sixteen. She sits astride her horse like a man, wearing white fur trousers under her white fur skirt that dips and drapes like a saddle cloth over her horse's back.

And now they are under the gates of Fourstrong. Though the castle itself, bulking protectively above its little flock of houses, is built to withstand war, siege and earthquake, the township has no proper fortifications. Instead, the houses (most of them only two storeys high) huddle together in a crude square, turning their backs on the mountains, packed close against each other for safety, so that any foe is faced with a continuous jagged line of stone, with here and there an arrow-slit, here and there a diminutive turret. The town gate is set between two houses taller than the rest, which serve in time of trouble as defensive towers.

The girl raised her slender white sleeve and the guard on the parapet of the open gate doffed his helmet and cried (his sentence freezing as he spoke it, and dropping like fragments of ice through the crisp air):

'Enter milady! We are glad at heart to see your safe return!'

And with a warmth that almost melted the frost, he turned his pike to the ground and beckoned them in.

It was a tiny township. An old man brushing his doorstep, a young mother shaking her duster out of the window, a bunch of children throwing snowballs at the gate of the castle, so that it was studded with little white explosions like stars on a shield.

'Do you like our snow-witch, milady?' they chorused, wheeling like a flock of geese as the girl approached.

A statue of snow, its long white skirt splayed out to the ground, four rough lumps of quartz for buttons, a carrot for a nose, a moth-eaten black wig and a tall red pointed hat that somebody had found in an attic. An old broomstick leaned down beside it, gap-twigged, uneven, caught in a furry arm of snow.

'Oh yes,' said the girl, reining up. 'But why is her nose so pink?'

'Because it's so cold, milady,' the children chanted. 'Because it's *freezing*!'

'Quite right,' said the girl, feeling her own nose ruefully. 'But what will you do when she melts?'

'Princess Catchfire!' breathed a little boy, his eyes wide, popping with admiration. 'When the snow princess melts, we'll still have the real you!'

'For cakes,' said Catchfire, smiling, spinning a big gold piece into the air. Yellow of summer, floating and turning. The little boy fumbled in the wet snow and had it, for his friends stood back, they knew it was his.

'Bless you!' cried Catchfire. 'And mind you share it out!' She turned into the castle courtyard.

'I'll share it,' said the little boy. 'Promise you!' And the children trooped off towards the cake-shop, falling into line respectfully behind the five-year-old who had Catchfire's gift held safely, warm between his palms.

Catchfire, smiling still, swung off her horse in the stableyard, patted him and let him go to the grooms. A single friendly snowflake kissed her on the nose. Then another poised lightly on her bottom lip. She put out a pink tongue and licked it away.

'It's going to snow again!' she called across the courtyard. 'I'm back just in time!'

A boy of her own age was advancing across the trampled snow. 'Catchfire, you speak truer than you know. It must be second sight that's brought you here at the very stroke of three!'

'Yes, for it's going to be a blizzard.'

'No, that's not what I mean.'

They kissed, then broke away excitedly, both trying to speak at once:

'Ewan, do you know what . . .?'

'Catchfire, at last it's the . . .!'

'Ewan, imagine what I've . . .!'

'Catchfire, can you guess who's . . .?'

'Hm,' said Catchfire, eyeing Ewan up and down. A slim lad of her own age, five foot eight at most, with a shock of fair hair, a pair of humorous blue eyes and wearing a leather jerkin, leather trousers and an old bronze sword swinging at his waist. 'Ladies first, I think. I've found something marvellous at Midnight – at the Necromancer's Castle. It could be the answer to our prayers.'

'Well, so could my news too! And mine won't wait. Will *yours*? Well, then!' he said with satisfaction. 'To the council chamber this very moment! We must see him at once!'

'See *who* at once, Ewan?'

'Why, the ambassador! The envoy from Feydom! He's here at last, after five long months. Let's hope he brings good news!'

Catchfire hesitated for a moment. 'Very well, my tale will have to wait, for it'll be long in the telling. But . . . an envoy from Feydom, eh? Don't start without me. I'll follow you up. First, you see, I must put on a veil.'

CHAPTER TWO

Two Messengers from Feydom

'Boy,' said the wizard Caperstaff, leaning forward and fixing the envoy from Feydom with his two sharp eyes, 'this message of yours is most unfriendly. You claim King Ewan's crown. You keep his mother a hostage in Feydom. And you blame our magic for the famine that destroys you. Yet we have offered you our aid. Does your master King Dermot still not know the facts?'

They were sitting in Ewan's council chamber high in the keep of Fourstrong. Roughstone walls, the bright-coloured banners of Kendark draped like tapestries across them. Torches smoking in their holders, a peat fire fuming in the grate. A long wooden table, crude and rough hewn, chipped out by woodmen's adzes from the heart of an ancient oak-tree. Smoke and boredom hung in the air, for the envoy's message, being a disagreeable one, had been couched in the floweriest of long-winded language.

Scantguise the ambassador was a young man in blue and white livery, peaky as a weasel, but with a contemptuous curl to his lip. 'The facts?' he said. '*What* facts?'

'Listen to me,' said Caperstaff patiently, 'For who's to say if our message was told you aright? You must hear the story and judge for yourself. And you must carry it back to the King.'

He leant forward again. 'Here it is,' he said slowly and carefully. 'Listen, boy. For you will tell this to your master.

'A little over a hundred years ago, your kings of Feydom lost the Crown of Unity, the crown that until then had linked your land and ours in peace and harmony. Soon after this mishap, the rule of Feydom became harsh and oppressive; Kendark groaned under the tyranny of your King, and our people gathered in rebellion against him. Under our leader the Necromancer, Lord of Midnight, we invaded your land. Well, I shall not go into the progress of that war. It is enough to say that Feydom threw out the armies of

11

Kendark in the end, and the Necromancer was killed. And then your wizards made a powerful spell among the ruins of Midriver. They held a ceremony in the underground tomb where the Necromancer lay buried, they thrust a sword through his dead heart – and they sacrificed a child upon his grave to hold the spell good with human blood for all eternity.'

'No, no,' muttered Scantguise, going pale and signing himself.

Caperstaff took no notice, but went on: 'They meant to close the gates of Feydom against us, so that no evil magic might invade across the frontier. Hobgoblins, dragons and suchlike. But the spell has shut your gates against all magic, whether good or bad. No wicked power can pass the frontier, true. But neither can any power for good.

'Well, that spell still keeps the Gates of Feydom closed. But you know that people's actions often turn out very differently from their intentions. Fear is a bad counsellor; and the man who bars his door and plugs his ears may defend himself against his enemies, but he prevents his friends from speaking to him too. The spell, as I say, has shut your gates against both good and evil. And that is why in Feydom the crops are dying and the people starving. How so? Because the waters of the River Hale have been lost, that carried the life-giving water from our land into yours. They have been blocked by the spell. At your gates they spill themselves into the bowels of the earth, and the river's bed runs dry. And why do you suppose the rain does not come? Because the powers of earth and sky have been locked out of your kingdom. The rain clouds drift around the north of Feydom, and empty their precious water upon *us*. And in Feydom there is famine.

'And that is why King Ewan generously asked your royal master if, with his permission, we might lift the spell. It is to save the innocent people of Feydom from further misery. We feel no hostility towards you. The war between us is over long ago. The Necromancer's grandson is dead. And Ewan is a Feylander himself; he was born and bred in Feydom, and his mother and his kinsfolk live there still. It is hard for him to see his own people dying of hunger.

'The evil, in short, is none of our doing. And we offer our friendship to King Dermot so that he may not fear to release the spell.'

Scantguise gaped at Caperstaff open-mouthed. 'But sir, your eminence,' he faltered, 'this cannot be true. To sacrifice a child – in Feydom! – it's unheard of! Our wizard Hoodwill is a *good* man. And he says that the Gates are old and worn, they are letting black sorcery through from the land of Kendark. The spell must be *renewed*, he says, not broken. And he appeals to you to call off the dark monster that sits now in the ruins of Midriver guarding the spell, and stops us from renewing it.'

Caperstaff frowned at him in puzzlement. '*What* dark monster?' he said. 'That's the first I've heard tell of any such thing. What sort of creature is it? Or is it just a tale?'

'Oh no, your eminence, no tale. We tried to restore the spell again only two months ago. And our men were' – the envoy shuddered - 'eaten by the dragon. Certainly they never appeared again out of the Chamber of the Spell. No one dares go near the place now. But we guard it from a distance, night and day, lest anything of darkness . . .' His voice faded, and he signed himself again.

'Nonsense,' said Catchfire impatiently from behind her veil. 'This talk of dragons! The dragon is a creature of Kendark, and the spell prevents her from entering Midriver at all.'

'No, lady,' said the envoy, shaking his head. 'You're quite wrong. Hoodwill knows. And *he* says . . .'

'That the spell is broken, and there is a dragon in Midriver,' put in Ewan. 'Well, I can see we shall get nowhere like this. *You* say the Gates are open. *We* say they are shut. *You* say there is a dragon. *We* . . .'

But Ewan never finished his sentence. The door behind Scantguise swung open, and the envoy leapt to his feet, clutching at his dagger. But he had no need to worry. A servant appeared in the doorway, bowing briefly and announcing:

'Sire, the ambassador of Feydom craves audience.'

The four Kendarkers gazed at each other in surprise. Then Caperstaff grumbled under his breath that dinner was surely going to be late now, and Catchfire tried to whisper to Ewan.

But he was getting to his feet, frowning. 'The ambassador of Feydom? But we have him here with us already!'

'It is a second ambassador, sire. Newly arrived, post-haste through the sleet and snow, and asking if his colleague is here already.'

13

'Well, well,' sighed Ewan, 'we wait five months for an answer, and then we get two in the same day. Very good, show him in.'

The new arrival stood in the doorway. From his collar to the toes of his boots he was coated in the mud of his journey over the winter roads. His cloak was still white with melting snow, and it dripped onto the floor, tracing out a circle of water around him. However on his head he wore an elegant hat with a white feathery plume, that he had evidently been keeping clean and safe in his baggage for this moment. He smiled now with all his teeth, and bowed, sweeping the hat off his head with a flowery gesture, bending at the waist and fanning his boots so that the dust flew and Scantguise sneezed violently. Then he straightened up and announced himself:

'Patspeak, Ambassador of His Royal Majesty the King of Feydom, to the court of His Royal Majesty the King of Kendark.'

'Splendid!' said Ewan in some surprise. 'This greeting is certainly more polite than the last, I will say. Has King Dermot changed his mind about me, then? His last messenger called me something much less complimentary.'

'Changed his mind?' said the new envoy, looking daggers at Scantguise. 'So this man has already delivered his message, has he?'

'Indeed he has,' said Ewan.

Patspeak sighed. 'Well, I made as good speed as I could. Through half the mud and snow of this misbegotten kingdom. Really, your roads,' he complained, fussing at the dried mud on his breeches. 'I had hoped to overtake him, but the going was so hard!'

'So your message is not the same as Scantguise's? Have you more welcome news to bring?'

'Yes, sire,' replied the new envoy, clicking his heels together and drawing himself up to his full height like an actor about to deliver a speech. 'From His Royal Majesty the King of Feydom, the Wavemaker, the Grain-Lord, Marshal of Battles, Scourge of Kennaught . . .'

'Yes, yes, yes,' said Ewan, cutting him short in mid-breath. 'No disrespect to King Dermot, but we have heard all this at least twice this afternoon already. If you will forgive me, I shall put direct questions to you. I shall start by asking you whether the King recognises my title to the throne of Kendark.'

Patspeak looked about him contemptuously. What? Was he not to be allowed to introduce his message in the proper formal way?

These Kendarkers were indeed ignorant of every civilised custom. Just look at them! This was the fellow who called himself King of Kendark – a mere sixteen-year-old boy. And as for his counsellors! A fat old wizard who looked as if his only interest in life was eating. A slender young girl no older than the lad beside her. And a painted savage from the north, whorls of bright red and blue sketched on his cheeks and forehead. His chest was bare too, and covered with intricate patterns. A pot-belly, a peasant lad, an ignorant savage and a girl. Why, it would be easier than taking cream from a cat!

'Yes, sire,' he answered. 'King Dermot welcomes the news of the Necromancer's death and his replacement with a monarch of Feylander descent.'

'Amazing,' said Ewan. 'Well, before we had seven noes. Perhaps now we are about to have eight yesses. Second: where is my mother, and is she being sent to join me?'

'Your mother is in good health at Midknow, sire. She will be reunited with you on completion of the little matter of the Gates.'

'Ah, yes, and what *about* the Gates?'

'The King my master will be delighted for you to open them. He suggests a meeting of Your Majesty and himself, along with your respective wizards, on the plains beside Midriver to arrange for the breaking of the Spell.'

'Another yes!' exclaimed Ewan in mock astonishment. 'But what about this monster that Scantguise spoke of? Does His Majesty expect me to . . . "call it off"?'

'Yes, sire, but that', said the messenger, dropping into the formal language of all politicians in all ages, 'will be entirely subject to the arrangements mutually arrived at by the properly constituted authorities in due course.'

'By Dermot and myself, you mean.'

'Exactly so. As will that other little matter which concerns us so nearly, namely the illness of the Princess Starfall, in which you promised also to use your good offices.'

'Yes,' said Catchfire, clutching her veil around her face, 'I'm sure we can do something . . . just as we promised.'

Patspeak frowned a little, and looked at her more closely. 'Lady,' he said, waving his hat again in all directions, and bowing like a jack-knife, 'have I the honour? I seem to recognise the enchanting

15

tones of . . .' Then he paused in puzzlement, his hat hovering halfway back to his head.

'No, no,' put in Ewan hastily, 'how can that be? You are new to Kendark, surely?'

'Sun'sgift, my lord!' exclaimed Patspeak with a shudder. 'What do you think?' And he pulled out a scented handkerchief and held it to his nose.

'Good, you accept, then,' said Ewan, taking no notice of the envoy's rudeness. (Though Knifeskin scowled through his bright war-paint, and tugged at his beard.) 'But the Gates must be opened first, you realise? For our magic will not work in Feydom till then.'

Patspeak bowed. 'My master is most sensible of the unparalleled kindness that his royal cousin does him. He is graciously pleased to concur with his royal cousin's request.'

'That language sounds a little formal, considering how things stand. His only daughter, the Princess Starfall, confined to her bed these last six months or more, speechless and unseeing like a soulless marionette! I hope', said Ewan, leaning forward in his chair, 'that His Majesty does not blame *our* magic for her illness?'

Patspeak's eyes shifted uneasily. Scantguise burst out, as if in amazement: 'What do you take us for? Of course it's your . . .' Then clapped his hand to his mouth in alarm as Knifeskin bared his teeth at him.

'Softly,' said Ewan. 'We must understand their point of view. They know nothing of Kendark, and men fear what they do not know.

'I might as well not give you assurances,' he added, turning back to Patspeak, 'for you will not believe them anyway. But nonetheless I promise you that we have cast no evil spell upon poor Starfall.'

'We are grateful for your assurance,' replied the envoy coldly, smoothing the breast of his doublet with one manicured hand, 'and naturally we trust your word implicitly.'

'Spoken like a diplomat,' said Caperstaff. 'But let it pass. The important thing is that King Dermot has seen sense.' He rubbed his hands together in his usual gesture of satisfaction. But Ewan could see an ironic curl at the corner of his mouth as he went on: 'So everything is agreed. Not a cloud on the horizon. Your master the King is the most wise and amiable of monarchs. It will all be plain sailing from now on!'

16

The ambassadors were escorted to the ante-room, where they sat sulkily, each blaming the other for the contradictory messages they had brought. And Ewan and his advisors talked it all over.

'It will not, of course,' said Caperstaff, 'be plain sailing at all.'

'No,' growled Knifeskin, 'I'm sure you are right. Even if the first of those two Feylanders' (he spat into the fire) 'had been overtaken by his friend – even if we'd never heard his message – Feydom is not to be trusted.'

'Treachery, you mean,' nodded Ewan. 'Well' (he sighed) 'I'm sorry to say it sounds very like it. We shall have to be ready for the worst.'

Knifeskin brightened visibly. 'War?' he said. 'We of the Frore, ancient bodyguard of the Kings, will be ready.'

'Well, well, it may not come to that,' said Ewan soothingly. The men of the Frore were an untamed people, invaluable in a tight corner; but they had to be kept firmly but politely in check. 'We shall hold counsel with the King on our own land, and be ready with our troops in case of treachery.'

'You're sure this is treachery?' said Caperstaff. 'Perhaps King Dermot has simply changed his mind.'

'Hoodwill has changed it for him, you mean,' said Catchfire. 'I have never known Dermot take his own decisions about anything. The Wizard is ruler of that kingdom.'

'Ah yes, Hoodwill, an untrustworthy fellow,' murmured Caperstaff. 'Never did enjoy his food.' And he rubbed his stomach and gazed out of the darkened window as if to remind them of the time.

'Don't worry, old friend,' said Ewan, 'you shall have your dinner this moment. For it is all decided. We shall raise an army, and march to Rockstrow to meet the King.'

'Yes,' said Catchfire. 'If only the King were ruler in his own land. If only we can get him alone.'

Ewan and Catchfire paused at the door to let the others go on ahead. 'Well, what do you think?'

'What do *you* think?'

'I think,' said Catchfire, 'you should listen to my news. I have made a discovery at Midnight. Who knows? It may solve all our problems.'

CHAPTER THREE

Catchfire's Story

'Mind you,' said Catchfire, tossing her head and pretending to pout, 'I'm not so sure that I *want* to tell you. You didn't listen to me out there in the courtyard, did you? You prefer your boring old ambassadors.'

'Oh, but,' said Ewan, 'that makes your story all the more exciting, doesn't it?'

It was after dinner that same night. They were sitting at the very top of the castle, in the wizard's chamber that was now Catchfire's own. A little pointed tower, poised above the darkness of the township, silent but for the gentle swish of snowflakes against its windows. The peat glowed cosily red in the fireplace; through the eight dark windows of the tower the jagged outlines of the peaks of Ironscale could be seen, still and ghostly in their sheets of moonlit snow.

'So all those old books of Necromancer's,' continued Ewan, 'they're turning out interesting after all?'

'Well, what do you expect? Our old enemy knew his trade, after all. His library is full of the strangest things, for he had ransacked all the wizards' towers in Kendark to stock it. Indeed, it's almost too well stocked, for I hardly knew where to begin.'

'Still, you've come up with interesting things already, haven't you?' said Ewan. '*This*, for instance.' And he held up his left hand, on which a little gold ring set with quartz crystal glittered and sparkled in the firelight.

'Yes, you must try that out,' said Catchfire eagerly. 'We've known about it for a couple of months now, and . . .'

'Well, there's all the time in the world,' said Ewan with a touch of uneasiness. 'You say yourself that one should never play around with such things just for amusement.'

'And talking of that, do you really *like* that place Midnight? I know it's got the Necromancer's library to recommend it, but . . . don't you sometimes wish you were back on firm ground at Fourstrong?' Ewan signed himself superstitiously. 'The castle of Midnight, the place of sorcery, the Necromancer's own dark tower – surely it's a creepy place, isn't it?'

'But Ewan, the Necromancer is dead. Well and truly dead. I have cleaned the place out from top to bottom. It isn't very big, you know. An army of maids, and myself in charge with a great big magic broom. And a shining bright spell in every room. You can see the broom *glow* as I dust out the corners. The shadows, Ewan, the shadows themselves are not as black as they were. No, really, it doesn't frighten me at all. You must come and see!'

'I will, I will . . . when I've time. But . . .'

'And you must come exploring with me!'

'Exploring? Is there some exploring to do?'

'There you are, Ewan, admit it! You're on the edge of your seat with suspense. Shall I put you out of your misery?'

'Yes, yes, what's all this about exploring?'

'Well, we'll leave that till later, I think, just to keep you on tenterhooks for a while. First I'll have to tell you all about the Necromancer's book.'

She paused, gazing into the glow of the peat-fire, collecting her thoughts, and then went on:

'It isn't just *one* of his books I've found. It's *his* book. The one he used as a sort of journal or log-book. It was hidden away in his tower room – by a sort of optical illusion. You remember that strange contraption made out of wires that hangs from the centre of his library, where you'd expect a candelabra? It doesn't seem to make up a shape at all, does it? Just a sort of wriggle of bent metal, all its ends sticking out like a dead spider, every angle a square one. Well, one day last week I was up on the ladder reaching for a book from the top shelf – when, I don't know why, I turned round on the steps. Perhaps it was because the sun suddenly peeped through the window and surprised me.

'And you know, I looked straight at the wire thing, and I saw – I saw that from the place where I was, and from only that place, up on the top of the ladder, level with the spider wires, the shape of them *made sense*. All the open ends of the wire looked as if they joined up, and formed the illusion of a wire box-shape hanging in the air. If you shifted your head to the left or the right, it didn't, it was nothing but a meaningless splutter of sticking-out wires. But from that one point it looked just like a cubical box. And as I gazed at it, very intrigued and wondering whatever it was for, the box grew glass sides, and I could see something inside it. A book!

'So I got down, you see, from the ladder, and went to get it. But of course once I was down from the ladder the box wasn't there any more, only a jiggle of empty wires, and the book had vanished. So I edged the ladder right up to it – you know, it's one of those step-ladders with wheels that you can move about. And I climbed up and stood right beside it just at the point where it looked like a box again.

'And I opened its door, and I took out the book!'

'Marvellous!' said Ewan. 'If only all witchcraft were like that! Go on!'

'I've got you interested now, haven't I?' said Catchfire, gazing at him with amusement. 'Well, there isn't very much in the book, and rather a lot of what there is is frankly horrible. The prisoners he captured. The things that happened to them. But every now and then there is something to think about, something to *know*. And it was there that I found two things!'

'Go on, go on!' said Ewan.

'The first – well, you remember the oakmonsters at Ironscale, Ewan?'

'How could I forget them?' said Ewan, shuddering. And he pointed out of the western window, over the mountains that shone like white gauze under their covering of snow.

'Yes, and you remember how we discovered that their relatives had all been enchanted by the Necromancer. And how he had left alive only those two big brutes who nearly did away with us both. Kept them alive to guard the passes of Midnight for him. Well, it's all related in the Necromancer's book, written down in his own spidery hand in the Old Tongue. Listen.'

And Catchfire quoted, in the harsh speech of the first inhabitants of Kendark:

'*Ath druons tetrokwa Menamenthons, ar iôn wikka nec moi dikti kwâ rupoimi Medhyariasa galarnam. Ar ed ewidet. Mena Keruna Trismiasa gwivam iois didasti. Kina galarnam sekwe.*'

'Which means?'

' "To trees have I turned the Moonmouths, because their witch will not show me how to break the Spell of Midriver. For she knows it. Only the Crown of Unity may give them life again. Here is the spell." And there follow the words of life written in the language of the wizards.'

Catchfire leaned back, smiling with triumph.

There was a silence as Ewan got to his feet to put another couple of peat turves on the fire. When he sat down again, holding his hands out to the glow, he was frowning slightly.

'It's exciting, sure enough,' he said. 'But can we use it? To raise the trees to life – hundreds of man-eating oakmonsters – why, they'd go rampaging across the length and breadth of Kendark! Who knows what damage they might do! No, it's out of the question.

'Unless . . . as a last resort.'

'Right. So what do you think of my second discovery?'

'Ah yes, I had nearly forgotten. What is it?'

'It is simply', said Catchfire, smiling again with some pride, 'five words. Five words tucked away in the margin of one yellowing page. Really, it's surprising I noticed them at all. But there they were!'

She paused, glancing at Ewan to see what effect her story was having.

'Only five words, and I don't know what they mean exactly. *Rúa Medhyaríasa, kelta dhurain Akmenoio.* "The secret of Midriver, hidden behind the door of Eversnow." '

'Yes, but Eversnow stands by the castle of Midnight. It is five hundred miles from Midriver. What can the connection be?'

'Well,' admitted Catchfire, 'I don't really know! But when I found those words, I called for my horse and went out searching round the slopes of the mountain in the snow. And sure enough, there in the hillside, tucked away out of sight in a gully full of bushes, I came across a little old door, rotting and green with moss. If I hadn't been looking for it, I would have missed it for sure, for it looks like nothing but a slab of broken stone. But there it is! The door into the mountain!'

'Did you try to open it?'

'Oh, I found it very hard *not* to! But no, I was saving it for you.'

21

'What self-restraint!' said Ewan with a mixture of admiration, mockery and even a touch of disappointment that there was nothing more to learn. 'Well! I only hope I'd have done the same for *you*!'

'I'm sure you would. But I admit it was a hard struggle, and my curiosity won't let me wait much longer. Tell me, when shall we go and explore? What about tomorrow?'

Ewan touched her hand and nodded. Then he shook his head. Then he got to his feet and walked over to the southern window, where he leaned on the sill and gazed out into the blue-black gloom where the dim shape of Eversnow reared up from the horizon, blotting out half the night sky. The plume of whirling snow that always flew like a flag from its summit looked dark now under the moonlight, but fringed with silver: an ambiguous promise of hope and failure. Ewan chewed his lip.

'Well,' he said at last, 'I don't think we *can* – not yet. It's a day's march to Midnight, and another day back. And we must be ready for the meeting with King Dermot. There's an army to be raised, and all our preparations to be made. I shall have to ride out along the rivers to assemble the troops. After that, well, – we'll see.

'But you know, I don't have much confidence in this door. Even if it does mean something, are you sure it'll really help us? After all, it's knowledge that the Necromancer himself had. And he, for all his trying, never succeeded in breaking the Spell of the Gates. You know very well that the magic of Kendark will not work in Feydom until the Gates are opened. And that applied even to the Necromancer himself, for all his knowledge and his power.

'No, Catchfire, first we'll raise the army. And then we'll see. Don't worry,' he added, looking at her crestfallen face, 'I promise you we'll find the time. Once the army has been set on foot – say in three weeks' time or so, we'll have a little holiday from affairs of state, just the two of us, and do some exploring.

'But I don't suppose we'll find anything. Just an old storehouse in the mountainside.'

CHAPTER FOUR

The Door into the Mountain

Nearly spring now. It was three weeks later, and though the snow still clung to the mountainsides, it was mainly gone from the valleys; so that the glens were clad in green, the peaks in sparkling white, like the colours of the flag of Kendark itself. Messengers had ridden out north and south, calling up an army from the towns and villages. A small army, for this was not a rich land, and even the biggest towns could spare only fifty or sixty men. So the force at Rockstrow would be merely a hundred and fifty archers, three hundred painted horsemen from the Frore, and a couple of hundred pikemen. And at Hammerdale in the south five hundred infantry with pikes and swords were ready to march if the moment came.

Hardly more than a bodyguard. But sufficient to protect them against treachery; for they were forewarned. And they meant to hold the meeting on their own land, where the magic of Kendark would ensure their safety.

At least there was plenty of time. For the meeting of Dermot and Ewan was still two weeks ahead. It was ten days' ride to the west. Ewan could allow himself a couple of days' rest. Indeed, he had arranged for it, just as he had promised.

'You see? We got here after all. The door into Eversnow! *You* said, Catchfire, that night in the tower at Fourstrong . . .'

'I know. I said we should never find the time to explore. Well, I admit I was wrong. Here we are, safe and sound.'

But Catchfire didn't sound particularly happy as she said this, and Ewan shot her a puzzled look. 'Don't tell me you've lost your nerve at the last moment? Why, you haven't given me any peace for the last five hundred hours! And now, when it's all settled and arranged, and here we are at Midnight . . . *moitos gwénasa, dharmos Ménasa,*' he teased her, quoting the old saying which means 'Women's changefulness is as constant as the Moon'.

On another occasion, Catchfire might have said something rude about this being the one proverb in the Old Tongue – indeed, almost the only phrase in that language – that Ewan knew. But for once she refused to rise to the bait. A small vertical line of worry creased her forehead as she said: 'A witch's privilege, Ewan. When I said I was worried about not getting here, well, I'm beginning to think it wasn't that at all. It was some other feeling. A sense that things were going wrong.'

'Going wrong?'

'Yes, the time, the moment. This place. Oh, Ewan, I don't feel happy about this door into the mountain.'

'Well,' said Ewan, amazed, but just slightly worried himself. After all, she had a witch's sixth sense. 'Can't you be more precise about it? What harm can come to us here, in our own land of Kendark?'

Catchfire did not answer. She gazed around her, bewildered by her own unease. Here at Midnight, the highest point of the glen, where the waters of the River Bane spilt glittering out of the great mountain lake of Skydeep, the snow had still not thawed. Valley and mountainside were carpeted in even whiteness, drifts fitting snug to the earth as a new-washed sheet to a bed. Above their heads a vast mountain wall reared up as if carved out of soft white marble. Eversnow, loftiest peak in the Western World, wearing always a smoking plume of snowflakes in its cap. So tall (men said) that it touched the sky. Behind them, not a quarter of a mile away, a tiny round castle stood between them and the silver lake. It was only a narrow ring of stone, a hundred yards wide, a perfect circle of battlements three storeys high. It had but a single tower, and that too was round, rising sheer from the castle's centre like a lighthouse, slender finger of granite. A simple ring with, in the midst of it, a wizard's staff of stone, pointing at the moving clouds. Catchfire's castle, whose name was Midnight.

'I'm being silly, Ewan, I know. We *have* to find out, don't we?'

'Of course we do. You've got your curiosity back, then? I hope so, for the sake of mine. Because there's our adventure waiting for us just a few yards away.'

He pointed one fur-clad arm at the cranny in the mountain facing them. A cleft at the foot of Eversnow where it met the drifts upon the valley floor. A tangle of dark bushes cowering for warmth within it. And, on the rock that hung like a keystone above the cleft, a dense creeper, outlined in silver, icicles glittering motionless from its branches.

'Well, now that we're here, let's at least take a look.'

The snow in front of them was smooth and trackless. There were not even the trident-shaped footmarks of any bird. Slowly they walked towards the mountain's foot, their fur-lined boots crunching in the crisp white snow. The silence was total. Except for the little dark creeper over the narrow gully ahead of them, whose icicles suddenly began to clatter and tremble like the chattering of teeth – or as if the bush itself were deadly cold. Strange. For there was no breeze.

Ewan shivered too. Perhaps Catchfire was right to be wary. Still, he was curious to know . . . ah, there it was now, half hidden behind a jumble of bushes. A wooden door, ancient, coated with moss, covered with dripping icicles.

They halted in the snow, and Ewan pushed against the door with the flat of his fur glove. Then harder. There was the splitting sound of rotten wood, and a panel fell out into the darkness behind. Ewan pushed again, and there was a crunch as something gave. The door sagged suddenly on its hinges.

'Shall I . . .?'

'I think you have already!'

True enough, the hinges, soft with long years of rust, had given way. Ewan put his foot against the door, and it collapsed on the instant, falling flat with a moist thud into the dark cave-mouth behind it. It was indeed very like an open mouth, for long silver icicles hung dripping from its upper lip, and others had fallen into the drifts of snow that had piled up knee-high below it, so that its lower jaw looked as if it were fringed with broken teeth.

'You see,' said Catchfire. 'A door into the mountain.'

'Yes, whoever would need such a thing? The Necromancer? Or does it date from long before him, long before he came to Kendark?'

'Well, shall we go and see?'

'I thought', said Ewan, gazing at her quizzically, 'you said we'd better not.'

But now that they had actually opened the door, and were gazing into the dark depths of the tunnel beyond, Catchfire's eyes were

25

aglow with curiosity. For reply, she pulled out the torch from her knapsack, and lighted it. It flared into a smoky blaze, and the mouth of the tunnel flickered back at them, the red light glinting off the smooth wet stone.

'I don't know why I felt nervous just now,' she said. 'Now we're actually here, I'm beginning to look forward to this little adventure. It'll make a nice exciting change before we have to have all that politics again.' She wrinkled up her nose. 'You must admit, Ewan, magic is so much more interesting!'

'Except when it gets *too* interesting,' said Ewan drily. 'Or too interested in *us*. But don't get enthusiastic yet,' he added, grinning. 'There may be nothing here at all.'

Catchfire could almost hear a tiny voice at the back of her mind saying 'I hope so'. But she closed her ears to it and said: 'Well, there's only one way to find out. I'll carry the torch.'

They entered the tunnel-mouth.

It struck Ewan as strange that the door of Eversnow, mountain of eternal whiteness, should lead into such night. The walls and floor of the cave were as black and smooth as polished jet, ground and burnished by waves, no doubt, long aeons before when the cave had been at sea-level. Its walls were dripping with moisture, and it was far colder in here than out on the sunlit snow beyond the door. It became colder still as, thirty paces inside the mountain, the natural cavern came to an end and was succeeded by a narrow passage that pierced horizontally right into the rock. They walked on cautiously, following the passage's gentle twists and turns till all sense of direction was lost.

At least ten minutes must have gone by when Catchfire paused and raised the torch high above her head, so that its red flame pierced further into the darkness. She pointed wordlessly ahead.

Steps.

They were cut out of the solid rock of the mountain's heart, but amazingly smooth and regular. 'And where there are steps,' said Ewan, 'the Necromancer means us to climb them.'

'Hush, Ewan,' said Catchfire with a shudder. 'And just when I'd got my courage back!'

In such a place, no spell is needed. Curiosity is enough. They hesitated only for a moment, then began to climb, counting as they went: 'One, two, three . . .

26

'. . . ninety-nine, a hundred, a hundred and one. And here we are,' said Catchfire in an I-told-you-so voice. 'Look, what is that but a door?'

'Well,' said Ewan doubtfully. 'It's certainly not natural.'

They had come out on a sort of landing, six feet wide and extending for six yards ahead of them. Its walls were rough-hewn out of the rock. But the end wall was of worked stone, blank and even as a plastered partition, formed out of a single slab of granite. It looked as if it had been slotted into place to close off the tunnel. Ewan ran his fingers round its edges. There was no nook or cranny at all: it seemed as if the door (if it was a door) had grown into, been made one with, the rough rock about it.

'We could try levering it open,' suggested Ewan.

Catchfire shivered, and shook her head. 'No, no, violence and magic don't go together. I can tell you, I shouldn't like to be the person trying to force this door. For look at the lintel.'

She raised her torch, and they both peered at the ancient script which had been carved into the naked rock just above the door. Four words:

'*Suadil. Ath trismiam yugoio,*' Catchfire read. ' "Be gentle. To the three-in-one of unity." '

'A vow? Or a prayer?' said Ewan, frowning.

'Well,' said Catchfire, 'this is one time when I don't know the answer. It's not a prayer, though. It means to the *place* of three-in-one. But what *that* means, I've no idea!'

'Then we'll try out your guess about the sword, shall we?'

Ewan pulled the sword Giftwish from his scabbard. And then they both drew in their breaths. For indeed, their guess had been right! The sword was shining, bouncing a shrill blue light off the cavern walls. Their shadows, thrown upon the roughstone, were doubled – two blue shadows cast by the torch, two red ones cast by the lambent sword. Truth to tell, the light that streamed from Giftwish was painful to the eyes. It was not that it was too bright, just that it struck somehow a discordant note, a sharpness transferred from the blade to the air around it. Ewan and Catchfire screwed up their eyes; but they were too excited by the change in the stone door to pay their discomfort any attention.

For it was as if bronze could float upon torchlight.

Giftwish's slender blade rose in Ewan's hand, buoyed up on the

27

stream of some invisible current that tugged it towards the centre of the massive stone slab. It was like holding in leash a hunting dog that had risen silently to its feet, pointing and quivering, pulling with gentle certainty straight ahead.

The door was changing. Its surface suddenly became hard to focus on: it seemed to stir into a sort of milky mobility, as if they were gazing not at a granite slab but at the liquid in a huge glass tank, dense with floating particles, which now began to settle as the liquid clarified, rarefied slowly into misty transparency. All at once they could see that the door was a yard thick, for the red torchlight filled it as water fills a sluice. Then it changed colour again, becoming darker as they saw right through it into the gloom beyond. The refraction of the torch's light in the foggy depths of the slab faded and went out. Instead of hovering like a pale red curtain just in front of them, it flickered now more distantly and thinly off the rough surface of a tunnel wall thirteen long paces away into the darkness on the further side of the door. Stone to glass. Glass to air. The door had melted like a mist.

Before their rapt eyes the tunnel opened up, only split now into two. For to right and left the passage divided, and ran away into the shadows on either side. They stood in fact at a T-shaped junction, and the passage they were facing was the crossbar of the T.

They smiled at each other, not so much in astonishment as in delighted awe. A mysterious and beautiful event, a little frightening too, though that added to its beauty. They felt like cheering – but not too loud! They felt also just a little like beating a hasty retreat. But only for a moment. For here they were on the brink of a discovery, and so far all their guesses had been right!

'Once a magic sword, always a magic sword,' breathed Catchfire, reaching out a hand to touch Giftwish. Softly. With respect. 'He's the key to more than one door, it seems.'

'Right,' said Ewan jokingly. 'We must try him out on some ordinary door one of these days.'

'You don't suppose that slab was just an illusion?'

'Well, if so, it was the sort of illusion I'd have broken my shoulder trying to force a way through.

'But listen!' he added with excitement. 'You know what this proves? Magic doors aren't built for no reason, so we must be on the right track!'

'Yes, and perhaps it explains the three-in-one. It must be the three tunnels that join just here.'

'How straightforward it is after all! Well, we have all day before us. Provisions too. Shall we go exploring?'

Ewan, you will notice, had swept aside all his doubts. In the amazement of this new discovery, he simply didn't pause to consider the creepy feeling that anything to do with Midnight gave him. And if Catchfire, who was wiser far than he in the ways of magic, was still haunted by any sense of danger, well, I'm afraid she decided to ignore it too in the thrill of adventure.

'Come along,' said Ewan. And he stepped boldly forward across the junction of the T. Catchfire clutched at his arm as if to hold him back – but she did not dare let him go on alone. She stepped with him across the invisible threshold. And, behind them both, the stone slab shimmered back into its place, closing off their exit. Air freezing to stone.

'Well, of course,' said Ewan. 'These doors always do that.' And he turned with Giftwish in his hand, to point it at the door again and open up the passage they had just come through. For, indeed, such doors always did exactly that: they closed behind you, opened in front of you in answer to the pointing blade of Giftwish.

But not this time.

Giftwish's glowing light had faded. It was nothing now but an old brown sword, like a long and slender leaf, autumnal bronze in the glow from the torch. Nothing magical about it. And the sword felt heavy in Ewan's hand, for the power from the door was no longer calling it forward.

The smile faded from Ewan's eyes. His mouth set in a grim scowl. Catchfire raised her hand to the locket at her throat, twisting it so that its facets glittered in the torchlight. She had gone quite pale.

'We can't get out,' she murmured. 'The door is shut and there's no way back!'

They gazed at each other in consternation.

'Bah!' said Ewan suddenly. 'What does it matter? These tunnels must lead somewhere! No doubt they come out on the other side of the hill. All it'll take is a little walking.'

'I wish I thought you were right. I don't like this at all. Why doesn't Giftwish work? There must be something wrong. Even against the Necromancer, Giftwish always worked.'

She reached out her hand for the sword. 'Here, let *me* have a try.'

She stood in front of the door, the sword poised in her hand. Nothing. It obeyed nothing but the muscles in her own arm. It stayed as dull and lightless as the copper-brown autumn leaf it resembled. It pulled only downwards to the floor, as ordinary prosaic swords do.

Shaking her head, she handed it back to Ewan. 'It's no good,' she said disconsolately. 'Ewan, whatever shall we do?'

They looked about them. Before them, a smooth stone slab, obstinately shut. No chance even of forcing it, for they had no spade or crowbar with them. To left and right the two dark mouths of the passageway, glowering, inscrutable, with not a glimmer of distant light to beckon them. The silence was absolute. They were locked away under the ground, darkness pressing in upon them on all sides.

'I told you so!' they both said in chorus.

'Yes,' they both said together in reply, 'but not at the same time as *I* did!'

They laughed, breaking the tension. There was no question of either of them blaming the other. After all, they had both agreed. Maybe it *had* been Catchfire's idea! But then Ewan had been only too pleased to have a day off from raising his army. And Midnight held secrets still which had to be cracked. They had both been quite clear about that. Besides, thought Ewan to himself, did I have to go rushing through that door like a boy of sixteen? But then I *am* a boy of sixteen, he thought with irritation.

'Take my hand,' he said. 'That's better. Now, which tunnel is the way out, do you suppose?'

Catchfire thought again of that earlier playful reference to the Necromancer. It was a nasty idea. That this might be some trap of his, planted in his book for any unwary enemy who might come after him. But she had better not dwell on the thought. She would keep her mind on the business in hand.

'Toss a coin,' she said. 'I've one in my purse. A witch's coin from back at Ashenfell. Look, here it is.'

'Good, you toss it, you're the witch.'

'Tails for the right. Matchcurse's head for the left.'

It came down left.

CHAPTER FIVE

The Mole

'I don't like this,' said Catchfire after some minutes. 'This passage is going downwards.'

'Well,' said Ewan, 'so does the one we entered by. It came out at the bottom of the hill, didn't it?'

'Yes, but if you go upwards, at least you must reach the light. And the torch won't last for ever.'

'Oh, we have another in my knapsack. Still, I must admit I don't like this much either. It seems to take a lot longer to get out than it did to come in. And what's that smell?'

Truth to tell, it was the smell that was the most disturbing thing. As they descended the gradual slope of the passage, it was getting steadily fouler. A rank odour like a fox's den, a mixture of dirt, decay and terror. And as they walked ever downwards into the darkness, something else began to bother them too. Catchfire paused, and held her finger to her lips, wordlessly. They listened, their ears pricked in the dense cold silence of this underground tunnel. And dimly, as if from far away, there came a sound.

'What is it, Ewan?' said Catchfire, whispering. 'The lake?'

It was gentle and rhythmic, like far-off waves sighing onto a deserted beach. Could a storm have risen over the lake of Skydeep?

'We must be getting near the opening,' said Ewan firmly, and pulled her on.

But, as they descended the passage again, the sound grew steadily louder, more animal. Catchfire halted abruptly. It was as if some part of her mind had made the decision to turn back, and had ordered her legs to stop walking. She said nothing out loud. She just *knew* they should go no further.

Ewan, holding her hand, had halted too. He could feel her trembling. Now he released her fingers, and walked cautiously forward a few paces, raising the torch above his head so that it

31

shone as far as possible down the dark passageway. Then he too froze to the spot. He could feel the hair rising on the nape of his neck.

Not daring to utter a sound, he pointed with his free hand. Silently, Catchfire nodded.

Ahead, not ten yards away, the passage was blocked. Not, this time, by a stone slab, but by something almost blacker than the darkness itself. Something soft and furry, faintly glossy in the torch-light, as dense and smooth as moleskin, like a huge rug of black fur stuffed into the tunnel ahead and blocking it from top to bottom. And as they watched it, the black pelt rose and fell, gently, rhythmically. It was breathing.

So that was the sound they had heard! Catchfire grabbed Ewan's hand and pulled him away up the tunnel. They neither of them dared speak a word, but simply bolted back up the stone slope, trying to make as little noise as possible. The torch swayed and flickered, so that weird shadows jigged and clutched at the walls and roof. As the torch swung, the darkness ahead of them wavered to and fro.

They did not pause for breath till they were almost back at the stone slab. Then they slid to a halt at last, panting, gazing at each other wide-eyed.

'What was that?' hissed Ewan in a whisper.

'I don't know,' said Catchfire, shuddering. 'And I don't mean to wait and find out. Come on. There's only one way out of here.'

At the slab, they paused for a moment in their flight, while Ewan tried out the sword again. But no. The stone door was as firmly shut as ever. Onwards was the only way.

Yet perhaps, once, before Giftwish mysteriously lost his magic power in the twistings and turnings of the Necromancer's secret tunnel, there might have been another exit. For, not twenty yards beyond the door that had trapped them here like hunted foxes underground, they came upon a second smooth stone slab, the mirror image of the first one; but this time set on the opposite side of the tunnel, and bearing on its lintel the words *Ath cafod gnôyasa*. Without much hope Ewan tried Giftwish again. Again there was no result. But Catchfire gazed in puzzlement at the carved letters over the door.

' "To the head of wisdom", ' she read. 'Did you notice? The

other door too. On the inside it bore almost the same message – *Ath kerdom gnòyasa:* "To the heart of wisdom." Ewan . . . what can it mean?'

'It means', said Ewan wrily, attempting a joke – though to tell the truth, his heart was not in it – 'that if we'd had any sense we'd have stayed the other side of the stone slab.'

Catchfire gave a pale smile of acknowledgement, and went on: 'Yes, and I'm worried. What if up ahead of us . . . what if all we find there too, at the top of the passage . . . is another closed door, with another inscription?'

They pressed on into the darkness, with increasing anxiety. But there were no more stone doors, either open or closed. The tunnel was sloping unmistakably upwards. And comfort was at hand. After a mere ten minutes – though those minutes dragged like hours – they both heaved a sigh of relief, and turned to smile at each other. A faint whiteness, as of the outside air, stained the tunnel's gloom. Saved! They'd be back at Midnight safe and sound within the hour! They rounded a last turn in the passage and saw . . . the light of day!

A normal, quite unmagical doorway this time. An arch of daylight cut out of the black rock. Made cautious by the experience they had just gone through, Ewan approached it slowly, taking care to accustom his eyes to the dazzle of sunlight before he peered out.

'Well?' said Catchfire. 'All clear? Which way do we seem to be facing?'

Ewan passed his hand across his eyes, and shook his head as if to arouse himself from some hallucination. He drew back into the tunnel mouth, and Catchfire raised her eyebrows at the expression on his face.

'Whatever is the matter, Ewan? You look as if you'd seen a ghost!'

'Catchfire,' said Ewan slowly, his voice husky with anxiety, 'just take a look out there, would you, and tell me if I'm going mad . . . or just dreaming,' he added grimly.

'You look quite pale, Ewan,' she said, touching his cheek. And then, as she in her turn looked out through the archway, she let out a little squeak of amazement. 'But the snow's all gone! And wherever are we? It looks like a ruined city! But . . . there's nothing like this up at Eversnow!'

Ewan stepped outside into the sunlight and looked up and around him. He went paler still. 'Look here, this is impossible,' he muttered to himself. He passed his hand over the carving on the archway. 'It's the same,' he said. 'And, Catchfire, come here, look up at that cliffside there and tell me . . . tell me, for heaven's sake . . . if you can see it too!'

'See what?' said Catchfire, craning her neck. 'It's an old ruined castle, isn't it? Strange, I agree, but not so strange as all that! We must have come out on some side of the mountain we've never seen before. But I thought there was nothing up there but the glacier?'

The archway they had come through led straight out into a little ruined street. The buildings about them were all roofless, and some of them had collapsed, so that blocks of stone lay scattered everywhere inside the houses and over the cobbled surface of the road. Further off was the shell of a massive stone gateway, its two flanking towers roofless and with great holes torn in them where the windows had once been, so that the gatehouse looked now like a gaping mouth surmounted by a pair of sightless eyes. Through the arch and beyond it lay a vast plain, stretching mistily into the far distance, with little woods and diminutive towns scattered across it as far as the eye could reach. Behind them, towering over the doorway from the tunnel, stood the huge shell of an old citadel – an empty shell, for all its stones had been cast down into the town beneath, and almost all that remained of the fortifications was the rock itself, hollowed out, cut away and shaped into the empty silhouette of a castle, standing out like a flat two-dimensional model against the mountain far behind it. You could see where the rooms had been, five storeys up, cut into the living cliff-face. But floors, ceilings, and all but the single wall that was the rock itself had been stripped away and thrown headlong down into the hillocks of rubble that strewed the ground.

As for the snow, it had vanished completely. The air was freezing cold still, but there was not a sign of snow anywhere on the ruins about them. Only the distant mountains, forty miles away to the east, stood out like a band of white paint against the clear blue sky.

Ewan felt for a moment the helpless terror of a man caught in an earthquake, as if the solid rock had begun to shift under his feet, and good reliable mother earth had been transformed into an untamed horse, rearing and bucking, determined to toss him from her back.

'Do *you* – do *you* know where we are?' he stammered. (For he was terribly afraid that this place was . . . but how could it be? And if only it were not!)

'Well, I – the other side of the mountain, it must be. Where else?'

'Catchfire, it's not, it's not. You see, I remember this. I've been here before. There can't be any mistake. Every detail of the place is etched into my mind, because I was anxious and afraid, and I took it all in so vividly that it's like a painting in my head. There's the spot where the rock scuttered down among the ruins. And that's where the raven flew startled up onto the battlements. And this is the door. That cursed door.'

'*What* door, Ewan? Whatever are you talking about?' But Catchfire too was pale, as a memory stirred within her mind as well.

'The ruined street. The deserted citadel. The door. The door that leads to the Necromancer's tomb. Catchfire, this is Midriver!'

'Oh now, look here, Ewan, it can't be. Midriver is five hundred miles away. Five hundred miles west across the glens.'

'Yes, I know all that, but where's the snow? It can't just have all melted away in half an hour like that. And where is the lake? Where are the mountains? And where is Eversnow with its plume of snowflakes? Can't you see, we're not in the same place at all!'

The dim memory that Catchfire had been desperately fighting off suddenly roared back into her mind like a wave sweeping away a child's wall of sand. A salt flood of memory – the ceremony at the Gates; the citadel standing on its rocky island, its empty silhouette of stone outlined against the distant mountains. She clapped her hand to her mouth. Tears came to her eyes. 'Oh no!' she said.

'Well, if I'm not right, if you know where else this place might be, – just tell me. I don't want to be a Midriver any more than you do!'

Catchfire turned back to the tunnel they had just come out of. In her turn she ran her hand over the strange carvings that ran across the arch. *Kina leceti Neicos, kladhyâ wertos. Aïnec Calos wiktu.* She looked at Ewan, her blue eyes dark with fear.

'The Old Tongue again,' said Ewan. 'What does it mean?'

35

'Ewan, you are right,' she said sombrely. 'This is the inscription over the Necromancer's tomb. "Here lies darkness, guarded with a sword. May this door never open." The words are written in the Necromancer's book. This is Midriver.'

She was silent. 'But how . . . but how did we ever get here? How is it possible?'

'It must be that door we opened just now,' said Ewan, scowling. 'Giftwish knew the way in.'

'But he doesn't know the way out. Of course. That explains it all. Once we crossed that threshold we were no longer in Kendark but in Feydom. And any magic that we bring with us from Kendark will not work.'

'Sun'sgift, yes! We stand here on the wrong side of the Spell.'

'And that was why I thought it looked like something *I'd* seen before too. Because, last year, Starfall saw the citadel from out there' (she pointed towards the plain) 'there outside the walls.'

'Five hundred miles across the length and breadth of Kendark,' said Ewan bitterly.

Both of them looked grim. Catchfire fingered her useless locket. Ewan sheathed his useless sword.

'It's no good brooding about it,' he said. 'We must make up our minds what to do. Now if this is Midriver, then there'll be guards about. That's what the envoy said. We must hide till nightfall, and then make our getaway. At least the frontier isn't far. We could make for Caperstaff's castle over the moors beyond the citadel. Once past the border we'll be able to use magic again. We'll be safe. But oh, how I wish I'd never stepped across that threshold!'

'Well,' said Catchfire, 'all is not lost by any means. But we'll have to hide in some safe place till dusk. Where do you think . . .?'

'Oh, the tunnel will be best,' said Ewan at once. 'I'll wager they never dare go near it.'

'I'm not sure that I dare go near it myself. That horrible black furry thing, sleeping down there. What if it wakes up?'

'Well,' said Ewan decisively. 'You hide now, just inside the tunnel mouth. I'll go and spy out the lie of the land. I'll find another hiding-place, just in case it *did* creep up on us from behind. And I'll see if I can get a sight of the King's guards. If there are any.'

So it was agreed. And Ewan slipped off into the ruins, hiding

36

behind dilapidated walls, ducking into porchways, advancing with slow caution towards the ruined gate ahead of them. Catchfire tiptoed back into the darkness of the tunnel, fingering her locket, her ears pricked for any sound from the depths of the rock behind her.

But nothing stirred. And fifteen minutes later Ewan was back, slipping in through the archway like a shadow. 'All clear,' he said. 'There are soldiers encamped on the other end of the bridge out there. And they're keeping a watch this way. But my guess is, they daren't come any nearer for fear of the thing in the tunnel. There's another encampment too, up there towards the moor, and two more on the eastern side, towards Hemdark. In fact, the place is surrounded. But I don't think we need worry. They'll be far too frightened to come in as far as this.'

'What about *me*?' said Catchfire. '*I'm* not frightened, I suppose? Can't we sit somewhere else while we're waiting?'

'Oh yes, I've found just the place,' said Ewan. 'Round to the left here. A sort of eyrie. And we can get out of it straight down to the tunnel if we need to.'

Indeed, the place was perfect. The little turret of a ruined house, with windows on every side. Here they could sit and, without being seen, keep a good look out on three sides of the citadel – west and south into the plains of Feydom, east over the March of Hemdark. They could eat their provisions, watch for movement out beyond the ruins, talk, and wait in safety for nightfall.

'But look!' said Catchfire, pointing to the south. 'There are lots of little encampments out in that direction. Do you see? Little plumes of smoke scattered across the plain. Do you suppose they're soldiers' bivouacs? Why, there must be dozens of them. Are they all there to keep watch upon the monster?'

'I don't know,' said Ewan, peering into the distance with some puzzlement. 'They seem to be all along the riverside, as if they were guarding the frontier of Hemdark. What do you imagine can be going on?'

'You don't suppose they're all waiting for us to arrive at our conference in Rockstrow in two weeks' time?'

'Yes,' said Ewan, 'it makes me think twice about that meeting. Perhaps we shall have to change our plans.

'But oh,' he added in annoyance, 'it's as if my fate brings me back always to the same spot! Here I am again, back at Midriver, hiding from King Dermot's troops, just as I was nine months ago. I don't like it, I can tell you. Once was bad enough. I could have done without this second chance to get caught.'

'Do you think', said Catchfire, 'we really need to hide at all? After all, you're the King of Kendark now. My – Dermot can hardly clap you in jail and execute you, can he? His brother monarch?'

'Ah well,' said Ewan, 'you may be half a king's daughter, Catchfire, but are you sure you know the ways of rulers? Spit you through as soon as look at you – if they get the chance, and if there are no witnesses, and if nobody could ever find out. Just think of it! What a perfect opportunity for him! I come from Feydom, remember. I may have found myself a crown in the mountains, but to Dermot I'm still nothing more than a peasant, a nameless fisher-boy from the coast, a serf over whom he has power of life and death. Remember what happened here last summer, here in this very place! I was chosen as Champion of Feydom, they told me, selected by destiny to renew the Spell of the Gates. And then it turned out it was all a cheat – trickery by the wizard Hoodwill. I was not to be champion at all, but the unsuspecting victim of a sacrifice. Oh yes, if they catch me again, how pleased they'll be! Hoodwill because I foiled his plans by escaping – so he blames me for the dark magic pouring into Feydom. And that posturing young cut-throat Fetch, the one who was set to kill me – he hates me like poison for not submitting to his sacrificial knife. And even Dermot himself won't have forgiven me for destroying the Necromancer.'

'But look here, Ewan, he can't be annoyed about that! After all, surely that was a good thing for Feydom too!'

'He won't see it that way,' said Ewan grimly. 'As long as Blackwish ruled in Kendark, then he was quite content.'

'Why ever so?'

'Well, because so long as Kendark was really to be feared, then he could keep all his people happy, saying: "Just think of the wickedness in Kendark! Stand together, ward off the evil, do as I say!" It's a marvellous way to hold a country together, you know, if you can pretend that someone threatens them.'

'Well, well, Ewan, and do you say you're a peasant's son? Where did you pick up that piece of wisdom?'

'I'm doing my best to learn, you know. Besides, peasants aren't quite as stupid as people think. They usually have a shrewd idea what's going on. It's just that they can't do very much about it.'

'Good, so the long and the short of it is that you think we'd do best to try and get away secretly. No giving ourselves up to the King's guards.'

'Well, can you imagine marching out there in all innocence, and saying: "I'm sorry, but can you direct me to Kendark? I've lost my way"?'

'Why not? I could pass myself off as Starfall, you know. The Princess. I look exactly like her.'

'Of course you do. But you wouldn't get back to Kendark *that* way! And as for me . . .'

'No doubt you're right,' said Catchfire, sighing. 'So we'll wait for twilight.'

'Yes. And then north towards Rockstrow, and Caperstaff's castle. As fast as we can.'

'Well, I'm hungry,' said Catchfire. 'Let's get some food inside us, shall we? We've got a long wait ahead.'

CHAPTER SIX

Smoke and Twilight

The afternoon wore on slowly. They gazed out through the little window to the east. In the distance beyond the crumbling citadel they could see the snow-capped mountains of Kendark, and below them the narrow green fields, the switchback hills, the scattered woods of the March. This was the wild border-country of Feydom, a strip of land thirty miles deep on the eastern bank of the River Hale – a countryside full of tiny castles, all its small towns and villages walled and defended against the wild outlanders from the east. A checkerboard of fields and copses, rugged and rolling as the sea on a windy day. Ten miles away behind the shoulder of a little hill, a coil of smoke was rising lazily through the cool winter sunlight.

They paid it no attention. There were so many fires out there on the plains to the south. Besides, as Ewan stretched, and shifted his position on the hard stone window-ledge of the turret, pressing the flat of his hand onto the cold stone to ease his stiffness, something else distracted his attention. A dull vibration, the faintest hint of a tremor in the stone, shivering up into his bare palm through the depths of the rock beneath him. Something like a low organ-note, below the range of hearing, sensed rather than heard. The citadel quivered slightly, then was still.

And a faint noise stole up through the earth towards them, into their bones, making them wince with discomfort. A squeaking noise, like chalk scraping against glass, like the sound of a mole in its underground burrow.

Catchfire reached for Ewan's hand. They sat there with bated breath, ears pricked for the faintest of sounds, hands poised on the cold stone window-ledge as if testing the rock for its steadiness.

But nothing happened. The citadel was silent again. The air was freezingly still. The cry of a bird came dimly through the air. But

40

the depths of the earth were motionless under their feet.

Catchfire shivered. 'The monster,' she breathed. 'It was moving. Turning in its sleep.'

Ewan nodded silently. He waited a long five minutes. Then sighed. 'Let's hope it doesn't start waking up.'

They began to talk again in whispers.

'Yes,' said Ewan, 'that's another thing that worries me. Now that we know there's that mole-like thing down in the ruins, is there any point having this meeting with the King? It blocks off the tunnel. The very tunnel we must enter to release the Spell. How are we going to manage it?'

'Well, neither can Hoodwill get through to renew it, can he? It's like one of those logical puzzles. We need magic to open the Gates. But our magic will not work till the Gates are open. Stalemate.'

'Yes.'

'So what do we do? Is there another entrance?'

'Yes, it comes out up on the downs near Rockstrow. But you see, that's no good because Caperstaff blocked it with a flood. That tunnel is full of water.'

'And meanwhile Feydom dies of thirst.'

Out in the March, the smoke was thicker now. The little hill looked like a broad squat chimney, pouring out dense black fumes into the pallid air.

'Well,' said Catchfire slowly, 'it looks almost impossible. Do you think we could let out the water? And come into Midriver from behind, through the back door?'

'I don't see . . . particularly with the Mole down there waiting for us.'

'All right, then solution number two. We persuade old Hoodwill to use *his* magic.'

Ewan grunted. 'Well, we shall try. But all these soldiers – I don't think he'll be easy to persuade.'

'What about the Trees, then? It's all that's left.'

'The knowledge of the oak-witch? Well, you know the objections to that.'

'I know, but if there's no other method . . . facing the impossible, any way is worth trying.'

'But, Catchfire,' protested Ewan practically. 'There is only one way to break the Spell, and that is to enter the tomb, to remove the sword and burn it to ashes. Catchfire, you must agree . . . we have to get into Midriver. And as long as the Mole is there we cannot. I can't see how the Trees can help.'

'Yes, it's the same with the door from Eversnow. Have you realised, Ewan? We could have done it, today, ourselves! We could have broken the Spell for ever, if only that thing were not coiled down there in its burrow guarding the passage.'

'Sun'sgift, yes! If the Necromancer had had the sword . . .'

'Giftwish . . . he could have simply stepped into that tunnel before the Mole arrived . . .'

'. . . and come out here, and destroyed the Spell. So *that* was his reason. Yes, I see it all now. *That* was the reason he wanted Giftwish!'

Over in the hills, the smoke was dense and choking, flapping like a dark grey blanket shot with threads of scarlet. Sparks soared through its dusky folds. A sooty canopy had formed above it, covering the woods and fields, staining the blue air grey. Ewan rose to his feet, and peered out towards the mountains.

'A funny time of year for a forest fire,' he said. 'Unless it's a village burning.'

'Well, whatever it is, no doubt they'll blame Kendarkish sorcery for it.'

'Makes it all the more necessary we get out of here without being seen.'

Ewan reconnoitred the ruins once again. There were two encampments of soldiers to the north, and another two on the east. He and Catchfire needed to go northwards, but on that side there was no cover, just flat fields stretching towards the distant hills, with hardly a hedge or a ditch to shelter them. They would have to leave the citadel by the south-east, where the woods were plenteous, strike some distance into the March of Hemdark, and work their way slowly round behind the cover of the March's switchback terrain, little hills and copses, till they were far enough north to be out of sight of the cordon of encampments.

Even when dark had fallen, the little clumps of tents would not be too hard to avoid, for a campfire burned in each one, and they could hear the soldiers chatting to each other and singing. Still, Ewan had carefully marked off their position in his mind's eye. It should be easy enough, he reckoned, once they had managed the first difficult fifty yards across the dry riverbed. For, once over this, they would be hidden by a patch of scrubby woodland that ran down to the very edge of the river. The only problem was, was anyone lurking on guard in that very patch of bushes?

So, during one long tense hour of twilight, Ewan kept careful watch upon it from a vantage-point just opposite. But there was not a sound from the copse, nor any sign of movement. And when one soldier from the nearby encampment wandered close to it, humming under his breath, passed under the boughs at the very edge of the copse and peered beneath his hand at the dimming shape of Midriver, Ewan became practically certain. If he had had any comrades in the wood, the soldier would surely have spoken to them. But he merely turned upon his heel, and sauntered back casually to his bivouac, to be greeted by conversation and a clatter of cooking pans. Good, if the guards were all having dinner, that would be an excellent moment. Ewan slipped back through the ruins and beckoned to Catchfire; and, as the darkness gathered, they crept carefully down the stony slope where once the River Hale had run, forming a natural moat around the fortress of Midriver; then they clambered across the boulders on the river's bed, and up the other side into the bushes. Here they paused, and listened carefully. But the sounds of merriment from the soldiers' campfires came to them just as before. There was no sign that the alarm had been raised, or that anyone had glimpsed them crossing the river. They set off into the night.

First they struck four miles due east through a succession of little copses, stepping as quietly as they could through the rough brushwood, heading towards the hills of the March. There was no difficulty in finding their direction, for the fire that had been burning all afternoon out in the hills there was still glowing fitfully, reddening the dark air above it, and acting as a beacon to keep them well on course. This was helpful, for, although the sky was clear and cloudless, the moon was new, and cast almost no light. It was a fine night for fugitives. And even if they had had no fire to go by, the stars were out and they could take their course from them.

Four miles into the March of Hemdark, they struck north-east through another little wood. They were starting to edge round the citadel of Midriver, circling it to the north, but always keeping four miles' distance between the cordon of soldiers and themselves. The wood came to an end, and they walked out along a grassy field, keeping always in the shadow of the hedge that bounded it. In fact there was little need for such caution, Ewan thought, for the hill rose steeply to their left, forming a perfect barrier between Midriver and themselves.

Good, he said to himself with relief. Safely away, without anyone noticing and sounding the alarm. But then, why should they? Who in their wildest dreams could imagine we were here?

At the end of the meadow another little wood loomed up like the mouth of a cave just ahead of them, a smudge of darkness blotting out the stars on the horizon. Somewhere an owl hooted. There was a rustle in the undergrowth, a badger perhaps, out on its nightly hunt. They paused and listened. But silence fell again. Nothing. Ewan nodded, pressed Catchfire's hand, and they entered the safety of the trees.

The owl cried again, and a bush swayed into his face. A weight struck him in the back, knocking all the breath out of him. He found himself lying on the ground, no time to draw his sword, his arms pinned painfully down by two dark shapes. A third shadow was standing over him, hissing in an urgent whisper some words in an unknown tongue.

'*Apármat' ioim, mannôs!*'

'*Sic!*' someone rasped in his ear. He could feel the harsh breath on his cheek. '*We thantos esi!*'

And a third voice over to his left, saying in an astonished whisper: '*Hai! Esti gwena, sa!*'

They were captured. But by whom? This was not the language of Feydom!

CHAPTER SEVEN

Hemdark

Beside Ewan, Catchfire's voice rose quietly in the darkness. *'Epioi swesi. Suadil, suadil, mannôs.'*

It was the Ancient Tongue these soldiers were using! Well, lucky that Catchfire could speak it, so Ewan strained his ears. The occasional word he knew. *Epioi* was the word for friends. But it was impossible to follow a whole conversation in a foreign tongue.

The tall man standing over them stepped back with a muffled cry of surprise. *'Esti gwena vo!* It is indeed a woman! Well, missy, what are you doing out and about in the woods of Hemdark at this time of night, eh? In wartime, too! And where are you from, eh, tell me that?' he hissed in a dangerous tone. 'Spies of Hoodwill's, I'll be bound!'

'Do I have the accent of Feydom when I speak the Ancient Tongue?' asked Catchfire proudly. 'No, we are not from Feydom.'

'Well, you speak fluent enough *Gwaséna*. That at least is in your favour,' admitted the leader. But he added grimly: 'What are you doing in these woods at night? Speak before we slit your throats.'

Catchfire was thinking as hard as she could. She knew that the folk of the March still used the Old Speech. But, whoever these people were, they had mentioned Hoodwill as an enemy.

'Suadil, epia!' she said again. 'At least find out whose side we are on first. We are not, I can tell you, friends of Hoodwill's. But who are you, if not his servants? Here, in the Kingdom of Feydom?' Whatever she did, she must find out who they were – and on whose side they stood.

The tall man spat into the bushes. 'Feydom is not a word I like to hear mentioned these days,' he said. 'But you are no Hemdarker, either, by your accent. Come, tell me quickly, where are you from?'

'Where should we be from but Kendark?' said Catchfire. 'And enemies of Hoodwill.'

'Spies then indeed? But spies against Feydom?'

Well, thought Catchfire, what an excellent claim to make! He's put the words right into my mouth. 'Just so,' she agreed.

The man pondered for a moment, gazing about him at the silent trees. It was plain by now that the wood was full of soldiers. Whispered greetings rose in the Old Tongue from all sides, as the others came up to join the handful of sentries who had captured them. What was this? A raiding party of some kind? Against the Feylander guards at Midriver, perhaps. Then what was the fire they had watched burning all afternoon? Perhaps that too had something to do with this mysterious 'war' that the tall man had mentioned.

'Well,' he said at last, 'I can't spend time on you now, whoever you may be. Bidwell, Speedfew, take their weapons and guard them with you. Bind their hands. They may be who they claim to be, or they may not. But we can't afford to take risks. Back with you to the horses, and escort them to Slashbuckle at Tetherheath. Don't be afraid to wake him if need be. He'll know what to do with them.

'And as for you and your friend, lady, if it turns out that I should beg your forgiveness for tying you up and delivering you to Slashbuckle like two packages, then I beg it in advance. But you understand, in a war we must take all possible precautions.'

'And our message to his lordship Slashbuckle?' put in Catchfire pointedly, inventing it out of her own fertile imagination. 'Will he be pleased to see two envoys from Kendark arriving trussed up like chickens?'

The tall man shrugged and turned away. 'Military necessity, dear lady. Slashbuckle will understand. I only hope *you* do.'

Twenty miles on horseback through the icy night, the stars glittering like sparks of frost above their heads. Twenty miles east into the March of Hemdark, their hands bound to the saddle-bows, and two fierce soldiers from the March urging their horses on. Catchfire explained what had been happening, for Ewan had barely understood one word of it, it being all conducted in the Old Tongue. As she began to speak, one of the soldiers interrupted.

'Now, lady,' he said in the Old Tongue, 'what's this? The language of the enemy?'

'Of course,' replied Catchfire. 'For that is what they speak in most of Kendark too. My friend, I regret to say, does not understand *Gwaséna*, and so I must explain our conversation to him.'

'Ah, I see,' said Bidwell. 'I thought for a moment you despised our tongue, like those damned Feylanders out on the plain there.' He spat expressively, then went on with satisfaction: 'For my part, I can't understand a word of their cursed lingo. Can't get my tongue round the sounds!'

Well, thought Catchfire to herself, let Ewan wait for a moment. This sounds interesting. 'You say they *despise* our tongue?' she asked. 'What makes you think that? It is the old language that our ancestors, theirs and yours, used to speak long centuries ago.'

'Lady, we still speak it in Hemdark,' replied the soldier. 'And for my part I think the Feylanders sound more like beasts of the field when they speak. Squeaking and croaking like frogs, I call it. As for the things they do, that's more like beasts than men, too.'

'How so?'

'Didn't you see the village of Halterdown blazing? Stained the sky black with ash, it did. All the mothers and their babies killed. My brother's children, cut down by Hoodwill's murderers.' He passed his sleeve across his face, and Catchfire saw that he was weeping, the tears running down into his beard.

'I am deeply sorry, friend,' she said in a hushed voice. 'Wait, let me explain to my companion.' She turned to Ewan and told him rapidly what the soldier had just said.

'Sun'sgift!' said Ewan in disgust. 'What is Hoodwill doing now? Massacring his own people!'

'Tell him you're sad for him,' said Catchfire.

'But I can't talk the Old Tongue,' said Ewan.

'Tell him . . . oh, tell him an old phrase out of the legends of the wizards: *Dakruons kapo merons marâ.*'

Ewan repeated the words, stumbling a little over the strange syllables. 'What does it mean?' he hissed back at Catchfire.

'It means: "I have more tears than the sea." '

'I thank you,' said the soldier huskily. 'But it won't bring back our babies, will it?'

'But what is this war about? How long has it been going on?'

'A mere month ago, lady, it started. Because our crops had grown. We have the little streams running down off the mountains of Kendark, you know. But Hoodwill said it was witchcraft, because our corn grew and the land of Feydom was barren. In league with Kendark, he said we were. What's more, he said our language proved it. He said it was the language of darkness, the Ancient Tongue of the dragons and monsters of the Forbidden Kingdom, and should be blotted out from human memory. He sent his men to Saddlemount our capital, and read out a great proclamation, two hours long, in which he forbade the Old Tongue to pass the lips of men. It was the language of devils, and he would root it out of the Kingdom.'

'What nonsense!' cried Catchfire, appalled. 'Were our ancestors goblins and devils? Here, listen to this, Ewan.' And she rapidly translated for him.

'And that is the story of the war,' concluded Bidwell. 'They burn our villages. They kill anyone they find who cannot speak their own accursed tongue. And the children – they above all talk only what they learnt at their mother's knee. I tell you, the Feylanders are brute beasts, not men.'

'Tell him that Kendark will be with him,' said Ewan. 'I shall send my troops to aid Hemdark. We will chase Hoodwill and his savages into the sea.' Catchfire could hear the anger in his voice.

She hesitated, 'Is it wise, Ewan, to make such promises? What of the Royal Council at Rockstrow in a fortnight's time? If Hoodwill hears that Kendark is aiding the Marchmen . . .'

Ewan bit back his indignation. 'True, but you have committed us yourself already, haven't you? You said we bore messages to Slashbuckle. I know that anger is a bad counsellor, but look at it like this: we shall see in two weeks' time if Hoodwill means to let the Gates be opened, and if he knows a way to open them. Then either our magic will be restored within the frontiers of Feydom or we shall know that talking reason to Hoodwill is pointless. One way or the other, we shall protect Hemdark. With sorcery or with soldiers.

'For this murder is not to be borne,' he said, bursting out hotly again.

Catchfire turned and translated Ewan's promise of help to the soldiers.

'Well,' said Bidwell slowly, 'perhaps your story is true after all. I hope we have not roped you up too tightly.'

'A little looser would be welcome,' said Catchfire, massaging her wrists.

They came to Tetherheath well after midnight. It was a small town set upon the crest of a hill, so that in the starlit darkness the hill looked as if it had grown towers and battlements out of its own black earth. As they approached up the slope, it reared up before them, blotting out the glittering dark crystal of the sky, its walls fifty feet high against the night. Bidwell dismounted, and pulled at the rope that hung by the massive gateway. At once, it seemed, the ramparts bristled with spears, and a shout came from above:

'*Stâté! Kwôs itha gwanti? Epiôs we antiôs?*'

'Friends!' replied Bidwell. 'It is Bidwell of Halterdown with two prisoners under safe escort. They are to be well treated. They bring us news of help.'

'If you are Bidwell of Halterdown, then say the password.'

'*Scistu scirros!*'

'Enter, friend.'

And when the door had been opened to admit them, and then hastily slammed shut again at their backs, the guard who had cried from the gate stepped up to the prisoners, frowning.

'And what of these two?' he said. 'Can they say the password too?'

'No need, friend, they are outlanders. If their tale is true, they bring us aid from Kendark.'

'Ah, but *I* can,' said Catchfire, tossing her dark head. 'My friend here does not speak our tongue, but do you want to hear *me*?'

'*Vanti!*' said the master of the guard sceptically.

'Then – *scistu scirros!* And health to Hemdark.'

'*Kálya!* Health!' said the guard respectfully. 'Spoken like a true daughter of the March. But why are they tied up, Bidwell? Loose their bonds. We shall lead them to Slashbuckle together, you and I.'

'Now what was all that about?' asked Ewan, as they followed the men into the dark alleys of the town. 'A password? And what a strange one!'

'Well,' said Catchfire, 'I suspect it's chosen for a reason. Tell me, can you say it?'

'Well, I can always try. *Sistoo sirrous.* How's that?'

'Spoken like a Feylander, Ewan!' said Catchfire, laughing and sticking out her tongue at him. '*Sistoo sirrous*, indeed! Come now, where's your double rolled "r" and your guttural "kh", and that tricky little "s" in front of it, so that you have to rasp out "skh! skh!" in quick succession! I'm right, you see, it must be chosen because no Feylander could ever get his tongue round the words.'

'Hm, I see,' grunted Ewan, not very pleased at her mocking his honest attempt to pronounce the unpronounceable.

CHAPTER EIGHT

Slashbuckle

Slashbuckle, Captain of Hemdark, was a tall young man with nervous blue eyes and a remarkable inability to keep still. When aroused by the watch, he had obviously been sleeping fully clothed, for his doublet was creased and unkempt. But, despite his weariness and the lateness of the hour, he was prowling up and down as if he found the big room too narrow and confining. When Catchfire and Ewan came in, accompanied by the two guards, he paused in his restless pacing for a moment, and scrutinised them both carefully.

'*Dwénil gwentoi medhyanoktin!* Well met at midnight!' he murmured at them ironically. '*Aï ándai álterai!* May your shadows ever grow taller!'

'Yours too,' said Catchfire politely.

'And what a slender shadow you have indeed, lady,' said Slashbuckle. 'Surely too slender a shadow for a spy. But doesn't your friend speak too? For two spies you make a strange pair: one a woman and the other mute.'

'Ewan is by no means mute,' said Catchfire. 'It is just that he does not speak the Ancient Tongue. Indeed, few Kendarkers do now. He speaks *Gwanéva*. May I ask if you do so yourself, for if so our conversation will move more easily?'

'Indeed I do,' replied Slashbuckle, dropping into Feylander speech at once, and turning to Ewan with a cautious 'Health!' Polite rather than heartfelt.

'Health!' responded Ewan. 'Well, I must say that is a relief. But I really must learn the Ancient Tongue. I have felt like a deaf man these last few hours.'

Slashbuckle was pacing the floor again. He reached the shuttered window, and spun upon his heel. '*Now*,' he said, as if trying to catch them out, 'your credentials, please!'

Ewan smiled at him confidently. After all, he had thought all this out during their uncomfortable journey here on horseback. 'Certainly,' he said. 'But you realise of course that we have no parchment with us. That would have been too risky, had we fallen into the hands of the Feylanders.'

Slashbuckle's restlessness spilled over for a moment into anger. 'Then what proves you are who you claim to be? Admit it: you are spies from Oltonath, the Wasted Land of Feydom.' And he advanced four paces down the room towards Ewan.

'We have His Majesty of Kendark's own royal seal,' replied Ewan, calm and unruffled – for naturally he always carried it with him. He took it from his finger now, and tossed it across the room at Slashbuckle, hoping to surprise him in his turn. But the tall man caught it neatly.

'Hm,' he said, narrowing his eyes at the ring, 'how am I to know this is not a forgery?'

Ewan looked offended. Then beamed at his adversary. 'Well, sir,' he said, 'it's take it or leave it. Tell me, do you *want* help from Kendark?'

'Of course. But how am I to know you are empowered to offer it?'

'You don't,' said Ewan. 'But listen to me. If we're not telling you the truth, what harm can we do you? And if we *are*, ah then, what a dreadful mistake you'll be making if you throw us into prison here, and we never get back with our message to Kendark.'

Slashbuckle stood still for an unusual minute, thinking. Ewan watched him carefully. That went home he said to himself. Good, I have the upper hand.

'It's the chance of help', he went on, 'against no chance at all. Come, you have everything to gain; you'd do best to trust us.'

Slashbuckle nodded slowly. His brow cleared. 'Well, let's talk in comfort,' he suggested, putting on a hospitable air and gesturing to two chairs by the fireside. He himself drew up another. But hardly had he done so before he was up again, striding across to the door. 'I accept your offer. But what precisely . . .?'

Ewan and Slashbuckle got down to military details, while Catchfire sat and listened, noting that the Marchman was warming to them as the minutes passed. For when he told again of the massacre at Halterdown, Ewan went so visibly hot with anger that

Slashbuckle paused and – despite his own grief and rage – smiled for a moment cordially at them both.

'I see you are honest people.' And he offered them his hand to shake. 'But now, as to the help you can send us . . . ?' His voice hovered on the uncompleted question, and his mood became suddenly sombre again.

'My lord, I . . . the King of Kendark parleys with Hoodwill in two weeks' time. He will insist that the attacks on Hemdark shall be stopped. If Hoodwill does not hear reason, he will send you the men of the Frore, who are his own personal bodyguard. Three hundred horsemen. It is all that Kendark can do, for our folk are but few and scattered. Nor can we act sooner, for the Froremen need time to gather and ride to Rockstrow.

'Now, you will have to treat your allies with care. With honour and courtesy, as I am sure you will. For they are a wild people. They live on horseback and carry their leather tents with them wherever they go. But take my word for it, they may wear paint like savages, and be sometimes quick to anger, but they have the manners of princes. They are peerless and upright friends, and they have one other great thing in their favour: for they speak your own tongue, Gwaséna. There should be no misunderstandings.'

Slashbuckle nodded.

'But I must make just one stipulation. This help is promised you on one firm condition. That you and the men of the Frore do not invade the plains of Feydom. There must be no sacking of towns, no burning of villages. I . . . our king has his own reasons for insisting on this point. But those are our terms.'

The Marchman was silent for a moment. Then he got to his feet and shook their hands for the second time, even more warmly. '*Vatur*,' he said. 'It is spoken. And we must all drink a toast to this alliance.'

'Bidwell,' he said to the guard, 'could you see to it? A bottle of the best vintage. And sit down and join us yourself. This is the best day for our fortunes yet. Oh yes, and before you do, hand back their sword and dagger to our guests. From this hour on, Kendark and we are allies.'

Ewan fastened Giftwish thankfully onto his belt again, and they all settled down by the fire with a glass of dark Hemdark wine glowing in their hands.

'Caperstaff's own,' murmured Ewan, winking at Catchfire.

'So they tell me,' said Slashbuckle, swirling the wine in his glass, and tasting it with appreciation. 'I have never visited Rockstrow myself, but I know that our vintners do. So you know the wizard Caperstaff, do you?'

'None better,' said Catchfire. 'A wizard who is buoyant of heart and buoyant of shape.'

'Unlike Hoodwill,' said Slashbuckle, taking another sip of wine as if to kill the bitter taste of the name in his mouth. 'But what do you expect? Hoodwill is *mannos sen ándavi*.'

'Yes,' said Catchfire, 'I know the phrase: a man without a shadow, that is without a soul. One of the dead.'

'Well, that is no doubt the usual sense of the words,' said Slashbuckle. 'But do you not know how the rumour goes? The saying, it seems, for once is literally true. I hardly know how to credit it. But they tell me that *Hoodwill has no shadow*. The sun's light shines through him as if he were made of glass.'

Ewan shuddered. And he and Catchfire both pressed their hands to their hearts in the sign against evil. 'But – a man without a shadow? How can that be?'

'I do not know,' said Slashbuckle, signing himself in his turn. 'But since he has lost it he seems to live in a world of total certainty. He has no doubts, no stirrings of compunction. No pity (as you see) for Hemdark. Which is why we have had to raise the flag of rebellion. You heard our password . . .'

'Sistoo sirrous,' murmured Ewan, hesitantly.

'Yes,' said Slashbuckle politely, but wincing. 'It means "Let the axe cut" or "Let the axe decide". And also "Let it divide us". But the division between Feydom and the March is none of our doing. Since the monster appeared – oh, a year and a half ago now – since it first rose out of the earth at our own castle of Windscathe, and destroyed the garrison, Hoodwill has started to murder his own people.'

'Ah yes,' said Ewan, pricking up his ears. 'The monster. The Mole, we call it.'

'And we, Erebor, the drill. It seems it is a strange creature. The soft is hard to it, and the hard soft. Every now and then it stirs in the ruins, and burrows through the ground to devour people. Why, I have myself . . .' He checked, and gazed at them sombrely.

'But it is ill luck to speak of such things.'

'Still, I should like to hear,' said Catchfire. 'For we mean – if it is possible – to break the Spell at Midriver. And Erebor prevents us, for it guards the entrance tunnel. So we need to know what manner of beast it is.'

Slashbuckle signed himself, and his voice sank to a whisper. 'Very well. The wizardry of Kendark, I know, is powerful. May it prevent my words from being heard beyond this room. I will tell you the story.

'It was at the *Amrai Púrasa*, the Days of Fire, when a candle is lit in every house, and the fires burn in every hearth to restore the cheeks of the pale winter sun to redness. At the same accursed moment when Hoodwill's minions came to Saddlemount to read his proclamation in the town square, and to ban us from speaking the language of our ancestors. Two hours long, that proclamation was, and the folk stood shivering in the snow, guarded by Feylander soldiers, lest they shut their ears to Hoodwill's abominable words. But in the end that day gave us courage, for the people said afterwards that it was not the will of the gods that Gwaséna should die.'

Slashbuckle brooded a moment, then went on. 'I was myself forced to stand beside the town hall steps, for I was Captain of the Watch. Besides, I did not know what Hoodwill planned, or I should have been far away that day. Well, the messenger of Hoodwill unfolded his parchment – a fat little self-important man, he was – and read aloud from it for two long hours. And – imagine the folly of it! – he read aloud in Gwaséna so that the folk should understand! While we stamped our feet in the snow and blew upon our hands and cursed the name of Hoodwill under our breath. But, friends' – Slashbuckle paused dramatically – 'he never finished reading. For the gods punished him!'

'What happened?' breathed Catchfire, her eyes wide with curiosity.

'Even befalling an evil minion of the wizard's,' said Slashbuckle, shivering, 'the thing is not pleasant to relate. Just as he had reached the high point of his speech, reciting the penalties that would fall on us if we broke the King's commandment, he hesitated, looked uneasy, and the words began to halt and stammer on his lips. Then he stopped speaking altogether, and went pale with fright. Bending down, he gripped his right leg in both hands, trying to tug it up from the ground – as if his boots had become rooted to the stone flags. For a moment his guards did not move to help him: they were puzzled, amazed, worried perhaps.

'And then he began to scream. I hope, my friends,' – and drops of sweat stood out glistening on Slashbuckle's forehead as he spoke – 'I hope that I never again hear screams like that. Even though the man was a Feylander, a mind corrupted by Hoodwill's magic, I pity him. It was as if the very bones were being sucked out of his legs into the ground, while the man fought and struggled with his body, striving to wrench himself away from the spot he stood on.

'He screamed aloud for a long time, poor man, while the guards ran to lever up the paving-stones with their spears and release him from the clutches of the earth. But they were already too late. Ugh! I will say no more . . . except that when all was over the messenger lay across the steps like a suit of clothes without a man inside them, like a puppet of straw or a gutted fish. For the Mole had indeed sucked the very bones out of his body. And when the paving-stones were raised from under his feet, there was a neat little hole through each stone, one inch round, a perfect circle, and the holes went down into the solid rock below like the burrows of a worm.

'We saw nothing else. Erebor came and went like a shadow. A darker shadow than the darkness of the rock itself.

'But that is enough. It is not good to speak of such things. *Pera siet Melkadya!*' And Slashbuckle signed himself again.

There was a long silence. Catchfire touched her locket, and then she said: 'I promise you. If the wizardry of Kendark . . .'

'Let us drink to that,' said Slashbuckle. He drained his glass, like a man trying to forget.

Night again, and the ice had an iron grip. The fields of Feydom were coated with a dim whiteness that looked like a dusting of snow, but was really a thick frost, settled on every brittle twig, every withering blade of grass. A ghostly landscape, sheeted in crystalline grey, shivering half between dark and twilight. The air itself was keen to the touch, as if the narrow sickle of the new moon, shining in the blackness above them, had filled the night with an invisible sharpness. They spoke softly if at all, for the air was so taut with cold that the least sound carried far.

Ewan and Catchfire had been riding all the hours of darkness, they and their tiny escort of half a dozen Marchmen. For the early part of the night, no problems faced them. The frontiers of Hemdark, the hills that bordered on Kendark to the east, were held by Slashbuckle's men. And their progress was steady enough. But the problems came after midnight, with the crossing of the empty bed of the River Hale, up to the north beyond Midriver. For the deep gorge of Pathpitch began where the waters of the Hale emptied themselves into the earth at Heartspill Force. There was no crossing the gorge – not for horses, at any rate – up beyond the waterfall. So for ten miles or so, they must ride out across the plains. Into the land of Feydom. And who could tell if the soldiers of the King were not on guard, even at night, watching for movement from Midriver, or, more likely, for marauders out of Hemdark?

So, now they were in Feydom, they slipped quietly, eight silhouettes on horseback, from the shelter of one little wood to the next, but turning always northwards, towards the safety of the moors and Caperstaff's own domain of Rockstrow.

It was hard to say just how far the frontier was. But they must be getting close now. The woods were nearly at an end and, on the near horizon, a dark backcloth of hills could be seen, misty in the frost-laden air.

Catchfire swayed sleepily in her saddle. Ewan pressed her hand. 'Look, it must be almost the last small wood before the heath. We're nearly there!'

'Oh, Ewan,' said Catchfire, yawning, 'how good it'll be to see Caperstaff's cheerful face again. And to be back in Kendark. On the right side of the Spell. I feel so . . . defenceless here. I can't even catch those faint quivers of foresight, you know, that allow me to *sense* things, like a melody heard at a great distance. But there's no such music here. Feydom' (she shuddered) 'is a dead land. All reason and surface, hard and opaque. You can't see *down* into things. No magic!'

'What bothers me', said Ewan in a matter-of-fact tone, 'is what we are going to do next. Yes, it'll be good to see Caperstaff again. And maybe he'll have some welcome advice for us.'

They had come to another little wood. The branches spread before them like grey-white tracery, clenched in the iron frost. An arcade of trees like a phantom archway, and behind it the wooded ground rose towards a tiny mound at the centre of the copse. From a distance the trees had seemed, in the frostly starlight, like a huge ball of down, a wood-sized thistle-head of seeds, hoar-grey, ready to fly at the slightest breath of wind. From within, it was a canopy of twining grey branches, a lattice-work of silver filaments, an arpeggio of twigs. Starlight and the sharp sickle moon shone off them like water-drops on gossamer.

'No, I'm none too happy', Ewan was saying, 'about Rooftree Forest. It's all too much of a risk.'

Like a spider's web woven by old Spinshade himself! A net of glass, weighed down with leaden orbs. Bidwell, leading the troop, had turned to the right to avoid two large oak-trees. They were skirting the grassy knoll in the centre of the wood. The stars seemed unnaturally near, not far out in space above the branches of the wood, but big, bright, peering close like the eyes of informers. How the frost glittered! It was almost like torch-light in the King's own banqueting-hall, only white, dazzling. Ewan put his hand to his face to shield his eyes from the glare. Ahead of them a horse neighed in fear. And Ewan distinctly saw, from underneath his hand, the trunk of a tree edge towards them and then stop. Instinctively, he tugged at the reins. The whole wood was moving, shifting, reforming out of the darkness into some other shape. The faint dappled light of the night sky on the grass was becoming shiny and regular like a pattern of wet cobblestones. The blackness of the sky seen in swathes and bows through the curving branches was stiffening into hard edges like the shape of battlements. The great oak-tree to his right turned suddenly to stone.

'Halt!' came a voice, as in a dream, from an immeasurable distance. Had the oak-tree spoken?

It had straightened itself in the air like a man suddenly jerking awake as he sits drowsing in his chair by the fire. Its trunk was a curving wall, a tall stone tower. And its silver branches opened backwards like the arms of a man yawning – and stuck there in position, the lines of dim white starlight marking out a circuit of battlements, catwalk, the enclosing walls of a castle courtyard.

'Halt!' came the voice again, as if from within his own mind. 'There's an arrow trained . . .'

The horses ahead were wheeling and turning. Lanterns shone

rom the trees on both sides of them. Only there were no trees any nore.

'Surrender, Marchmen! An arrow is trained on every heart!'

The wood had turned itself inside out. The trunks of the trees ad become grey stone towers, the branches had changed to spears. The thin dark lustre of the sky had thickened to a milky lantern-ight, hanging from the walls of a narrow stone courtyard. Ten feet o the left, ten feet to the right, stone walls. A big oaken gate shut ight behind them. On the battlements around crouched the sil-ouettes of soldiers, each one aiming an arrow straight at the little and of horsemen caught in the pit of the cobbled yard. And on the ower to Ewan's right, a misty figure in a long white cloak stood olding his wizard's staff aloft like a candle, white fire sputtering rom its tip.

'Surrender!' he cried in triumph. 'Traitors to the King of eydom, throw down your arms! Or not one of you shall leave this astle alive!'

CHAPTER NINE

Snarewood

The wood had been a delusion, a Feylander ambush, a trap of stone and sharp bronze blades. The Hemdark soldiers raised their hands and surrendered, and the men of the garrison circulated among them, taking their weapons. It was as if the cold of the night air had soaked like an icy water through their clothing, making their muscles limp with fear.

'And I said there was no magic in Feydom,' said Catchfire bitterly. 'It's a lesson in tempting providence.'

'What do we do now?' muttered Ewan as he handed his sword, reluctantly, to the Feylander guardsman at his side. 'This is a pretty mess.'

'*Bren amrain, gel andain*,' agreed Catchfire. (Which means 'Out of the frying pan into the fire', or rather 'Burn in the sunlight, freeze in the shadow.' For fear is the coldest sensation of all.)

But they were not finished yet. Catchfire had a last card to play. And – who knows? – it might be an ace. 'No, don't you dare,' she cried to the guardsman who stood now beside her, his hand held out for the little jewelled dagger she always carried at her belt. 'Don't touch me! I am the Princess Starfall, and *I* give the orders here!'

And, rising in her stirrups, she called out across the courtyard, imperiously, as one who was used to having her orders obeyed: 'I am the Princess Starfall, and here upon the King's own business. You will release my escort and let them go in peace. We ride by royal command and you will answer to the King my father if you hinder us in our rightful errand.'

The Feylander soldiers, who had appeared at every saddle-bow to receive the weapons of the surrendering Marchmen, paused in indecision, looking about them. The guards on the castle walls, too, looked doubtful. A few of them lowered their bows and glanced at the wizard who stood on the tower at their right. There was a pause.

The face of the wizard, hidden in the shadow of his hood, was a patch of dark absence. But his confident tone seemed to desert him too. His voice sounded suddenly boyish as he answered hesitantly:

'It's such a dark night, your – Your Highness. Starlight and a sickle moon. I'm sorry if . . . But how was I to know?'

Then he collected himself. 'Your Highness, if you are truly she, I invite you to enter the great hall, where the light is better, and we may receive you' – he went on, with the confidence of someone returning to well-worn formulas – 'with the honour that your station deserves.'

Catchfire hesitated in her turn. 'Very well,' she agreed at last. 'But in the meantime guard my soldiers well. Let no one touch a hair of their heads, or his life will answer for it.'

And, turning to Ewan, she whispered: 'Wait for me here. It is best if *I* am recognised, and *you* are not.'

Not that anyone here, she thought to herself, is likely to know Ewan. Still, better safe than sorry. And she followed the wizard's flowing white cloak up the steps of the central keep, and into the brightly lit hall. There she stood proudly in the full glare of the torch-light, while the wizard threw back his cowl, shook his brown hair free, and gazed at her respectfully.

'So?' she said at last, as he guarded a persistent silence. 'Am I not indeed Lady Starfall, just as I say?'

The figure in the white cloak before her was a young man with shifty brown eyes that seemed to communicate uncertainty rather than cunning. 'Well,' he faltered, clearing his throat unsuccessfully, 'you do seem – that is, you look exactly – well, I've only seen Your Highness at a respectful distance, and there are – ahem! – certain problems. You must be aware yourself . . . How is it that you are here on the borders of Feydom, apparently in good health, and yet, when I saw you last, you were ill with the magic sickness, lying still as a stone in your bed at Midknow? I am glad to see Your Highness has made such a wonderful recovery,' he added hastily, and clutching his staff tightly as if to support himself against impoliteness to royalty, 'but how can it be? Some wizard from . . . ?' His voice stammered to a halt.

'Why, exactly so,' said Catchfire gaily. She was in a tight corner, she knew, and she improvised, drawing freely on her imagination. 'It is Caperstaff's doing, wizard of Rockstrow. You must realise', she said rapidly, crossing her fingers against the untruth, 'that I know nothing of magic. So I cannot tell you just how. But he sent a messenger to Midknow, to the King my father, with a remedy against the evil. The remedy worked, as you see, for I awoke from my nine months' sleep, and here I am. But it seems this is just a brief surcease. To be sure of being whole again, and free for good of the evil spell, I must travel to Rockstrow and undergo the care of Caperstaff himself. And that is what I am doing now.'

The young man made a sour face over Caperstaff's name, and stood shaking his head in doubt. 'Well, you seem to . . . it's quite a likely . . . but really, it's not my place to decide.' (This, rather thankfully.) 'You see, Your Highness, I am but Hoodwill's apprentice – oh, I can do a few bits of magic, as you saw, but this is a *political* matter,' he explained in reverential tones.

'Besides, I don't have to,' he added more cheerfully. 'Hoodwill himself is here. And *he* will know the answer.'

'Nightshade!' muttered Catchfire to herself. 'Here's a hard nut to crack. Hoodwill himself! Still, when you have a good story, it's best to stick to it. Though I only hope the story *is* good enough.'

There was a moment's awkward pause, while they waited for the older wizard to arrive. The young man shifted from foot to foot, though he was happier now that all responsibility was out of his hands. From the yard outside came the neigh of a horse, and the distant jangle of a harness. The grey of dawn was dimly visible for the first time through the tall windows of the hall. The torches hissed and shuddered in their holders, then all their flames dipped and swayed as if in obeisance, as the little white figure of Hoodwill entered, stepping rapidly, frowning like a question mark.

'Well, Mazewit, what's all this?' he said, his voice crackling with annoyance. 'Don't you know better than to disturb . . .'

His voice died in his throat as he caught sight of Catchfire, standing there straight as a birch-tree in her silver-grey mantle. 'Your Highness,' he muttered, and went down on one knee before her. Then straightened, his frown darkening. 'But this – but this is impossible,' he murmured. 'Are you Starfall indeed or is this some new trick of Kendark sorcery?'

'No trick,' said Catchfire, 'but simply myself, as you see me.'

And she told her story again, her eyes fixed on Hoodwill, noting how he was taking it.

He was taking it badly. He tugged impatiently at his beard, clicked his tongue over the mention of Caperstaff. Finally, shaking his head as if in sorrow over some silly jest, he waved her to silence.

'This is impossible,' he declared. 'Caperstaff's doing? A wizard from evil Kendark? How can that be? Do you claim he is a friend of ours? My dear young lady, your story just doesn't make sense. Yes, yes, this is a matter of witchcraft, but not the kind you're pretending.'

And without warning raising his staff in the air over Catchfire's head, he cried out: '*Dík-twam, maïa! Prován tínam mórcam wéram!* Show yourself, shape of illusion! Reveal your rightful form!'

Catchfire smiled and tossed her head. The spell had no power over her, for she was as she appeared. She was Starfall's twin, and indeed far more than her twin. Here was no lie; and the spell against deceptions and disguises missed its target.

Hoodwill's eyes were troubled as he lowered his staff. His gaze was fixed on Catchfire's confident smile, and he muttered through his pale lips: 'No, not a shape of the mist. You are as you seem to be. Then what . . . But no! If you are Starfall indeed, what are you doing so far from Midknow?'

'I have told you,' said Catchfire quietly. 'I am on my way to . . .'

But Hoodwill cut her short. 'There is something here', he muttered, 'that I don't understand. But if you are not an illusion then what are you? What is clear, oh crystal clear, is that your story makes no sense. Perhaps you are indeed the princess, but roused from your magic sleep by the very witchcraft that threw you into it; and now that same spell is calling you back like a sleepwalker into Kendark, into the power of its evil sorcerers. You know not what you do, you are bewitched.'

'It is not so,' insisted Catchfire. 'It is as I have said . . .'

'Well, no doubt we shall see more clearly when we question your escort.' He turned to Mazewit. 'Have them in. Under guard. One at a time.'

Catchfire sighed. 'The King my father', she began, 'will not be pleased . . .'

'The King your father', replied Hoodwill, as calmly baleful as a snake, 'will do as I advise him.'

Catchfire's little escort from Hemdark filed before them one by one, staring sulkily at Hoodwill as he questioned them, and refusing to utter a single syllable. Even when Hoodwill (for all wizards know and use the Ancient Tongue) turned with distaste to interrogating them in their own language, they still gazed blankly through him, and kept their lips obstinately closed. Hoodwill grew angrier and angrier. He banged with his staff on the floor, and his voice became softer and more dangerous. As his questions droned on over the tight-lipped silence, dawn began to rise through the windows of the keep. Its chill pale light cast pointed shadows on the further wall, and the torches were guttering.

Then a lazy voice spoke from the shadow of the archway behind them. Movement. A lacy gesture of white. And, stepping out from behind the arch, there came, elegant in jet-black velvet frilled with white ruffles, and with a white-plumed bonnet on his head, a boy of Ewan's age. His doublet was embroidered with his coat of arms, a shield of white with a battlemented tower and the silhouette of a gallows etched in black across it. When he spoke, he too spoke softly.

'Put them to the question,' he said. 'A little pain – that'll bring their tongues to life.'

The boy indeed, thought Catchfire, her heart sinking, looked very like Ewan. The same yellow hair, the same blue eyes. But this boy's cheeks were pale, his eyes languid, his lips set in an expression of contempt. She knew him. He was present to her mind in Starfall's memories. A figure at the Court of Feydom, one of the young noblemen of the kingdom. And Ewan's deadly enemy. Yes, this was . . .

'My friend!' exclaimed Hoodwill. 'I'm glad you're here. How much have you heard?'

'Well, there's not much to hear, is there?' said the young man, fingering the little jewelled bodkin he held in his hand, testing its blade against his thumb. 'If ever I saw a bunch of insolent rogues . . .'

'But as for you, my lady, surprised as I am to see you here, I am overcome with joy,' he said coldly, dropping to one knee before Catchfire, gathering the hem of her cloak in his hand and kissing it.

'Sir,' she said, equally coldly, twitching her cloak away from his fingers. 'I am aware that I know you. But this greeting seems, if anything, too warm.'

'Milady,' he protested, rising to his feet, and toying with his little dagger again, 'how could it ever be too warm, when . . .'

But Hoodwill silenced him with a wave of his hand. 'Hush. Don't tell her anything. Let's see if she really does know you. That might help to prove . . .'

And he turned to Catchfire, with the exultant air of someone who has caught a suspected criminal contradicting herself. 'Well,' he said, 'now you can show us all that you are who you claim to be. If you really are the Princess Starfall, you know this young man. *Who is he?*'

The question hung triumphantly in the air. Even the soldiers from Hemdark pricked up their ears and listened. A last torch flickered desperately, and died with a spurt of flame.

But Catchfire answered at once, in spite of the fear in her heart: 'Fetch, christened Fendspite, son of Barterfaith, Lord of Spylaw.'

A look of disappointment spread over Hoodwill's face. He stroked his white beard and shook his head. 'I don't understand it,' he said unhappily. 'She seems to be . . .'

'Who I say I am,' replied Catchfire. 'And now that I have proved it to you, I should be obliged, in the name of my father the King, if you would guide us on our way. You have no further reason for detaining us here, and my health demands that I should reach my destination soon.'

For there was still hope, she told herself desperately. Fetch and Hoodwill knew Ewan; they could not fail to recognise him. But he had not yet entered the hall to be interrogated. If she could only persuade them before he was called in.

But Hoodwill had forestalled her.

'Not so fast,' he said. 'It may be as you say. But there is still one of your escort whom we have not seen. You will not deprive us of that pleasure, I suppose, your – Highness? I may not get to the bottom of this,' he muttered, 'but, Sun'sgift! I shall try!'

And he turned to his guards and called for the last man to be brought in. Ewan.

Catchfire fixed her eyes upon the arched doorway. Blue space. The light of morning. And through it walked Ewan, not exactly unsuspecting, but still unaware of the enormity of the disaster that now faced them. His shadow came before him, long and slender in the early morning sun, laying its dark finger across the threshold of the door like a prediction of defeat. Catchfire watched him enter through a blur of tears. She fought them back. Since this was the last time she would see him, she must see him clearly. For there was no chance that Fetch and Hoodwill would let him live.

Ewan paused in the doorway. His eyes widened, peering into the darker light within the hall. Where was Catchfire? Ah yes. And on her right . . . And on her left – Nightshade! What tale would he tell now?

As for Fetch and Hoodwill, a sigh of recognition breathed in unison from their lips. The enemy of Feydom. The destined victim of the spell of sacrifice. Here, in their hands, unarmed and at their mercy.

'Well, well,' whispered Fetch into the silence, 'the so-called King of Kendark. I am so *very* pleased to see you again. And so much sooner than we thought! You are indeed the little fool I took you for, putting yourself into our hands like this.'

But Catchfire's voice rose clear as a bell over his words. She would brazen it out to the last. And she would tell Ewan the gist of the story he must know before it was too late. 'Yes,' she sang, 'Ewan was the messenger sent with magic to release me. He it is who escorts me to Rockstrow for the spell to be lifted by Caper——'

'Shut her mouth,' hissed Hoodwill violently. And Fetch clapped one hand to the back of the witch-girl's head, the other to her lips. Then leapt back with a yelp of pain as she bit deep into the palm. He clutched his injured hand, swearing to himself.

'She-wolf! Snake-spawn! You'll pay for that, I promise you! Even if you *are* . . .'

Catchfire's voice sang on like a bird, telling her story. And Ewan, though shaking with anger against Fetch, listened carefully. So that was their line, was it? A good tale, certainly. But he was afraid it would not be much use now.

'Put them to the question,' spat Fetch, still wringing his bitten palm. 'Didn't I say so before? Torture the truth out of them, that's the only way with such lying vermin as these.'

'Well, well,' said Hoodwill, 'perhaps you are right.'

But at this point, and to everyone's surprise, the shy little wizard's apprentice spoke up, tripping a little over his words, but sure of himself again, as he had been on the walls an hour before, when his magic staff had charmed away the illusion of the frosty wood, and had revealed it for what it was, a castle of stone lurking in ambush. 'No, no,' he stammered, waving one limp hand in front of him, 'you must not do that.'

'And why ever not?' said Fetch, as astonished as if the mantel-piece had suddenly started to express its opinion. He glared poisonously at the young man, trying to will him into silence, to send him running out of the door in terror.

The apprentice quailed, but stood his ground. 'For a very good reason,' he said, his eyes turning in fright away from Fetch, and then, as he caught sight of Catchfire, gazing thankfully at her. 'Pain is a human sensation that vies with magic. You see, my lady,' he said, as if appealing to the witch-girl, as if speaking only to her, 'it's the strength of life, of a living consciousness, that powers the spell, that holds the veil of illusion in place across this castle. You must not torture these people. Their pain will draw so deeply on their lives that it will shatter the illusion. The castle will be revealed for evermore as what it really is.'

'Yes,' put in Ewan, 'an ambush, a place of treachery.'

Fetch swore again to himself, but did not insist. Instead, he turned to Catchfire. 'Very well,' he said, 'but as for you . . .'

Catchfire had thought they already knew the worst. Her story had failed not through its own weakness but because this castle held Hoodwill and Fetch, almost the only people in Feydom who would not wish to believe it, because they did not care about poor Starfall. And because they knew Ewan. So now defeat was certain. Defeat and perhaps death. But this, she thought, as she listened to Fetch's words, was almost worse than anything.

'. . . as for you,' he was saying, 'you may be the King's own daughter, and my affianced bride . . .'

Ewan, though swordless, moved forward a step. His voice was angry as he said, 'Take that word back, Fetch, or I will ram it down your throat.'

Fetch laughed in his face. 'My *lord*,' he said, sweeping off his hat in a mocking bow, 'you have no will. You are mine now, mine to do with as I like. And so is the Princess Starfall.'

Despair in her heart, Catchfire tried one last argument. 'But my life and health, my lord? If I do not go to Rockstrow, to the wizard Caperstaff . . .'

'Your life?' said Fetch. 'Your life and health? What do you suppose a princess to be, but a pawn in the game of power? To tell the truth, I'd as soon be married to you, lying like a dead thing on your bed of sorcery in Midknow, as be wed to a living, moving princess. Sooner, in fact, for dead princesses don't bite. Do you think I am interested in *you*, Your *Highness*?' he asked, mouthing the title as if it were an insult. 'Of course not, it's your kingdom I want. So much the better if your story's true. So much the better if you don't get cured. Good riddance to a vixen.'

Catchfire turned to Hoodwill. She clutched at the locket on her breast (though its magic properties, she knew, had no chance of working here). She appealed to him with all the power of her dark blue eyes: 'And Starfall's life? And the Spell of the Gates? The dying land of Feydom? Are you not afraid you are making a terrible mistake?'

Hoodwill frowned at her in puzzlement. 'A woman, a mere slip of a girl questioning my wisdom? Even if Kendark *held* the answer, it is evil, it is the land of darkness.' Then his thin lips became thinner still – a smiling slit of self-satisfaction. 'And as for my making a mistake, how could I be in the wrong?' he wondered.

He laughed suddenly. 'Of course, you do not realise! Well, well, that is easily cured. Just watch: keep your eyes on me.'

And haughtily, icily, he moved to the centre of the great hall.

The dawn was now high. Through the tall windows of the keep, the morning sun threw golden patterns on the floor, long pointed spears of brightness. Hoodwill stalked to the base of a pentacle of light, and stood there proudly, his left hand poised above the flag-stones.

'My intentions are pure,' he said. 'My mind is clear. How could I be in error?'

And then: 'You fools, do you not see?'

It was true. The rosette of light, stencilled out on the floor by a windowful of sunshine, lay bright upon the paving-stones, as clear behind him as before. His white robe shone like a lantern; he glowed like a prophet in a stained-glass window, a two-dimensional cutout devoid of the least fringe of shade. He cast no shadow on the floor.

CHAPTER TEN

The Road to Spylaw

It was as they had suspected. The fort of Snarewood had been newly garrisoned in preparation for the coming Royal Council on the borders of Rockstrow. It had been originally one of a necklace of little castles built by King Dermot's great-grandfather a century before, to defend his lands against further incursions from Kendark. But his Royal Wizard, Witfix, had turned it into the semblance of a wood, so that invaders could be ambushed from behind. Usually it was left almost empty; for the fewer who knew about it the better. But now that Dermot and Ewan were to meet at the frontier, Hoodwill had crammed a huge force of three hundred soldiers into its narrow walls. Surprise would work for them, he had thought; Ewan could be persuaded to hold the conference either in the shadow of the castle's leaves or at least close by, so that a sudden raid would capture him and drag him back in chains to Feydom. And indeed the trap had snapped shut sooner than they knew.

And then what had they intended to do with him? Well, what did they intend to do with him now? Fetch had been boiling for revenge; he had demanded Ewan's own sword Giftwish, so that he might murder him there on the spot in front of Catchfire's very eyes. But Hoodwill had held up a warning hand.

'No, my lord, that is not the way it must be. Certainly he is the appointed victim of the sacrifice; and you, Fetch, are the appointed butcher. But magic has its laws; the forms must be observed, and the boy's blood must be shed at Midriver, when the moon is full. Or else the Spell will not be refreshed. Lord Fetch, you must be patient just a while longer.'

Fetch clenched his hands upon the sword in disappointment. Then he looked more cheerful. 'Ah, but that will still give me time for the other matter. I shall ride for Midknow with Her Highness at once; and we shall see if this is really she, or some Kendarkish impostor. For if the princess is still in Midknow, still lying speechless on her bed . . .' He licked his lips.

Yes, thought Catchfire: that was precisely the problem. For Starfall her twin, she knew, did indeed lie all this while in Midknow, as unconscious as a soulless automat. And what would Fetch do when he discovered that? But there was nothing for it: that very morning, Fetch detailed twenty soldiers to accompany her on the three days' ride to Midknow. If she was indeed the princess, then he wanted her safe at the capital to await their coming marriage. If she was not the princess, well, Fetch would cross that bridge when he came to it.

As for the six soldiers from Hemdark, Catchfire and Ewan claimed in chorus that they were renegades, and had thrown in their lot with Feydom. Fetch wanted them hanged on the spot, but Hoodwill was more cautious; he had them put under guard till he had investigated further. Ewan, of course, had to be found a prison to himself. And Hoodwill refused to have Fetch take him into his charge, for he knew that the young baron wanted immediate revenge. No, it was better that Ewan stayed at Snarewood – it was but a few hours' march from the place of sacrifice. In the meantime, six soldiers were moved out of a chamber overlooking the stableyard on the first floor. And because the room had not been designed as a prison, and its two windows had no bars across them, Hoodwill placed a spell upon the door; an eight-foot chain was screwed into the stone wall, and Ewan was attached by both his wrists to it. Standing, he could see out of the window right into the stableyard. From there, sick at heart, he watched Catchfire and her escort set out for Midknow through the great oaken gate. She blew a kiss to him as she went; and the eyes of both were wet with tears.

So it had come to this! But three short days ago she and Ewan had been safe in their own little castle of Fourstrong. Two days ago they had embarked on the disastrous adventure of the tunnel. And now here they were, both of them helpless prisoners of the land they had sworn to help – and Ewan threatened with certain death. Despair lay heavy on her heart as she rode out through the gates of Snarewood.

As she passed under the archway, the ringing paving-stones

turned suddenly to soft grass; and loopholes of sunlight began to shine through the stone walls of the gatehouse as they faded to a dapple of bark and air, transformed into the arching boughs of two giant beech trees. Catchfire turned in the saddle. It was not that the castle had vanished, she knew; it was just that from a point midway through the arch it no longer looked like a castle. In its place there seemed to stand the same little beehive shaped wood that they had entered only that morning. An illusion of wizardry; but from the outside there was no way of telling, save perhaps that the wood formed a surprisingly regular circle on the grass. Its stone had melted into air and leafless branches. No sign remained of the treachery that had destroyed their hopes.

What disquieted Catchfire most was (ironically) that Fetch had after all decided against riding with them. He had 'business to finish', he said, and had shouted to his captain-at-arms to go on without him. He would follow next day. Catchfire felt a pang of fear: did he intend any harm to Ewan? Hoodwill, she knew, would prevent this if he could, for Ewan was vital to his precious spell of sacrifice. Still, there was nothing she could do. And she rode now beside Mazewit, who was being sent back to Midknow too, with Hoodwill's instructions for the King.

For now their plans were entirely changed: there would be a great ceremony at Midriver; and some of the wizard's magical devices had to be brought back from the capital for the sacrifice ten days hence.

'You are happy to serve Fetch and Hoodwill?' asked Catchfire. 'The cruelty of the one, the blind certainties of the other?'

'*Sic!* Hush!' said Mazewit in alarm, immediately dropping into the Old Tongue, and glancing around him at their escort. '*Nec toia sek!* Don't say such things! These are Fetch's hand-picked men.'

'Well, and isn't it interesting,' said Catchfire with some irony, 'that you wizards are not averse to speaking the Old Tongue when it suits you, but you object to the folk of the March doing so!'

'Oh, but that,' said Mazewit, gazing at her wide-eyed, 'is none of my business. That's a political matter, and I am a mere wizard.'

'Doesn't Hoodwill concern himself with politics? And isn't it a question of right and wrong? Are you in *favour* of war and massacre?'

Mazewit shrugged his shoulders. 'I'm a searcher after truth. Life

71

is so *messy*, you know; there are no straight roads through life. Pure *galya*, on the other hand – a wizard's knowledge – that's a different matter. It's clear and pure, it has no ambiguities. Besides,' he repeated, 'it's none of my business. I simply obey my orders.'

'So you *do* disapprove of Fetch, after all,' said Catchfire, with even more irony in her tone. 'Some roads are more crooked than others, you must admit.'

Mazewit looked extremely unhappy, but refused to answer.

Catchfire sighed, and changed the subject. She asked wrily: 'What of Hoodwill's shadow, then? How did he come to mislay it? A man must surely be careless to lose his own shadow!'

Mazewit looked offended at her lack of respect for his master. 'Oh no, milady, it is a supernatural assurance of his goodness.' And he told her the story we have already heard, how Hoodwill's spell had gone amiss and he had lost both shadow and reflection in his magic mirror.

'So you see, milady,' he ended proudly, 'Hoodwill is a man of perfect whiteness. There is no blemish to his purity.'

'Well,' said Catchfire, 'that is not how the story reads to *me*. A man without doubts of his own rightness? Could anyone be more dangerous? You know what they say in the Old Tongue. *Mannos sen ándavi* means a dead man. For the shadow is an image of the soul. Now tell me, Mazewit,' – and she dropped her voice and signed herself – '*where has Hoodwill sent his soul?* Into what mirror land of opposites?'

Mazewit went pale, but kept his lips closed, eyeing Catchfire with dismay.

'Into what darkness,' she went on, musingly. 'Ah yes, I wonder. Two years ago, you tell me?'

But what she wondered she did not say. And in any case, Mazewit put his hands to his ears. 'That's enough,' he said, 'that's more than enough. I will not hear any more . . . blasphemies against my master.'

'Silence,' said Catchfire bitterly. 'Is that your only argument?'

They had left the country of little woods behind them now, and come out onto the broad agricultural plain of Feydom, which stretched all the way west from here to the ocean of Eventide. The earth, strangely, looked both burnt and frozen; it was cracked and dry under a dust of frost. For there had been no rain for a year, nor even any snow. And never the shadow of a cloud to soften the chilly glare of sunlight. A wide plain, spreading as far as the eye could see, with no more wrinkles than a grey table-cloth, prone and helpless under a towering weight of cold, malevolent air. For the sky was a stubborn, somehow an irritating blue – it nagged at the nerves like some unnatural colour, like a note of discord just below the threshold of hearing. And though the sun shone steadily on it gave no warmth; it seemed to have lost its vitality, as if it were no longer the true sun, shining proudly with immortal light and heat, but some ordinary fire of sticks and coal, burning itself out with spendthrift unconcern. Winter, with no hope of spring. Even though her witch's power was locked out still by the Spell, Catchfire could feel that this was a dying land.

For two days they travelled, past fields full of starving cattle, an occasional carcass lying dead by the roadside, already picked clean by hungry crows. The villages they passed through were full of pale and listless children, their eyes wide and dark, sitting on their doorsteps watching the soldiers pass. They played no games, not a word did they utter, but simply stared at the riders as if with unseeing eyes – except in one village on the border of Fetch's own domains, where one little urchin bestirred himself at last, and picked up a stone to throw at the column of soldiers. The last archer in the line turned in his saddle and raised his bow.

But Catchfire stopped him. 'Don't shoot,' she cried. 'Or you shall answer for it when I am Queen.'

The soldier stayed his hand. But he scowled at her blackly, and muttered under his breath.

Yes, this was a dying country. It was as the Marchmen had called it – Oltonath, the land destroyed. Only the soldiers themselves were well fed; and that was through robbery, as Catchfire saw when they paused in a couple of villages to plunder what little was left in the farmers' barns.

As they neared Spylaw, they saw the first signs of plague – an empty village; five doors with a black cross daubed hastily across them; and every living soul fled, one knew not where. The soldiers reined in their horses in fear, making the sign against evil; and Gruefleck the captain-at-arms led them out of the infected air at a gallop. They gave this village a wide berth; and the men were pale under their helmets as they continued on their way.

'It is the famine,' said Mazewit, white as a sheet. 'Disease follows it as surely as death follows an arrow in the heart.'

'But the ancient spells against plague?' said Catchfire. 'Surely . . .?'

Mazewit shook his head. 'We have tried them. They no longer work.'

'You see,' said Catchfire, 'by closing the Gates, you have cut yourselves off from help.'

And now ahead of them a little black rock, pyramid-shaped, stuck up out of the smooth flatness of the fields. Astride it rode a castle, the same sable colour as the rock itself. And the pointed roofs upon its turrets stood out in gloomy silhouette against the sun as it set above the Western Ocean, a dark red orb, swollen and inflamed. For it was the evening of their second day out from Snarewood. And this was Spylaw, Fetch's eyrie on the plains.

'And here you will stay, Your Highness,' said Gruefleck with grim politeness, 'till my lord returns from Snarewood. For we cannot have you seeing the King if my lord is not there to supervise your meeting. In the old days, I recall, you used to twist King Dermot round your little finger.

'And here you will stay too,' he added to Mazewit. 'For I do not know what you would say of Starfall to the King if Lord Fetch is not there to give a true account.'

As she entered the castle, Catchfire glanced up at the sinister stone crossbar sticking out of the gatehouse right above the archway. She shuddered, for she knew what it was – a gallows-knob.

'Aye,' said Gruefleck, noticing the direction of her gaze. 'I'm sad to say it lacks its tassel. Well, no matter. Lord Fetch will soon renew it once he is back.'

The castle of Spylaw too had no argument but silence.

The witch-girl was shown up into the best bedroom of the castle, a big stone chamber lined with tapestries that hung high in the western wall of the keep, five hundred feet above the plain. The canopy of the big four-poster bed was all decked in Fetch's grim coat-of-arms – the black tower and black gallows on a white ground. She was given a terrified little serving-maid to wait on her, and told that she must not stir from this room till Fetch returned. The door was guarded and, well, she might or she might not be the princess, but Highness or no Highness she was a prisoner till his lordship said otherwise.

Fifteen miles to the west, the sun had set behind the great white rock of Midknow. There stood King Dermot's castle, sinking into night. And as for the east, where Ewan lay in prison, and where the wild land of Kendark reared its mountains up to touch the sky, she could not even look that way. Spylaw's black walls of volcanic stone, ten feet thick, locked her away from even the wistful sight of freedom.

But not from the thought. Tears ran down Catchfire's face as she gazed out into the falling darkness.

CHAPTER ELEVEN

Chains and Crystals

Fetch's black castle waited for its master to return all through that night, the next day and the day after. Catchfire could see nothing of the entrance to Spylaw from her prison. It was only towards evening on the second day that she heard, at last, a clatter of weapons from down in the castle's depths, a bustle in the corridors of the keep, and anxious shouts from the guards outside her door. Finally her little serving-maid burst in, all big brown eyes and a fluff of alarm, to give her the news.

'His lordship, oh, his lordship is back. All the way from Hemdark in one day. And oh dear me, he's *very* angry!'

Then she squeaked with fright as the stamp of booted heels was heard in the passage outside, and hid herself behind the curtains of the four-poster.

Fetch threw open the door with such force that it swung right round and hit the wall with a crash. He stood fuming at the threshold, glaring at Catchfire with bloodshot eyes. He was no longer his usual cool and elegant self. Sweat was dripping down his face, and his clothes were filthy with the grey dust of the roads of Feydom. But his face was pale and, despite his towering rage, he swayed with weariness as he stood there in the doorway. There was a silence. Now he was here he did not know what to say.

At last he growled: 'Well, at least you're still safe under lock and key.' And stood there glowering.

At the rim of his helmet a bandage, now foul with dust, could be seen covering his temple. From underneath it an angry red bruise extended over his cheekbone. Catchfire felt a sudden pang of hope: outside the window she could hear, for the first time since she had come to Feydom, a bird singing. Over and over again, six notes like a question.

'Why, what's the matter?' she said sweetly. 'Isn't everything going according to plan?'

Fetch stamped on the floor, then held his head in pain.
'Kendarkish sorcery!' he swore.

Ewan, left alone in his prison back in Snarewood, had not long
remained sitting on the floor and brooding. Something would have
to be done. He inspected the chain that tethered him to the wall.
They had bent two bronze bands tightly around his wrists, and it
was impossible, try as he might, to squeeze his hands out through
them. The chain, also, was too much for his strength. But the thick
bronze ring that fastened it by a long spike embedded in the wall –
ah, that was perhaps a different matter. He examined it carefully.
Pulling directly at it was worse than useless. Still, it had been a
hasty job, and who was to say? If he applied pressure at the right
angle . . .

Slowly and carefully, he wrapped the two ends of the chain
round the ring in the wall. Clockwise, so that he could bear down
towards the right. Then he gripped the ends of the chain in either
hand, just beyond where they met the bands that enclosed his
wrists – for using his wrists to exert pressure would be impossibly
painful. Pulling outwards at the ring was no good at all. But if
he tried to turn it in its socket in the wall . . . besides, this
was the direction in which he could apply the greatest leverage. He
bore down hard towards the right, struggling to exert as much
pressure as he could. Panting. Beads of sweat stood out on his
forehead.

Nothing budged. Well, he would try the other direction.
Widdershins for luck. He unwrapped the chain again, listened for a
moment to see if there was any movement from the guard outside
the door, then twisted it round the ring the opposite way. Now!
Another try. Heave-ho! And Ewan fought once more to turn the
long spike sunk in its socket in the wall.

After five minutes he rested again. Well, it was hard, but there
was nothing to be gained by sitting here and bemoaning his fate.
Up again, Ewan! Try and get your shoulder against the chain this
time! Either the ring will move or the chain will break!

It took him half an hour of violent leverage, panting and
heaving, his shoulder clamped into the bend of the chain. But then
at last, suddenly, with a thrill of hope, he felt something give: the
spike was moving in the wall. He worked at it slowly and carefully,

forcing it first one way and then the other. Yes, it was true! The spike was coming free!

Then he heard steps in the corridor. He checked that the spike still looked as if it were firmly in its socket, then sat on the floor, looking as despondent as he could.

It was only his jailer, a small scowling man named Grudge, bringing him his midday soup. Ewan did not try to engage him in conversation, for he was eager to get on with the job of freeing himself. Though to tell the truth Grudge didn't look as if he cared for talking, anyway.

When he had gone, Ewan checked that indeed the spike had been freed. He drew it right out of the wall, then inserted it again and moved it to and fro, so that it was easy now to pull it out or to jam it back in and make it look as if it were still firmly fastened. With his hand he cleared away the powdered stone that had fallen, brushing it into the cracks between the floorboards.

Well, so far so good. But what would he do now? At least he overlooked the stableyard; there were sometimes horses waiting saddled there. Perhaps he could jump from the window . . . and during the day they never bothered to close the gate, for what was the point, with an invisible castle? Still, the exit was guarded by two armed men, and he would be conspicuous with this eight-foot chain dangling from his wrists. If only there were some way of getting rid of it!

There was another thing that worried him too. Hadn't he heard Hoodwill placing a spell on his prison door, earlier in the day? Well, he would face that problem when he came to it. And perhaps the window had been overlooked.

As he sat there thinking it over, the spike plugged back into its socket so as to make it look, to anyone entering the room, as if he were still safely shackled to the wall, he suddenly heard whispering outside the door. Ewan got to his feet and stood pressed against the wall, trying to listen. For he felt a slight sense of unease. After all, why should anyone bother to whisper, unless . . .? Surely that was Fetch's languid voice? Ewan felt a stab of fear. He placed his right hand firmly on the bronze ring, and stood there poised.

There was a clink of coins from outside the door. Someone's footsteps moved away down the passage. The bolt scraped back in its socket . . . and Fetch entered the room, grinning. Ewan gazed at him without expression, his heart thumping in his chest, his hand tight upon the ring.

The young baron closed the door stealthily behind him. He was dressed as for a dance or a wedding – elegantly black and white, a cape flung over one shoulder, ribbons and feathers in his hat, and at each wrist the crisp carnation of a ruff. But at his wrist swung Giftwish in its own worn leather scabbard.

'Looking after you well, peasant lad, are they? What comfortable quarters, too,' he sneered, casting an eye over the bare and empty room. 'I'd have thought a cow-shed more suitable myself, but there, I don't suppose a yokel like yourself has any complaints.' And he took a step towards Ewan.

Ewan said nothing, but braced himself. If Fetch came a hair's-breadth closer . . .

'I have, though,' went on Fetch. 'You escaped me once, remember? Back in the tunnels under Midriver. Well, I don't intend that to happen again. Twelve days in prison here, for a slippery customer like yourself? Not a good idea at all! Why, I should never forgive myself if you wriggled through my fingers once again. No, little fool, I mean to make sure of you this time.'

'But the sacrifice?' said Ewan, watching him as a mouse watches a cat.

'Wizard's mumbo-jumbo,' said Fetch. 'Useless rogues like yourself are two a penny. Let Hoodwill find some other gallows-meat to play his games with. We'll settle the account now. Start saying your prayers, whelp.'

His hand went to his sword.

Ewan moved like lightning, arm and body flexing in one supple swift arc of motion as he slipped the bronze ring clean out of the wall and, crouching, clasped his hands around the chain six inches from his manacles, so as to control its swing. Fetch stepped backwards in alarm, unarmed for a moment; both his hands fumbled at his belt, his right hand firm on the hilt but his left hand groping for the unfamiliar scabbard. Nightshade, why wouldn't it pull free? Ewan swung the eight-foot chain like a whip, hard back behind his right thigh. It gave him a four-foot length to strike with, plus the ring and the bronze spike that swung from its end. Fetch, caught off balance, had still not got his sword out.

The chain whipped back towards Fetch's chin and, as he tried to

duck aside, struck him full on the temple. There was a sickening
dry cracking noise. And Fetch sprawled upon the floor, the back of
his head striking the wall as he fell.

He lay still, blood welling from his temple.

Ewan stood over him, panting. He got Fetch under the armpit
and dragged him two yards to the door, propping his unconscious
body against it so as to hold it shut in case anyone had heard and
might try to enter. Then he unbuckled his enemy's belt, and
fastened it, scabbard, sword and all, around his own waist. Ah,
that was better. What luck! He had his own sword, Giftwish, once
again!

But there was no time now for self-congratulation. He must work
quickly. This treacherous attack had been a blessing in disguise.
For though he was not exactly Fetch's twin, still they had much the
same blond hair, the same blue eyes, and much the same height
and build. Besides, it would solve the problem of that cumbersome
bronze chain.

Ewan tugged Fetch's doublet over his unconscious head. It was
blazoned with the young baron's coat-of-arms, and would make an
excellent disguise, at least for the few short minutes he would need
one. Better still, he could slip it on over the chain so that it was
entirely concealed inside his sleeves and beneath the back of the
tunic. For good measure, he picked up Fetch's feathered hat from
where it had dropped on the floor, and clapped it onto his own
head.

But as for Fetch himself, was he dead or just unconscious?
Should he kill him where he lay? No, no time for that now. For,
looking over his shoulder into the courtyard, he could see a black
horse standing waiting, saddled for a journey. Perhaps it was
Fetch's own. And the outer gate lay open!

Ewan tugged the dead weight of his enemy's body a yard into the
room again, pulled the door carefully open, and gazed out into the
corridor. No one. Fetch had bribed the jailer to leave them alone.
Well, casual assurance, that was the behaviour to adopt. He shot
the bolt to on the outside of the door. And strode off down the
passage with an air of calm unconcern, but keeping his hand as
casually on the hilt of his sword.

The jailer was nowhere to be seen. Perhaps he had even fled the
castle altogether, for who could say what Hoodwill's anger would

be once he found that his prisoner was murdered? But there were four soldiers chatting in a corner of the stables, and two more guards on the gate. Well, there was no need to worry. With Fetch's surcoat on his chest and Fetch's cap on his head, what cause could there be for suspicion? Forcing a lazy nonchalance into his movements, Ewan sunk into the saddle of the horse that stood there waiting, gathered up the reins and urged it calmly towards the gates, saluting the two guards who stood there with the same contemptuous gesture Fetch himself would have used. They saluted him back, crashing the butts of their pikes into the flagstones.

Sun'sgift, it had worked! He was past them and out into the freedom of the fields!

Ewan clapped his spurs to his horse's flanks, and away to the north around the castle walls – which looked now, he had barely time to notice in his haste, like nothing more than a clump of woodland, homely and unremarkable among the peaceful meadows. Snarewood, the place of treachery!

Why, Fetch's murderous attack had been an unlooked-for blessing after all! It had been almost an act of generosity – the present of a sure disguise and the return of Giftwish, key to Midnight.

To Rockstrow! But was it to Rockstrow he should go? Catchfire was only three hours departed on the road to the west, and if he hurried . . . But what could he do alone against a troop of twenty men? He was wellnigh certain to get himself killed, playing chivalrous games of that sort. And his death would serve no one, least of all Catchfire. No, it made more sense to make for Caperstaff's castle as fast as his horse would carry him. There he could send an urgent message to the King at Midknow – see what diplomacy could do. And yes, however dangerous it might be, he would set their other plan in motion now. The trees – it was the thinnest of chances! But if the Spell could be broken, then Catchfire's magic would be restored. And she would be safe, even from Fetch and Hoodwill.

If it could be done! If it could be done at all!

But Ewan wondered, as Fetch's black horse galloped onwards through the sunlight, rejoicing in the freedom of his fluent hooves, why Hoodwill's spell on his prison door had not prevented him from passing through. Could it be . . .?

'And as for you,' said Fetch furiously, but wincing at the pain in his head, 'I've a good mind to string you up on the spot. My gallows-knob looks lonely without its tassel, and it's long since a girl swung her pretty young heels over my gateway. A high place,' he sneered, 'so right for a Highness!'

Catchfire still had her little dagger concealed in her clothing. She placed her hand upon its hiding-place now, but answered quietly: 'The King my father is a weak man, I know. But there is one thing he will not brook, and that is the murder of his daughter.'

Fetch glared and spat. 'I shall wait till I see,' he said ominously, 'but no longer. Tomorrow – to Midknow. And woe betide you if you are not the Princess.'

He stood there brooding, biting his nails.

'That peasant brat . . .'

'He spared your life,' Catchfire pointed out. (Unwise of him too, she thought to herself.)

Fetch looked at her as if this only added insult to injury. 'Yes, and what is he plotting now? I don't suppose . . . Why yes, we have Mazewit in the castle, after all. He might as well earn his keep.'

'Fetch Mazewit!' he roared at the serving-maid, dragging her out by the hair from her hiding-place in the bed-curtains. He aimed a kick at her as she ran squealing out of the door.

'I must know where he is,' groaned Fetch, holding his head, as if it were hatred and not his wound that caused this stabbing pain.

Mazewit went from room to room of the keep, humming and hawing. 'Not suitable,' he complained. 'The window – the shape of the room. And it must look out to the east.'

Fetch fumed with impatience.

The right room, when at last they found it, was a tiny circular chamber at the top of a turret, with a narrow pointed window that looked out towards the Kendark mountains, or would have done had it not been already night.

'But will you be able to see?' said Fetch, irritably biting his nails, as Mazewit unwrapped his wizard's belongings and selected a smooth crystal ball and a curious silver stand with four legs carved into the likeness of an eagle's claws.

'See? Of course. The moon is ideal. So is starlight, naturally. Now, *sunlight* on the other hand . . .' And Mazewit paused in his preparations to give Fetch a careful lecture on wizardry. Fetch groaned and clutched his head.

But at last all was ready. The crystal ball was placed on its circular stand in the middle of a small table. The candle was put out. Fetch and Catchfire (her hands bound, for Fetch understandably did not trust her) sat at two of the three chairs, and Mazewit settled himself down in the third, peering into the crystal and muttering under his breath in Sorcerish. There was a long silence.

By this time their eyes had grown accustomed to the crescent moon's pale light shining through the window behind them. Dim pools of whiteness lay upon the polished table, and a glimmer of moonlight picked out the shape of the varnished wardrobe in the corner and fell upon the closed surface of the door like a faintly luminous mist. Now, slowly and surely, these pallid reflections were being drained out of the room; it faded, faded into an absolute darkness, as the moonlight was all drawn out of it and concentrated, focused, condensed in the centre of the crystal, as if it were a vacuum sucking the light out of the air. As Catchfire watched, even the dull glitter of the wizard's eyes went dark. The room and its occupants sank into utter blackness, and all that could be seen was a tiny sphere of light the size of a silver coin hanging in the depths of the crystal. A candid, brilliant whiteness, suspended in space, as if it were a tiny sun a mere inch in diameter, blazing with a frosty glare, but lost in a sea of distance so remote that no other light ever penetrated there. And now it seemed as if it were moving – moving through trackless space and carrying them with it. All sense of time and place was lost as the three watchers gazed fixedly into the little sphere of light, and were swept onwards with it through the wastes of night. Catchfire gripped the edge of the table. Yes, it was still there, but she was not in the tower room any more, but being swung through empty steppes of starless sky in pursuit of the crystal's tiny silver sphere.

No sense of time. And yet the ball of light they followed sped and sped onwards without pausing, through silent oceans, dreary centuries of darkness. A sense of immense nothingness began to oppress her. Speed without a moment's respite, on and on, and never a solid shape to cloud its milky whiteness.

Yes, her sense of time was returning. How long had they been sitting here? Fifteen minutes? An hour? It was impossible to say. She began to feel deeply uneasy.

For Mazewit had performed the spell correctly. *Ex caelo lumen - exsorbe - ex orbe nomen - argento speciem caela - ex nocte omen -* and so on to the final words: *Decela nomen celatum - Evanum regem.* There was no error; the words of the formula were right. So what was wrong? Why did the light in the crystal sphere not pause somewhere and hover in its flight, circle like a bird and float down to settle, to focus on Ewan in Rockstrow, or in Hemdark, or wherever else he might now be? For the movement of the crystal, restless, ever onwards, seeking and not finding, proved - Sun'sgift, what did it prove? A disaster beyond imagining!

Mazewit shook his head in disbelief. He whispered to Fetch, softly, so as not to disturb the spell: 'You say he escaped? Then where is he now?'

'You know what I said,' replied Fetch impatiently. 'He cut and run. He's in Kendark somewhere. Can't you see him?'

'Well, no,' said Mazewit, scratching his head and stammering with uncertainty. 'He's nowhere to be - not a sign - the light, you see, the window on distance, it should come to a halt, it should focus on the person named, wherever he may be. But this continuous movement, it's almost as if . . .'

'As if what?'

'There's only one explanation. If the crystal cannot find him, he's not to be found.'

'Don't speak in riddles, man. What do you mean?'

'I mean he has escaped you, my lord. Somewhere, somehow, in these last four days since he fled from Snarewood, some accident has befallen him, some danger of the road. If the crystal cannot find him, he is nowhere on earth to be found. Ewan is no longer in the world.'

CHAPTER TWELVE

The Road to Midknow

'I don't believe it,' said Fetch, harshly. 'My enemy – out of reach of my vengeance? It's a blow too hard to bear. It cannot, must not be true. Are you sure the spell was rightly cast?'

Mazewit bridled. 'Rightly cast, my lord? I know my business, I assure you. And there can only be one reason for it. Ewan is a dead man.'

'Bah!' went Fetch. And the glow in the crystal vanished with the force of his exclamation. The light swam up again in the little tower room. They could see each other once more.

'All this hocus-pocus with crystal balls and enchantments,' Fetch grumbled. 'It simply goes to show it's a lot of nonsense. To tell the truth, I've never believed any of it. I want proof, proof, do you hear me?'

'But, lord,' said Mazewit, waving his hands in the air, 'how *can* I prove it? If Ewan's not there to be seen, then how can I show him to you?'

'Wizards!' growled Fetch. 'Impractical to a man. Why, you fool, it's quite simple. Get it to seek out someone else. Show me somebody you know is alive.'

'Who, lord?'

'Why, fool, anyone you like. Show me Hoodwill, or Caperstaff, or, stay just a minute! Show me my cousin the Lord of Threshold. Yes, yes, that's a face I know as well as I know my own. Bidewile, Lord of Threshold, the grain-town on the borders of Kennaught.'

'Very well, my lord.' And Mazewit applied himself again to his spells.

Catchfire too had been hoping – but oh, for such different reasons! – that something had been wrong. With Mazewit's spell, or with himself as a scryer, or even perhaps with the little room they sat in.

But no! Once again the little crystal ball gathered the moonlight into itself, sucked it down into its depths, into that little spherical window that swam like a cold white comet away, away into the darkness of endless space. Once again Catchfire lost all sense of time as she watched the movement of this tiny crystal moon, and felt the tower around her disappear, and seemed to float in space like a planet or a star herself. But this time the darkness was not endless. Suddenly, as the silver sphere moved, shapes could be seen growing dimly through its light, trees and towers etched into its silver circle, bulging like the distorted reflections in a convex mirror. It was the eye of an eagle stooping on a castle keep, drawing nearer and nearer a pointed window, peering in through the glass, hovering there. And then alighting with the softness of a feather on the window's marble sill.

It was as if they were standing just inside the window of a castle in a small room with a ceiling of beams, and rich tapestries on the walls. They could make out the pictures on them: a battle, a parley, a treacherous alliance. But what took all their attention were the figures in the centre of the room.

Two men shaking hands, one tall and blond, dressed in Fetch's own coat-of-arms, the other in a black surcoat with a crimson blazon. Around them half a dozen soldiers, some in outlandish costume, others in the colours of Feydom. The two men in the centre of the room were talking now, smiling and nodding. The blond man gestured the other to a chair, and both of them sat down, still deep in conversation. No sound could be heard. If only they had been able to lipread, though! For the image in the glass was as clear and well defined as if they had been there themselves, only tiny, like witnessing a parley between elves.

'There,' said Mazewit. 'I do not know your cousin. But who is that? Perhaps you can tell me.'

Fetch, leaning forward in his chair, peering at the illuminated scene in the crystal, let out a roar of anger. 'Nightshade!' he screamed. 'What trickery is this?' And he raised his fist and smashed it with all his force into poor Mazewit's face. The young wizard went sprawling on the floor. And the picture in the crystal vanished on the instant like a snuffed-out candle.

Mazewit picked himself up, sniffing and groaning, not daring to rise to his feet, but staying there crouched on all fours in the darkness.

'But – but, my lord,' he protested shrilly, 'what is the matter? I – I showed you Lord Bidewile, didn't I? Surely that was him?'

'Traitorsoul, grubwit, wishmonger,' swore Fetch into the darkness. 'Of course it was. You fool, didn't you see what was going on? I can tell you, I've had enough of your wizard's tricks and evasions. An invention of your filthy mind put into the crystal there! Lies, deceit and fraud!'

'B–but, my lord, what . . .?'

Fetch's voice was soft, like someone talking to a child – but a child that he hated with a steady, evil passion: 'My cousin, Bidewile, holding court in his own castle of Threshold. And those men with him, who were they? As if you don't know! Soldiers from Kennaught, you clown! This is the last time I ask advice from a wizard. The army of Kennaught invading Feydom! And my cousin committing treason! A slander, I tell you, an obscene slander!

'Well, you can go to Midknow with me tomorrow, and play your sorcerer's tricks on the King. No doubt you'll take *him* in. But as for me, this is the last time, I promise you, I'll let a wizard past my gates. Liars and deceivers, every one of you!'

Well, if Mazewit and Fetch were at loggerheads, what did Catchfire care? It was Ewan she feared for. What had happened to Ewan? He had escaped from Snarewood, certainly, she had Fetch's word for that. She could hardly believe that some accident had overtaken him on the road to Rockstrow. The trouble was, what had he done after that? It was all very well for Fetch to refuse to believe him dead; but she, Catchfire, had only too clear an idea of the dangers he might have had to face. Suppose he had set off to break the Spell of the Gates, had tried to discover the secret of the oakwitch, and had been killed by the oakmonsters themselves, or been sent by them on some fatal errand. Or else, if the secret of the Trees had turned out useless, could he have entered the tunnel of Midriver again, in a desperate attempt to save her, and been killed by Erebor? As she lay in her bed that night, lonely and afraid, unable to sleep, these visions of Ewan's death kept turning in her head like the repeating images of a magic lantern. Fear. It's just fear, she said to herself again and again. But then, again and again, with a horrible sinking of the heart, she relived the endless flight of the crystal sphere. For how could it lie? Where, in this world or out of it, was Ewan now?

On the following morning, five long days since their capture at
Snarewood, Catchfire sat at her window, staring out over Feydom
to the west, where the white walls of Midknow shone in the sunlight like a mirage, and the blue air spread its cold sheet over the
countryside, bright and blinding as the sky above a desert. On the
parched grass below her lay the shadow of Spylaw, its massive walls
and soaring turrets etched in black like the silhouette of some
horned two-headed monster. As the sun rose slowly, ever higher in
the sky, the shadow shortened gradually, and ceased to point the
black daggers of its towers at her father's palace; it shifted, shifted
to the north, shrinking as it moved. And the shadow became ever
denser as it shrank. It lay on the ground like night, like a ragged
black pit cut deep into the yellow fields.

She planned what she would do when Fetch returned, as he
surely would before the day was out, with the news that Starfall
still lay sightless and unhearing on her bed in the King's own
palace – returned to threaten her with death. Well, she still had her
little dagger, seven inches of razor-sharp bronze. And she would
plunge it into his heart – or maybe into her own if it came to that.
A dismal ending to their story.

But then, if Ewan was really dead, what hope was left for her?
His escape had so raised her spirits. For they did after all have one
last chance. She had told him the Spell of the Trees; he had re-
hearsed it carefully these past three weeks. And had not the
Necromancer written in his book that the oakwitch knew the secret
of the Gates?

Yet what if Ewan were dead? Mazewit, a fool in some things,
was no bungler when it came to magic. The scene he had shown
them at Threshold proved that his scrying worked. It was true, she
thought to herself with surprise, people talked about hearts *aching*.
She had always imagined it was just a thing that was said, a figure
of speech, a familiar turn of phrase. But now she could feel it was
really so; her own heart ached in her breast like a death-wound.

How long would it be before Fetch got back, she wondered. Two
hours in the going, he would be, and on the way back – well, he
would be likely, being Fetch, to come at a gallop. She had little
more than the time from now to the midday meal. But, to tell the
truth, she wished the minutes past. The slow movement of the
shadow of Spylaw towards the north was all too leisurely. Almost

he hoped for Fetch's return. For then things would be settled, once and for all.

'Oh lady,' came her little maid's voice from the room behind her, 'is it true that the men from Kennaught have invaded? That's what all the soldiers are saying.'

'I'm very much afraid that it is,' said Catchfire, turning round. 'But there's no need to worry, you know. The army of Feydom will beat them back, you can be sure.'

Threadseam must be reassured, she said to herself. But in truth, with Feydom weakened by its long famine, had it the strength to repel the invader? She doubted it. And she thought of Mazewit's words on the way to Spylaw: plague follows famine. Invasion too. The wolf eats always the weakest lamb of the flock.

Threadseam hardly looked consoled at all. She twisted her hands together anxiously. 'And do you think he'll be there by now? And when will he be back?' Catchfire knew she was talking of Fetch. And she thought, with a twinge of sympathy, that the girl was almost as terrified as herself.

'Why, Threadseam, don't trouble your mind about that,' she said, struggling to summon up a smile of comfort. 'Whatever happens, *you're* not to blame. Remind Fetch that you're . . . one of my jailers.'

'Oh lady,' wailed Threadseam, 'I don't want to be your jailer!'

Catchfire gazed back into the room at her maid's pale, frightened face. For all her words of comfort, the shadow of Fetch's return lay heavy on her mind. Fear and night. His mindless violence. She clenched her hand on her breast where her dagger lay concealed and, as if responding to the darkness of her thoughts, the room itself sank into deeper shadow.

The cloud of her anguish dimmed the walls, grey fear pressed down from the dark beams above her head. Or was it a sudden mist across the sun? And what was that sound she could hear, faintly, like a whispering of grass in the wind? She had heard nothing like this since she came to Feydom. The light in the room was greyer, certainly but somehow softer, more luminous. The wind outside, rushing, rushing, but with a smooth and steady note that no wind could ever sustain, a liquid murmur of relief. And the air stealing in through the window behind her had a gentle touch.

She turned with a sudden pang of hope to the open casement.

The sky was sighing with pleasure. The fields outside were shining like a silken counterpane. Raindrops hung glistening from the lintel of the window, and its sill was soaking wet.

It was raining.

Catchfire stared out through the window, stock-still, open mouthed, too amazed to utter a sound. It was as if soft grey swathes of drapery had been drawn across the landscape, wavering and shifting slightly like curtains in a breeze – a cloudburst of curtains, a drapery of waterdrops, a downpour quivering and moving, blotting out the white rock of Midknow fifteen miles away, wraiths of dim water dancing in the soft grey air.

'Threadseam? Do you see? *Is it true?*'

'Why yes, milady, I – I can hardly believe it. Rain!' She was hardly less astounded than Catchfire herself.

'But this is impossible! The Spell . . .'

No, but that must be it. The Spell of the Gates – it must have been broken! Someone, somehow had entered Midriver. Was Ewan still alive, then? Hope and joy stirred together in Catchfire's heart but she hardly dared to think their names. She shivered slightly but not from cold or even, now, from fear.

It was as if her lost sixth sense had been given back to her. Like a shudder up and down her spine, a renewing sense of reality, a feeling of being again entirely herself, here, where she stood locked in this chamber high in the keep of Spylaw, a bright candle in an ocean of darkness. Ewan! She had better not hope too fiercely, for the crystal cannot lie! But her senses were awake again. Outside the door she could hear her two guards whispering. She knew there were two of them; it was as if she could see right through the tapestries, through the wooden panelling, through the three-foot stone of her chamber wall.

'Milady?' whispered Threadseam nervously. 'Are you all right?'

'All right?' said Catchfire, forcing her voice to speak softly despite the jubilation in her heart. 'Why' – gaily – 'I've never felt better. Never in my sixteen years.' She caught her little maid by the hand. 'Hold to me, Threadseam, just hold to me, and I'll have you out of this darkness for ever. Tell me, can you ride?'

'Ride, milady? But why ever? Well, yes, since you ask me. I'm a peasant's daughter, as you know.'

'Good, then fetch your cloak.'

Threadseam fluttered away into the adjoining room. And Catchfire strode to the wardrobe, flung it open and drew out a pale grey riding mantle with silver clasps hammered into the likeness of foxes' heads and a hood of white fox's fur. She swung it across her shoulders.

'Quickly now. You never know when Fetch may be back.'

And the two of them stepped through the door.

The pair of guards in the passage halted in the middle of a sentence, their mouths open. They gaped at Catchfire as if they had seen a ghost. 'What do you think you're doing, missy? Back in the chamber with you, and quick about it.' Their hands clenched on their swords.

Catchfire took no notice. Her hand was at the locket at her throat. She twisted and turned it, making it beam soft sparks of light down the gloom of the corridor.

'Shrinkbold! Sneakfeat!' she said, wringing the ugliness out of their names as she sang them aloud like notes of a song. 'Hear me!'

They both stood motionless, staring at her. Their mouths opened, their lips replied: 'We hear you.'

'You will let us pass.'

'We shall let you pass.'

'You will forget you have seen us.'

'We shall forget we have seen you.'

'You will not look inside my chamber.'

'We shall not look inside your chamber.'

And they stood there like statues, frozen to the spot, as Catchfire, taking her maid by the hand, led her wide-eyed and dumbfounded straight past them down the corridor and on to the broad stone staircase which led to the stableyard and the outermost gate of Spylaw. They walked down the stairs in unison, their cloaks floating out behind them, like two little galleons in full sail, a grey and a brown sail together. As they passed, down the stairs, into the great entrance hall, out through the doors of the keep, into the stableyard, and finally away past the black doors of Spylaw and over its echoing drawbridge, they left, everywhere behind them, Fetch's servants standing like puppets on a string, gazing into empty space, dangling in the air of the castle like folk in a fairy-tale, turned to stone in the act of challenging Catchfire.

Outside it was pouring, a steady unremitting rain from heaven. The black and white glare of sun and shadow had been blotted out, softened to compassionate grey. And the parched earth sighed with relief as the first rain for a twelvemonth fell, fell upon the stubble, filled the furrows and cart-tracks, soaked into the thirsty ground, seeped away into the roots of the grass, to awaken and revive it. The air was blurred with tumbling rain, and the walls of Midknow in the distance were now invisible, sheeted and concealed, softly huddled away behind the gentle curtain of wetness.

Catchfire and Threadseam put up their hoods, wrapped their scarves across their faces; and their horses fled through the pelting rain like wraiths carried westward by a tempest, like shadows flickering behind a mist of falling water.

To Midknow, to the castle of the King, and to poor enchanted Starfall's bed of stillness.

Behind them the frozen figures in the castle stirred, gazed with a puzzled air about them, passed their hands across their faces, struggled to remember. But no, there was nothing *to* remember. Now what was it they had just been doing?

CHAPTER THIRTEEN

Witshift Castle

Caperstaff was out in his orchard pruning the cherry-trees when Ewan arrived. The wizard's plump cheeks crinkled into a smile from one ear to the other, but he showed not the faintest sign of surprise.

'A splendid little tree, this one,' he said, clambering back down the ladder and shaking Ewan's hand with enthusiasm. '*Maurillos*, they call it in the Old Tongue. It's not an eater, mind. But so delicious cooked in the oven with honey for a sweetener and crumbs of good brown bread on top. I really must have it done for you some time. Last year you were far too early. And this year,' he added innocently, 'even earlier.'

'Caperstaff,' said Ewan suspiciously, 'do you know where I've just come from? All afternoon at full gallop?'

'Well, what do you think, Ewan? Do I know, or don't I?' He placed a pudgy hand on the boy's shoulder, gripping it with surprising firmness.

'I know something,' he admitted. 'But don't speak a word. A serious talk without refreshment? Unthinkable! A glass of wine, that's the thing. And perhaps, since we're on the subject, the merest sliver of cherrycake.'

Caperstaff's merest sliver was a slice the size of two brawny fists. Ewan, however, didn't feel like either wine or cake. He swirled the drink around in his glass disconsolately, and gazed through the window of the wizard's tiny dining-room. For it looked out upon the plain of Feydom, where Catchfire rode with her captors through the barren lands to Spylaw Castle.

'Now,' said Caperstaff, 'you may think I'm wasting time. But . . .'

'No, old friend. For I cannot act without thinking first. And I sorely need your advice.'

'Well, two heads are better than one; and tossing the thoughts to

and fro often kneads them to a better shape. But first let me tel
you what I know, for in all honesty it is little enough. I try, yo
see, to keep a watch on the borders of Rockstrow, and naturally
use' (said Caperstaff modestly) 'what little skill I possess with th
crystal ball. So I was up in the tower scrying this morning and, t
my amazement, I saw Catchfire riding under guard toward
Midknow, and later yourself on a black horse, riding this way a
full tilt. That is all I know. But I suspect – am I right? – som
treachery of Hoodwill's, for there is a magical barrier set up amon
the woods at the frontier. I cannot pierce that barrier, for the Spe
at Midriver weakens my powers. So you must tell me what ha
been going on.

'Is Catchfire indeed a prisoner? For that is a calamity! And ho
did you come to be there at all, the two of you? I think you hav
some explaining to do.'

Ewan told Caperstaff everything that had happened to him an
Catchfire since their entry into the tunnel two days before. Th
wizard listened with great attention, smiling with delight at th
start of Ewan's tale, but clicking his tongue and shaking his head a
the story proceeded.

When Ewan came at last to the shackles he wore, the wizar
raised his hands in horror. 'Sun'sgift! Why didn't you say s
before? Come, we must have them off you at once!'

'No time now,' said Ewan, brushing his suggestion aside. 'I ca
visit the blacksmith after we've talked.'

'Come, lad, you don't need a blacksmith. What do you think thi
is for?' And he picked up his wizard's staff. 'Roll up your sleeves.'

Caperstaff touched each manacle with the tip of his staff, sayin
as he did so:

> *Vindicis vinculis vincti*
> *Vincula vincit vindicta.*

At the point where the staff had touched it, each bronze cuff brok
sharply across, and peeled back upon itself like a leaf curling in
bonfire.

'There!' said the wizard with pride. 'The easiest spell in th
world – except for *saying* the thing, of course!

'And now go on.'

Ewan struggled out of Fetch's tunic and his chain. 'That's all there is to tell. I am here, as you see. But what of poor Catchfire? She is in terrible danger. For once it is found that the princess is still in Midknow, Catchfire's ruse will be seen through. And then what will Fetch do to her?'

'But are you sure you did not kill him?'

'How can I say? If only I'd put my sword through him to make sure! But somehow, a defenceless man . . . Besides, I was in rather a hurry at the time,' added Ewan, smiling somewhat ruefully.

'So you were, but I only wish you had made certain of him. As long as he lives he is a danger to Catchfire's life.'

'Yes, and I can hardly forgive myself for not riding at once down the road to Midknow to rescue her.'

'You are more use to Catchfire alive than dead. No, no, you acted very sensibly. *Listam kamoio máravam seswertha*, you have kept the hem of your robe from the sea. From here you can send an ambassador to Dermot, support Catchfire's story, insist that the King sees her himself. You can offer him a ransom. Money, corn, who knows?'

'Yes, and today is surer than tomorrow. Is Tatterbeg here? He would make the ideal messenger. I would trust him with my life and Catchfire's too.'

'Excellent! We will send him and two others. We will despatch them by the northern road, so they do not risk falling in with Fetch's men. And at speed. They must be at Midknow before Catchfire can reach it. A hundred miles. They could be there by tomorrow night.' And Caperstaff rang the little bell by the chimney-piece.

Thirty short minutes later, this business duly settled, and Tatterbeg and his two companions already saddling their horses in the stableyard, the wizard poured himself a second glass of wine.

'And now,' he said, 'somehow I feel you have another plan to discuss. If my poor old wits can be of any use . . .'

'Your poor old wits', said Ewan, 'have guessed quite rightly. And ah, how I shall welcome any advice you have to give me!'

'For this is how I see things. Our embassy to King Dermot may work, or it may not. It would be best in any case to have a surer method of saving Catchfire. But there is only one certain way.'

'And that is to break the Spell of Midriver.'

'Exactly.'

'But how do you propose to do that? No one can enter Midriver now, either to renew the Spell or to release it. Or do you know of any other way?'

'No, all I have is one small hint – and a large dose of optimism.'

And Ewan related how Catchfire had found the Necromancer's book; how it was told there that the oakwitch knew the secret of the Spell; and of his own doubts as to the wisdom of freeing the giant trees from their enchantment. 'I have always told myself it is the one good act old Blackwish the Necromancer ever performed. For by planting them all in the forest he protected his people against them.'

'Perhaps, since it was Blackwish who planted them, they were after all less evil than we think. But in any case, there *is* a way! Do not forget you are talking to a wizard. I can tell you how to imprison the Trees within bounds. For, if they break those bounds, you can turn them again into motionless leaf and timber. I will give you the formula.'

Ewan's brow cleared, and he smiled for the first time since he had entered the wizard's castle. 'Caperstaff, you are a friend indeed. Perhaps I shall drink a little of this wine after all. For you set my mind at rest!'

'Well, two heads are better than one. But there are still difficulties. How will you find them in Rooftree Forest? It is vast and trackless. So you must first seek out the giants at Ironscale, for them to guide you to the spot. But these distances are immense. Three weeks on horseback at least. And you have only a day or two's grace. Hm,' said the wizard thoughtfully, 'what about a pair of seven-league boots? I should have a set lying about the castle somewhere.'

'Yes,' said Ewan, 'but do you have a pair that would fit me?'

'Now, now, lad,' said Caperstaff, seeing Ewan's eyes on his waistband, 'it's my *feet* they were made for, not my midriff. I don't know if you've noticed, but I take quite a delicate size of shoe.

'Still,' he went on more seriously, 'it presents a problem. Even magic wears out, as you know. And my seven-league boots may take you to Ironscale, certainly. But not much further.'

'Ah,' said Ewan excitedly, 'but I may have the perfect solution. Catchfire, you see, discovered also how to use this ring.' And he held up his left hand. The crystal shone and sparkled on his ring-finger. For, though night was beginning to fall, the weather was fine and dry. Not a cloud in the sky, and the day had been blue with sunshine. So naturally the crystal shone clear and white in its setting.

'Say no more,' breathed Caperstaff, gazing at the ring. 'I understand. And it is marvellous news! A secret I did not even know existed. Yes indeed, what an exciting way to travel! And, using a wizard's foresight, I should predict – why! it's the transportation of the future!'

'So you agree?' said Ewan. 'It seems a tiny peg to support so great a hope. Will the ring work? Will the Trees give me their help? Shall I be in time? Besides, to break the Spell from outside Midriver! It is the most desperate of tasks! I must be mad even to hope for it. *For it is impossible.*'

'Well,' said Caperstaff, 'people have been hoping for the impossible since the dawn of time. According to the old legends they sometimes even achieved it. Of course *we* do not live in such times. But when there is only one chance left, then – Sun'sgift! – that chance must be taken! Besides – and here is the crux of the matter – who *knows* what is impossible?'

A silence fell. And Ewan thought to himself: well, some things are certain. I am, and Catchfire is. Yes, he thought, with a sudden glimmer of hope: we are both more real than what we know or do not know.

'Poor Catchfire,' he said. 'I should set off at once, this minute.'

'Don't worry, lad, she'll be safe for a day or two. And you cannot leave till you have learned what you must learn this evening. You shall spend dinner rehearsing it. *Kwan drus lipeti, wesra dhalsati*: while the tree still lives, spring will be green. And perhaps it's a good omen that the old saying speaks of a tree.'

He rose to his feet. 'But let us talk it over while we eat, for a good dinner will put courage into you, and the better the food the greater the courage! Goose in confit, now, how would that suit you? A goose preserved in its own delicious sauce. Hm, I'm quite looking forward to this evening's business.'

And he rang for his cook.

CHAPTER FOURTEEN

Whirlwind

Ewan and Caperstaff were up well before dawn the next day, and already riding out of the gates of the little castle before the sun's first rays had touched the snow-topped mountain of Greyscape above them. A grey and chilly dawn. Far to the east, however, the clouds were purple and rosy pink already, and there was a mist hovering close above the grass around their horses' hooves, so that it seemed as if they were stepping through the shallows of a soft grey sea of vapour. Clouds above them, mist below, they seemed to be floating in the air rather than riding upon solid earth. The occasional trees were floating too, like little ships with their masts and rigging bare, their sails all furled, at anchor in a bay of icy steam.

Caperstaff reined in his horse and pointed. 'A magic tree! This is a friendly place.'

They dismounted, and their two guards were told to look after the horses at a safe distance. 'Blindfold their eyes,' said Caperstaff. 'And remember, whatever you see, do not come to our help unless we call you. And do not run. Be ready to calm the horses. Remember, it is a *friend* we go to meet. Whatever happens, I say again, there is no need for fear.'

The guards stationed themselves a good two hundred yards away. Meanwhile, a little fire of dry rowan sticks was built in a hollow a few yards from the tree. Caperstaff lit it with a spark from his wizard's staff, and the smoke began to seethe and coil from it as if the ground-mist itself had caught alight. Ewan stood with his back to the fire and gazed towards the Forbidden Mountains to the east. There lay Eversnow. And from there the sun would peep over the mountain-summits and shine its rays full in their faces. The pink light of dawn was already stealing down the slopes of Greyscape behind them, leaving great purple rifts and gulleys of shadow in its crevices. Ewan slipped the weather-ring from his finger and held it in the air, peering through its narrow golden circle with one eye closed, holding it against the edge of the distant mountains where the snow could be seen beginning to glitter as the sun rose behind it. The words of the Old Tongue came with a sort of clumsy assurance from his lips:

> *Gwentu pura sweloio, etmen warunoio,*
> *Gwentu kerdhos ámrasa, korpos ándasa,*
> *Gwentu kratya nevoio, galsos meldhoio,*
> *Gwen . . .!*
> (Come fire of the sun, breath of heaven,
> Come heart of daylight, body of shadow,
> Come strength of the cloud, voice of the lightning,
> Come . . .!)

The line of silver turned to crimson. A single ray shot over the mountain crest and stabbed like a burning arrow straight at Ewan's eye. He winced and closed his lids.

And the crest of the mountains from where the sun had shone went suddenly dark. The dawn had changed its mind, and it was night again.

But only for a moment. The distant shadow that had, for an instant, cut off the sun's light, was shifting and spreading their way. It was as if, just behind the grey and purple ceiling of clouds above their heads, a blackness was flying, like a flock of a thousand dark birds, winging its way at immense speed over the distant mountains straight towards them. A chilly breeze sighed out of the east. And the darkness slowed and came to rest, hovering in the sky directly above their heads.

A darkness that was also a wind. But not the normal sort of ice-laden wind that blows out of the north, horizontally from the cold sea of Frozenglass, and threatens to rip your cloak from your shoulders and toss you aside into the nearest hedgerow. But a vertical wind blasting down out of the sky from above them, ripping at their helmets, pressing their bodies down into the earth. Under its superhuman force, their knees gave way, and they found themselves crouching on all fours upon the ground, staring up wide-eyed at the vast black shadow that seemed to embrace the whole dome of the sky above them, and was now falling, falling

over them, stooping upon them like an eagle seeking out its prey.
Only this creature of the air was of unimaginable size: its wings had
a span of two hundred feet or more; and they were shaped like those
of a bat. Its jaws were those of an enormous reptile, a grinning row
of sabres, its open maw crimson as flames against the jet black
lustre of its body.

It landed, however, as softly as a black snowflake; and the gale
dropped to an eerie stillness as its wings arched high above them
like a vast gloomy barn. They felt dwarfed, naked, insignificant.
Even Caperstaff, for all his wizardry, signed himself. As for Ewan,
he clutched onto the cold wet tussocks of grass to prevent himself
shaking with fright. Behind them, the horses whinnied and shifted.
The men calmed them, though their voices too were hushed and
shaky.

It was the dragon, Whirlwind, lord of the clouds and rain, himself the colour of a storm-cloud, with wings two hundred feet
across and a tail that, if he should choose to crack it, would shoot
forked lightning.

'*Kwa dharsya!*' he roared. And his voice was like the harsh
bronze trumpets of Kendark, like wind and waves together beating
on the shuddering cliffs at Moorskiff. As the blast of hot air went
by from his mouth, it plucked Caperstaff's metal cap from his head
and flung it away down the hillside. 'What boldness! Never in the
Necromancers' time did even *they* dare to call me! And not ever
lying flat upon the ground at the sight of me? Come, we must cure
that!'

And, drawing a breath like the draught sucking into a furnace,
he puffed at them both, knocking them sprawling on the earth like
two little scarecrows in a gale.

Prostrate on the wet grass, Ewan thought it was time he said
something. 'Greetings,' he stammered, 'great lord of the air. We -
we bring you remembrances from her majesty the earth-dragon -
and from the King of Kendark.'

The dragon's amber eyes lit up like three-foot lanterns. His voice
moderated, fell from hurricane-level to that of a mere storm. 'From
Earthquake my wife?' he bellowed. 'Do you presume to claim . . .?'

'Why yes, we do,' said Ewan, still prone, but thinking that if the
dragon lowered his voice again he might even try to sit up. 'I do
not know whether mere mortals such as ourselves may make so

bold. But we are friends of Earthquake's and . . .'

Ewan pressed his face to the grass again, as another hot blast of rage went by from the dragon's jaws.

'Friends of Earthquake's! What presumption! How old are you, boy? Sixteen short human years, I should judge. And friendship, among dragons, takes five hundred orbits of the sun before even the first rough clawshake. You say you *know* her?'

And the dragon laughed. The earth shook, and Ewan and Caperstaff's teeth rattled like dice in a box. The rowan-tree behind them bent and straightened itself like a dancer, and the cinders of their little magic fire fled scuttering away into the marsh-grass. But truth to tell, thought Ewan, the dragon's laughter was a gloomy sound. It was as if, behind his reptilian contempt, there lurked a sort of sadness.

'Yes, lord,' said Ewan firmly. 'We know her. The witch Catchfire and I. For we have her dragon-ring, and . . .'

The dragon clamped its great ten-foot jaws tight shut, and glared at them both like a pair of yellow lamps. Two threads of smoke blew sighing from its nostrils. Slowly, carefully, it furled its wings, huge black bat-shaped sails. Its voice became softer again, this time no more noisy than a strong wind. And like a wind, it was a melancholy sound.

'Come, that is different,' he said pensively. 'It was *you*, was it, who . . .?'

'Yes, it was we who called up Earthquake. And she, my lord, befriended us. I do not know', said Ewan tactfully, 'whether men can befriend dragons. But certainly it seems that the other way around . . .'

'Well, I know the story,' replied the dragon. 'For Taivimbra, of course – Earthquake, as you call her – has told me everything. But if that is so,' he added, narrowing his eyes so dangerously that the yellow glow of them on the grass went quite out for a moment, 'why is she not here? And where is her ring? And where is the witch princess?'

Ewan thought that he might get to his feet at last. He did so, brushing the damp grass from his hands and his bearskin mantle.

'Lord,' he said, 'she is a prisoner, alas, of evil men in Feydom. And we appeal to you in our great need, as the most powerful creature in the Western World . . .'

The dragon was the image of Earthquake herself – except for his wings, for she, being an earth-dragon, had none. Only, unlike her, he did not glitter like the many-coloured crystals of the earth, but was black as a storm, as coal or jet-stone. Slender scarlet veining ran among his scales like the patterns on black obsidian. But somehow his sheen was dull, gloomy like a dying fire. And when he spoke there was sadness as well as scorn in his voice.

'Your appeals mean nothing to me. Throwing yourselves on my mercy! Try that on my wife Earthquake. She is amenable to flattery. I am not. And I care nothing for you human beings. Why, I remember the time when none of you existed. And the world was a quieter place, I can tell you, then.'

'It will be a quieter place again soon in Feydom if you do not help us,' said Ewan. 'For the crops are dying, as you know, and the people with them. Yet, with your help, my lord, we mean to break the Spell that is destroying the land.'

The dragon gazed at them without expression. His huge tail, fifty feet long, swung threateningly like the black tail of a cat. But when he spoke, his voice was gentle. 'Little mousekin, your words make sense. Now please understand that I do not care if those Feylanders live or die. Kings and princesses, witches and warlocks – what absurd human pretensions! But the earth, the good fertile earth, ah, that is a different matter. And that Earthquake and I should be shut out from our own domain of Feydom by some petty human spell, is *lèse-majesté* of the most impudent kind. Good, I will help you. But not for your sake, little mousekin. I hope you understand

'Indeed, we do,' said Ewan, bowing his head. 'And words cannot express our gratitude . . .'

'Then do not try to make them. It is merely wasted time. But come, we must have an introduction. You are Ewan, you say? And I am Wheviros, which is to say Whirlwind in your newfangled tongue. Now, what can I do to help you break this Spell?' And the underside of his body lit up along its whole length, hopefully, like live coals glowing in a fire.

Ewan explained about the oakmonsters and his need to release them from enchantment, and the dragon listened, the sheen on his jet-black scales growing duller as he did so.

'Well, well, little mousekin, that is all very well,' he said at the end. 'But what has all this to do with me?'

And now, Ewan thought to himself, comes the difficult part. How will his highness Whirlwind take this? Will he be flattered, amused, disbelieving, or will be blast us in fury with his red-hot breath?

'Well, you see, my lord,' he said cautiously (for he wanted to let Whirlwind work it out for himself), 'I need to go first to the giants' castle at Ironscale; then to Fourstrong for the Crown; and finally to Rooftree Forest. And these distances are vast. By the time I have travelled there, the spring will already be far advanced. And we are in urgent haste.'

Whirlwind whistled like a wind in the eaves. His carapace began to glow dark red again, like black coals heating in the furnace. His eyes shot yellow flame, and his breath began to smoulder. But instead of feeling insulted, he decided to register amusement.

'I see,' he said almost cheerfully. 'Never in all my thousands of years . . . Such impertinence! And from one so young!'

'My lord, it is with all the respect in the world', said Ewan, 'that we ask this. For there is none but yourself alone who can carry me so far and so fast.'

'Boy, boy,' groaned the dragon, 'do you think I am a ferry-boat?'

Goodness! thought Ewan to himself, so he has a sense of humour after all! And now he'll agree, and the battle is half won already!

Well, Whirlwind hummed and hawed, but Ewan could see that the notion amused him. 'All right, all right,' he said. 'You shall have your journey. But you'll have to strap yourself on, you know. Tight. And cover your face from the wind. And mind you don't start to complain once we're up in the clouds there. If you don't like it, it's by your own choice, remember.'

Ewan nodded.

'Well, then, back to the castle with you, and find something to harness yourself to my back with. Good leather straps should do the job.'

'Lord,' said Ewan gently, 'we have them with us already. See, here in my packsaddle.'

If a dragon's breath can be taken away, so was Whirlwind's now. He gasped, and the little rowan-tree ten yards away swayed dangerously. 'The impudence of these mortals! You mean to say you had worked all this out beforehand? Sun'sgift, it's beyond belief! Well, well, Earthquake always did say you had something about you.

Why, you treat me almost as if I were one of your own kind. It is almost a compliment. Not quite, of course, because only dragons are qualified to pay compliments.'

And so Ewan was saddled to the dragon's scaly neck, and whirled away into the grey and icy sky, muffling his face in warm furs against the piercing blast.

And the soldiers rode wonderingly back to Witshift Castle with Caperstaff the wizard, to relate to their fellows how they had seen Ewan raised up into the skies on the back of a jet-black dragon, calling and waving. And how the snow ten miles away on Greyscape Mountain was melted by the dragon's breath. And how the rowan-tree put forth red berries on the spot, in the dead of winter. And how the treetops of Capdale Forest had burst into flame as the dragon passed.

For soldiers always love to exaggerate.

CHAPTER FIFTEEN

Ironscale

The dragon's huge wings beat and beat like a coal-black wind – on and on, four hundred miles due east through ice-cold air that brought tears to Ewan's eyes, froze the fingers in his thick fur gloves, and tugged at him like an arctic current, struggling to tear him from the dragon's back. Seven thousand feet into the pale air soared Whirlwind, for he had the stony ramparts of the Forbidden Mountains to cross. And, with every hundred feet he rose, the air burned colder through Ewan's furs, and the breath gasped thinner and more rapid in his lungs. The whole of his new-won kingdom could be seen now spread out below him from the dark forest of Capdale in the north to the southern mountain chain of Icescar. And, in the deep and shadowed gorge under the lee of the forest, he could see the River Bane, running black under its precipitous wall of cliffs. They had come this way just seven months ago, he and his little troop of desperate men, winding through the forest towards Ashenfell. But then it had taken him two weeks to reach the first stone bridge across the river.

An hour and a half passed. There was a drip at the end of Ewan's nose that had frozen to an icicle and, despite his furs and the fiery warmth of the dragon's body between his knees, he was shaking in every limb with the bitter cold. His helmet too was lined with fur, but he still felt as if the very thoughts in his brain had turned to ice. They were turning south now towards Ironscale, the land to the north-east of the Forbidden Mountains, and below them lay the little River Headlong, straggling away to the west like a trickle of molten glass. Not far from here he and Catchfire had turned across the bridge and ridden on towards Midnight through the deserted landscape, where not a village, not a house stood – save for the giants' lonely stronghold, set upon a mountain peak. And there it was now, the one habitation in all this bleak wilderness, a square shape sitting on the mountain-crest like a little black dice upon an ice-floe.

Ewan fought to rouse himself from his cold stupor. He raised a gloved hand to shield his eyes from the rush and whistle of the wind, and peered down.

The black square on the peak was growing bigger and bigger with every beat of the dragon's powerful wings. And they were dropping now. Soon he was close enough to see the few stunted trees that stood scattered along the riverside, as if only half sketched by the pen of a hasty artist.

The giants' castle was crude but massive. It consisted merely of four walls with a tower at each corner, a drawbridge and, within, a vast keep like an outsize barn. Ewan knew that, from the giants' point of view, it was but three floors high; but to a normal man it had the scale of a fifteen-storey building. The whole rough fortress was built of tree-trunks laid one on top of the other or hammered like posts into the rock. And it reared up two hundred and fifty feet from the mountain's flat, bare summit.

The dragon sank to rest just outside the drawbridge, his paws raising barely a flurry of snow, so soft was his landing. His body of black obsidian veined with scarlet shone out upon the whiteness like a silhouette. And he was so warm after the flight that where his claws rested on the snow, it at once began to melt.

Ewan found he could hardly undo the straps of his harness. He tumbled from the dragon's back, and lay numbed upon the snow. Whirlwind stared at him coldly.

'Well, mousekin,' he whispered, 'I warned you it would be hard. I wonder how you human beings can survive the world's weather at all! But wait. Turn your face away.'

And he breathed over Ewan's cold body, hot air sighing from his throat like the blast from a red-hot oven. Ewan took off his fur coat and warmed himself in the heat.

'*Gwéryas, Whevira,*' he gasped, as the circulation came back into his frozen feet and hands – though the sensation was rather painful.

'Why, you are learning,' said the dragon impassively. 'That is my own language!'

'Well, a man should at least know how to say thank you. But it is almost all I know.'

'Good, shall we see if the giants are awake?'

'Yes. I see not a sign of life. Are they at home?'

'They must be,' said Whirlwind. 'With my eyes I can see a shrew twitch in the grass from five hundred feet. I could not miss such great lubberly clodhoppers as these. No, don't you understand? Don't you know what season of the year this is?'

'Why, early spring,' said Ewan.

'Still winter on the mountains here,' said the dragon. 'They hibernate, didn't you know?'

And as Ewan was silent, he added impatiently: 'They sleep all winter long. They are oak-trees, you know.'

'I see,' said Ewan slowly. 'Then what shall we do?' His heart sank. 'Is it possible to rouse them?'

'Not with *your* little voice,' said the dragon. 'No, no, I'll do it. What do you think the voice of spring is for, but to awaken the dead?'

Ewan thought of the gentle trumpet of the flowers. But the dragon's voice, when it came, was not gentle. He raised his long sharp muzzle – ten feet of sharp-fanged hunger – and roared, so that the castle shook, plumes of snow fluttered from its towers, and the whole mountain-top shuddered in the organ-note of his voice. 'Thighbarn! Bloatbrawn! You laggards, you layabeds! Up! Up and greet your visitors!'

The snow settled. Silence fell. From within the castle not an answering movement. The passing clouds cast gentle shadows on its ramparts.

'Shall I burn the gate down?' suggested Whirlwind.

'I'm afraid that might be impolite.'

'Hm,' grunted the dragon. 'They're not the politest of people themselves.'

'True,' said Ewan, remembering their narrow escape from the giants seven months before. 'But there must be some other way. Couldn't you fly up and look through the window first?'

'Hardly worth the trouble for a couple of boors like these. But very well.'

He sprang into the air, placed his forefeet on one turret and his back feet on another, tilted his head on one side, and lowered his great yellow eyes to peer in at the darkened window of the keep. Ewan waited in the snow, stamping his feet and clapping his hands together to keep warm.

'Cobwebs and spiders!' grumbled the dragon from two hundred feet above him. 'The floor knee-deep in rubbish. But no giants. Let's try another window.' And he shifted his stance, stepping with the delicate precision of a lizard – almost too fast for the eye to follow – from one tower to another.

'Aha!' he rasped. 'Found! Well, well, why didn't I notice that before?'

For now that their attention had been drawn to it, they could see that one of the towers at the castle's four corners was *snoring*. That is, it was vibrating gently, and a soft, almost inaudible growling sighed from its roots in the earth. R-r-r-r-r . . . dying away into a silence. A minute passed. And then came a sound like the soughing of a wind, rising in volume, becoming harsher, lasting at least two minutes, then dying away in its turn. The tower quivered again, but to a different note, and flakes of snow swirled gently from its battlements. Silence once more.

'They're asleep in there,' said the dragon with satisfaction. 'Well, they won't sleep for long.' And he opened his mouth, its two jaws snapping apart at almost one hundred and eighty degrees like a pair of scissors. And roared again. The wooden tower bent like a tree in a wind, and shook. But there was no response from inside.

'Will they wake?' asked Ewan in worried tones. 'After all, it isn't quite spring yet.'

'You are right, of course,' said the dragon from far above. 'But ach! The Spring is here now, looking in through the window at them.' And he dropped his great jaws open again and bellowed for a third time.

'A roaring spring,' smiled Ewan. And a spring of gales and splinters. For the window of the tower shattered under the pressure of Whirlwind's breath, blown clear across the room in a smash of breaking glass. The tower's snoring was cut off in mid-rumble and huge sounds of alarm came from within. There was a crashing and thumping like a pair of haycarts overturning. And a moon-sized face appeared at the empty window, blinking its great eyes owl-like in the thin blue daylight. On catching sight of the dragon, it shrank back immediately into the shadow of the tower room, its dismay comic for such an enormous creature. Good! They had roused the giants!

'You laggards, you sluggards, you layabeds!' rasped the dragon with infinite contempt. 'Up! Up with you! Slumbering the day away when you have friends come to see you!'

A grumbling and roaring came from inside the tower. Its walls shook again to the sound of heavy feet descending the stairs within. The gigantic face loomed into view again – but now much nearer – peering over the ramparts above them. A face the size of a wardrobe, and covered with an indescribable tangle of hair, green and matted like ivy on a church wall. Its owner pushed clumsily at it, trying to clear it away from his eyes and mouth. Evidently, in his long winter's sleep, the green hair that sprouted from his head and chin had grown like a bramble patch right across his face. He tugged at it now, ripping it apart like a man peering through under-growth, picking fragments of broken glass out of it as he did so, and brushing petulantly at the cobwebs that trailed from it. At last his great mouth came free, opening and shutting like a green wave.

'Nightshade!' he cursed loudly. Then stopped, clearing his throat with a sound that reminded Ewan of the sea withdrawing down a pebbly beach. 'Spoiling our beauty sleep! Lizard!' he swore at the dragon. And roared for his brother: 'Thighbarn! Stir your treestumps, it's a thumbkin and a lizard for the pot!'

Another great matted head appeared beside him, yawning like a forest cave. 'Quietly, brother, quietly,' it rumbled. 'I doubt there'll be no cooking today.'

The dragon's windy laughter sheared the air. 'Right, Bloatbrawn, look about you. And mind your manners – supposing that you've got any!'

'Aren't you going to give a friendly greeting to your visitors?' added Ewan, laying his hand on his sword. 'Your friends who've come all of four hundred miles to pass the time of day with you?'

'Well, Thighbarn,' said Bloatbrawn, peering over the battlements, 'maybe you're right after all. Isn't that our own little thumbkin down there?'

Thighbarn picked a huge spider out of his beard and dropped it over the wall. 'Didn't the Necromancer do for you, then?' he asked wonderingly 'How come you're still alive and talking?'

Inside, in the giants' barn-like living-room, the story was quickly told. How Catchfire and Ewan (with the help of a little luck) had defeated the Necromancer; how they had found the Crown; and how Ewan was now ruler of the land.

'So that,' hissed the dragon, 'even if I weren't here – but I am – you'd better mind your P's and Q's, you two! Or it'll be lightning from King Ewan – or fire from my own warm mouth.'

'Nay, friend,' grumbled Thighbarn with a ponderous attempt at injured innocence, 'what do you take us for? Peaceful folks like us? We wouldn't hurt a hair of your head, little thumbkin, would we now?' And he nudged his immense brother playfully, so that he nearly went sprawling off his ten-foot chair.

The giants were as huge as ancient oaktrees, each leg twenty feet in height and ten feet round the thigh. Their heads (when they stood upright) were fifty feet from the ground, and their eyes as big as meat dishes. Their skin was as rough as the bark of a tree, and their fists were knotted like boughs. The hair that sprouted from their faces was the green of forest leaves. And the clothes they wore looked too as if they had been manufactured out of bark – the bark of a dead tree that had lain in the forest all winter and was now thick with green mould from the damp. Great brown mushrooms sprouted from the folds of their jerkins and from under each armpit. Bloatbrawn plucked one from out of his right hand pocket, and threw it into the fireplace so that it squashed and burst. Plainly, they never undressed, and had been sleeping in their clothes all winter.

In the veins of oakmonsters, it is sap that runs, not blood. Their limbs were built out of a tough woody substance. Like deciduous trees, they slept all winter and in the spring returned slowly to life, beginning to grow again at the leisurely pace of oaks, and never sleeping all summer long, till the first chilly winds of autumn began to turn them drowsy again. They had had a rude awakening just now. But then, it was nearly spring once more; and their slow wits were stirring.

Thighbarn creased his great forehead, till it looked like corrugated bark. 'But where's our little missy?' he asked.

'Catchfire is a prisoner in Feydom,' said Ewan sombrely. And he explained, for the third time in two days, how things now stood. How they needed to break the Spell of Midriver. And how, for that, they needed to discover what the oakwitch might know.

'So,' he concluded, 'we have come to release your kinsfolk from enchantment – if you can promise us one thing.'

'Our kinsfolk,' boomed the giants in gentle wonder. 'Our wives and children. And you know how to free them?' Bloatbrawn got up and did a little dance, shuffling about so that the dust flew and his brother Thighbarn sneezed like a small volcano. Then they both roared with laughter, and cobwebs and rubbish fell from the rafters above their heads.

'But only,' repeated Ewan more loudly, 'on certain conditions.'

'Conditions?' mumbled Bloatbrawn. 'What conditions? We had conditions before from old Spinshade. Didn't care for 'em, did we, brother?'

'Ah, but these conditions are quite different,' said Ewan reassuringly. 'We simply want you to go back and live with your families at Rooftree – and not, mind you, not *ever* to bother human beings again. No interfering with the men who live around you, no stealing cattle or sheep, no eating people or trampling on buildings. Just a peaceful life, keeping yourselves to yourselves.'

But what will they eat? he wondered to himself. They can't live on air.

'Eating?' said Thighbarn. 'Why, that's no problem, little thumbkin. We'll eat what we used to, before old Spinshade brought us here.'

'That's right, brother,' agreed Bloatbrawn, 'there's no trees here, you see.' He fell silent, as if all was now clear.

Ewan looked faintly puzzled, but the dragon intervened. 'That's right,' he sighed coldly. 'I thought everyone knew. It is hard to remember how long fifty years seems to a human being. Why, they eat trees. They plant and cultivate them, usually the kind that grow fast and furious like fir and spruce. No problem there – provided you can keep them to their promise,' he added darkly, glaring at the two giants.

'Oh, we'll keep our promise,' roared the two brothers. 'Don't worry, we'll do as we're told.' They nodded their heads in unison like trees in a storm, and sat there as quiet as little children in their chairs, hands folded, backs straight up, feet together – though these 'children' were fifty feet high and the size of two small hills.

'Oh please, little thumbkin, do it for us. You can trust old Bloatbrawn, you can trust old Thighbarn. Only free our kinsfolk.'

Towards the end of the morning, the citizens of Clatterbridge were amazed to see, bursting high into the blue winter sky from a point forty miles south among the mountains, an immense plume

111

of black smoke. It rose billowing through the cold air, woodsparks sailing upwards amidst it as if from a colossal celebratory bonfire. Like a galleon moored among the snow-white peaks of Ironscale, tugging at the hawsers, its timbers cracking, its red and gold banners flying and its huge black mainsail tossing in the wind, Headsever Castle was burning.

CHAPTER SIXTEEN

Birthwood

es, this must be the spot.

It was the following morning. Thighbarn and Bloatbrawn had been on time at the rendezvous, for, though it was three hundred miles to the south, that is a mere day's march for a giant. Thighbarn had stood at the margin of the forest, waving a whole tree that he had plucked out of the ground, and had led them another ten miles up the wooded slopes of Icescar, crashing his way through the tall trees as easily as a man treading through bracken. The dragon hovered above, ready to land when they reached their goal. Ten miles and twenty minutes later, there was Bloatbrawn waiting too, on the brink of a steep chasm in the forest floor, a nervous expression on his usually stupid face.

'Merkelda,' he said: 'Deathwood' – his great voice hushed to a mumble by his awe of the place.

For, gazing about him as the dragon came noiselessly to rest at the edge of the gorge, Ewan could see that the trees above the cliff were all knotted and twisted into grotesque shapes as if by a pitiless wind – or as if they had all turned their backs on the gorge below them in the terror of that moment, fifty years before, when the necromancer had raised his staff and transformed the Oak-people into mere stubborn wood and sighing leaves. Every tree within a hundred yards of the cliff-edge crouched cowering away towards the forest, its branches reaching out in prayer or panic – as if each tree had held its hands over its averted face so as not to see the moment of the spell, and had stood frozen ever since in the selfsame posture of dread. Some lay bent and twisted, almost prone, as if seeking to crawl away from the enchanted valley. With some, the whole trunk had fallen flat on the earth, and only in recent years had the tree struggled to climb skywards again, so that now it looked like a figure lying terrified upon the ground, and

113

raising its arms in a prayer for mercy. The glade was a tableau of fear.

And yet . . . when Ewan peered over the brink of the cliff, casting his eye over the valley full of oaks below him, there was nothing frightening about the scene. Tranquillity. Stormcocks busy with their nests in the branches. And here and there among the whorls of twigs, the arching boughs, a touch of pale spring green. For here they were many miles south, and the valley, though high upon the slopes of Icescar, lay warm and sheltered behind its ramparts.

'A good time,' he murmured, 'for a wakening.'

The dale spread southwards for a mile or more. And it was full of oaks, some of them mere saplings, others immense, a few of them twice the height of Thighbarn and Bloatbrawn. Sheltered among cliffs and towering forest slopes, there was a frozen stillness in the air. A perfectly ordinary scene, but somehow Ewan felt that this silence was not a normal absence of sound, more like a curtain drawn across a distant breathless whispering. It was as if they waited among dreams that could not be overheard, but which thickened and filled the air. This was indeed the place they had sought.

'Do you recognise any of them?' he said in a hushed voice to the giants.

'Oh yes,' said Thighbarn, nodding. 'Oh yes, little thumbkin. Just over there, that's Stormbough. And who those little trees are I can't say. Just seedlings. But that big one up there on the slope, that's Mistlefoot, maybe. And the pretty one there,' he went on with a rush (though a giant's rush takes time), 'that must be Galesooth.'

'Yes, yes, that's Galesooth,' rumbled Bloatbrawn. 'What a slender little oaklet she is, to be sure, only five foot round the waist. And the biggest one of all' – he pointed away to a great oak that stood half a mile away, towering above the rest, and had several rotting boughs hanging from its massive trunk – 'that must be Thousandring.'

'Our sorceress, brother,' said Thighbarn, respectfully. 'The wisest and oldest of us all.'

Ewan pulled the buckles free from his knapsack, and drew out a parcel of linen packed with wool. Carefully, he unwrapped it. A circle of shining metal, fashioned into the shape of a walled town, battlemented, surmounted by three arches of gold, and topped with a wizard's tower. The ancient crown of the Two Kingdoms.

The giants gaped at the sight, and hid their eyes.

As for the dragon, his eyes blazed. The yellow light fell glowing on the grass at the cliff's edge. He licked his lips as if with longing, his tongue lapping over his great dagger-shaped teeth. But he held himself in check. Reluctantly.

'The magic of the earth,' he sighed. 'Gold and sapphires from the rocks. Rubies from the core of the mountain. Power, little mousekin, power. I warn you, you had better not fail.'

But Ewan knew this already. His hands were shaking as he placed the Crown upon the soft green turf. Fear, he reminded himself with clenched teeth, is futile. It gets in the way. He fought to remain cool.

Squatting on the ground, he put out his hands to the Crown. Would it resist him? Surely not; for once before, at the Necromancer's own castle, the Crown had crouched in the grass like this, like a small savage animal with its own will and its own demands. And it had not failed him then.

Ah! He could feel warmth surging from it, as from a tiny golden brazier. He shut his eyes and concentrated, recalling the ancient words written in the Necromancer's book – Catchfire had shown them to him – and with them the Spell that followed, recorded too in Spinshade's own spidery hand. It was as if he could see them now, incised in flame on the inside of his closed eyelids. He began to speak. The spell to awaken the silent trees of Deathwood.

> *Donum dona*
> *Auram mentis*
> *Venti aura*
>
> *Aurem dona*
> *Aurum terrae*
> *Aurae gemma*
> . . .
> *Nec folio vireant volitante*
> *Sed manibus humanis*
> *Neque volent avicelli vagantes*

> *Sed mentes volentes vigentes*
> *Aventes agantes*
> *Advenite! Resurgite!*

And then indeed the silence deepened, as Ewan had felt it should, into a pitch-black absence of awareness. It was as if his words had touched on a space that opened between the flickering seconds, so that strange inhuman voices whispering between and outside the passage of time could at last be sensed. And through that space between sound and silence, the life-will of the trees now passed. A chink in the curtain of time, but sufficient for a breath of air to slip through the momentary opening – a breath not only in branches, but in the roots as well. The boughs of the trees stirred, and their roots shifted in the earth – blown out of inner stillness into the outer world of movement. The birds among the branches suddenly all rose together with a clatter of wings, so that the air for a moment was full of beating tawny feathers. The valley was in motion, a cloud of wings, a mist of plumage, a haze of shivering. And a great shout came from the centre of the dale, half a mile away.

'*Amra!*' it pealed. '*Amra ausía! Maco mevarn, credharn!*'

(Day! Shining day! I can move and walk!)

The haze that had been birds was now a tangled mist of hair. The whole valley seemed to tip and right itself. The trees had taken a step, groaning as their limbs tugged free of the deep black earth below them.

And behold! No longer oak-trees but a threshing forest of giant forms, two-legged, two-armed, with matted heads of leaf-coloured hair and huge green deep-set eyes. And a mutter and a roar, like woodland in the grip of a storm. A surge of energy from beyond, which had beat for fifty years against a screen of silence, and now suddenly burst through out of darkness into a dazzling, terrifying daylight. The earth shook as they shifted and swung awakening from half a century of sleep or restless dreaming.

'*Mora, mora! Antios leukasa! Ku esti, taiasa skotos?*'

(Nightmare! The enemy of light! Where is he, the darkness of the world?)

'Speak to them quickly, mousekin!' hissed Whirlwind close in Ewan's ear. 'Or they will destroy you!'

116

Ewan, transfixed by the splendour of this sight – all the trees tossing together, in a whirl of bewilderment and anger, hundred-foot oak-trees transformed into living beings and swirling like a crowd in a square, but throughout the length and breadth of a valley two miles long – Ewan, trembling in every limb, but proud at the power of the Crown, stirred himself, cupped his hands about his lips. The roar of the forest oaks was deeper than the deepest tempest. It rang from the cliffs like a chant of trumpets – stones falling from the cliff-top; earth splitting away from the sides of the gorge and scattering like dust into the depths below. Ewan shouted. It was like the thin voice of a sea-bird crying above the waves.

'*Réwa, réwa!*' he called, in the few good words of the Old Tongue that he knew. '*Kalya, filya 'ti lipa!* Peace, peace! Health, friendship and long life!'

The hurricane calmed to a tempest. Down below him, a mother oak picked up her sapling from the forest floor, and cradled him in her arms, sighing gustily. 'Boughblow,' she wailed. 'Boughblow, my little son.'

Her little son was twenty feet tall and had muscles like a blacksmith.

But Thighbarn and Bloatbrawn had taken a hand. There they went, sprawling down the cliff edge, down into the throng of trees below them. Shaking hands and bellowing with pleasure. 'Mistlefoot, Stormbough! Oakwaist, Maybole, our wives, our wives! And Windsap, my daughter!'

'*Réwa, Menamenthôs, réwa!*' came a tired and patient voice from deep in the throng of tossing trees. The 150 foot oak that the giants had pointed out to Ewan, far away in the depths of the valley, now stood before them – a brown face, the lined and knotted brow of an ancient oak-tree, scarred by long years of battering by the gale; one huge arm only, for the other had died in the winter storms twenty years before; a skirt of leaves falling to the ground, sighing and whispering as she moved on limping aged feet to the foot of the cliff.

'*Kálya, druwikka,*' said Whirlwind, bowing his scaly head.

It was Thousandring, the Oakwitch, whose wisdom Ewan had come so far to seek, and in the hope of whose advice he had roused the trees.

117

For the dragons were older still. But Whirlwind sailed his in
different way through the clouds, careless of men and their fate
Till the Spell of the Gates had threatened the earth's health, he ha
needed no human magic. But the oak-trees – they were different
Men were their affair. A menace, an ever-present danger. And th
knowledge of life and death was not scorned by them, as it was by
the immortal dragon of the sky.

'Greetings, crown-bearer,' sighed the Oakwitch. 'Tell us you
name and how we may repay you. The gratitude of the trees,
promise you, is not a matter of a few years only. Speak. And if it i
possible . . .

'But first, tell me' – gazing askance into the mêlée, where th
voices of the two giants rose in noisy laughter – 'whatever mad
you bring those two ruffians with you?'

Ewan explained.

'Well, well,' she said, lifting her eyebrows like two moss-cla
archways, 'so even *they* have had their uses!'

CHAPTER SEVENTEEN

The Door to Darkness

Another day, another morning. And every new rising of the sun brought danger nearer to Catchfire. It was now the third day since Ewan had escaped from Snarewood. And only this morning Fetch had risen from his bed, to ride at a frantic gallop across the dusty plains of Feydom to threaten her with pain and death. But, were it not for Catchfire, said Ewan wrily to himself, I should make no more journeys on dragonback. It freezes the bones within you, slows the very blood in the heart.

Midnight. The place, not the time of day. For it was morning, and the Necromancer's castle stood there calmly in the thawing snow, a ring of darkness in the white. Eversnow above its battlements was deep in purple shadow. But the sun had come up on the mountains opposite, across the lake of Skydeep. And they were misty white, shining in the morning sunlight as if illuminated from within by the pure white light of eternity.

All very well for them, thought Ewan. They have seen millions of years go by, and the thought of passing time does not disturb them. The grass grows year after year, the heather blooms, the bracken flicks out its spores from a myriad tiny catapults. A little dust falls from the mountains to settle in the valley. And the river carries it away. The mountains shrink, shrink. But only by an inch in a thousand years. Whereas we human beings – what we might have done by midday is a grief by one o'clock.

But first, despite my urgent need, a word of thanks and a farewell.

'For, Whirlwind, shall I meet you again?'

'I shall bring you the news of Feydom's release – *if* you succeed. After that, who knows? I am carried forward blind into the future as you are yourself.' The dragon had been going to say more, but he clamped his jaws obstinately shut upon the words.

Ewan bowed his head, then said: 'I am infinitely grateful . . .'

'Tcha,' spat the dragon. 'The facts are infinitely grateful. Words spill into the air and are gone.'

'But the words of the Oakwitch have not spilt into the air. I know what must be done now.'

'*Wéresi*. You speak true. But a word of warning. That sword you carry at your waist – Donnavow, the granter of wishes – will enable you to perform the impossible. But when you have entered the darkness and returned from it, and when in the years to come you think – as you surely will – of performing the selfsame act again, question your motives deeply before you do so. For what you are about to do now is to repair the balance of the world, that equilibrium that was destroyed by the wizard Witfix when he closed the Gates against all magic, good or evil. You will merely be restoring the earth to her true path. We dragons have an ancient saying: *Swelos stati, taia mevti. Tó ankai amvôn*. Which means: "The sun stands still, the earth moves. That is the need of each for the other." To tamper with the processes of life and death is a dangerous matter. After this day, think twice before you seek to repeat this action.

'And mind you let no food that is not of the earth pass your lips in the land of darkness. Or you will never set eyes on Catchfire again. That was the Oakwitch's warning.'

'I shall remember. May I . . .' Ewan hesitated. 'May I call you my friend?'

'That,' said the dragon, showing all his teeth, 'is your affair. It depends upon your future actions.'

And with this parting shaft, he sprang into the air. Coiled steel muscles, a snatch and downbeat of the wings, a black bat's shadow huge over the ground, and he was gone.

Ewan drew his sword.

Before him reared the black castle of Midnight, grim in the morning sunlight. He advanced towards its arching gate. And, like a slender branch borne airwards on a stream that flowed invisibly towards the gate of the castle, the sword Giftwish tugged upward in his hand to point at the centre of the archway.

The heavy oaken door shimmered as in a heat-haze. And melted. Ewan saw beyond it, as if through a window cut in the air itself, not the fortress's dark interior but a land of forest and hills, stretching away under the morning sunlight into the far distance. No mountains, merely small hills and sand-dunes; and the treeless emptiness of the glens had been replaced by dense forest. Another country, perhaps even another time. He stepped forward as if to enter it.

But, remembering the careful instructions Thousandring had given him, he halted with his feet on the threshold of the archway. The keystone hung now directly above his head. The crude stone of the pillars reared up on either side of him. He forced the hilt of his sword downwards against the resistance of the blade, and drew it in a circle round him as if marking out the archway's shape in the air. From right to left, as if to split the stones of the arch away from the very air that clothed them, he cut an arc of light into space, peeling the rind of appearances from what lay behind.

Where the point of the shining blade had been, a circle of light stayed hanging in the air – a light like the track of a falling star but which darkened, darkened to a fiery red, to dense crimson, and then to black.

It was as if he had been standing in pitch darkness before a closed door, through which chinks of light from the next room could be seen – as if someone behind the door were pulling it ajar slowly, slowly, so that the chink of light opened like a wedge in the blackness. Only the colours were reversed. Here Ewan stood in the light of day. But the dark line he had traced out in the air around him widened, widened with immense slowness like a door sighing open on a pit of night. And the scene of hills and forest swung aside to his left as if it had been merely an illusion, painted on a wooden shutter. The door to darkness! It slid open to the left. And was gone.

Ewan stepped forwards into the night.

But the darkness which, by contrast with the dazzle of sunshine from outside the door, had seemed total, was not so – as he could see now, his pupils dilating against the gloom. He could see the dim shapes of trees all around him, with fruit (at this season of the year?) hanging from their boughs. And every fruit was a lamp of golden light, suspended there, growing from the branches of the trees.

Nor was there silence – a sound of music in the air, harps and kitharas; a woman's sweet voice singing; a murmur of cheerful conversation. Faint shapes were moving everywhere in the dark woodland about him, in a rustle of dresses and a hush of laughter. As Ewan's eyes grew accustomed to the light, he could see that the wood was alive with human figures, walking and conversing in whispers. Over to his left was a long wooden table set out on trestles, and piled with food. The figures sitting there held silver goblets in their hands, that glimmered in the gentle light from the trees. At the head of the table sat a woman in a long green robe, singing and accompanying herself on a kithara. And, as the song came to an end, the diners burst out into smiles and gentle applause. A mixture of the two tongues, the old and the new together.

Ewan now saw that the clothing of the whole company was leaf-coloured, the pale green of spring, or the darker hue of conifers, russet or autumn red and gold. Their dresses were all light and flimsy, and none wore a cloak; for though a moment before he had stepped out of the chill winds of March, here it was mild and warm, as if on a pleasant evening at the height of summer.

He hesitated, then advanced, sheathing his sword, towards the woodland table. As he did so, the figures about him parted like ghosts to let him pass. They were of all ages, white-haired men and women, young men and girls and little children that ran giggling about among the trees, playing tag, and squealing with the excitement of their game.

'You can't catch me, Talisman!' And a little boy of seven came swerving through the trees straight towards Ewan, ducked aside at the last moment, and fled into the bushes. Behind him came a girl of nine, pink in the face with running. She stumbled and almost fell as she reached Ewan: and he put out his hands to catch her. She felt light in his arms, like a doll of downy wool.

'Talisman?' he murmured, wonderingly.

The little girl stood there gazing at him from dark brown eyes. A flicker of pain or fear seemed to gleam in their depths for a moment, and was gone. Then she smiled, as if taking a decision, and confidently put her hand in his.

'Talisman! Talisman!' the children sang, hopping on one leg or darting out from behind the trees to tease her.

Talisman tossed her head like a young lady deciding she was much too old for childish pranks like these. 'Choose someone else!'

she called over her shoulder. 'Can't you see I'm busy? There's a new arrival. Come and see the Master. The Old White Beard, *I* call him!' she said confidingly to Ewan.

And, her hand clasped firmly in his, she led him towards the trestle-table groaning under its weight of food.

Ewan felt hungry the moment he saw it. Mushrooms, hazelnuts, good warm bread fresh from the oven, peaches, apricots and plums. And silver-green wine, cool and refreshing, standing ready poured in silver drinking-horns. But he remembered Thousandring's advice, and pushed away the hands that offered it.

'No, no,' he said, 'I have food of my own.' And he reached into his knapsack for a crust of bread from his own land of Kendark.

The hands were all about him, pressing food on him, holding out cups full of wine, urging him to sit down and share the meal. It hurt Ewan to reject these friendly gestures, but he smiled and shook his head. 'I thank you, I am grateful for your hospitality. But I need your help, for I have business that cannot wait.'

At this the woman beside him laughed aloud. 'Business that cannot wait?' she wondered. 'Why, *here* there is no such thing! Business? And haste? And need? It must be the first time I have heard such words – since –' But she shivered, and did not complete her sentence.

The young man beside her frowned at Ewan. 'What do you mean,' he asked, 'reminding us of such things? Still' – his brow clearing – 'you are new here, I know. Come and meet Almelkalar, Healer of All Ills, Master of the Land of Peace.'

But the Master was himself already advancing down the table, his hand outstretched in greeting. Immensely tall he was, and straight as a poplar tree, though the hair that fell about his shoulders and the long beard rippling down his chest, were both snow-white. His eyes shone a kindly blue at Ewan, and his grip on the lad's hand was as light and dry as a fallen leaf.

'*Kálya*,' he said. '*Dwénil gwentos ath Taiam Dakruántasa.*' And then, as he saw that Ewan did not understand, he translated, in the guttural accent of those who speak Gwaséna: 'Health. Welcome to the Land of Sorrow's End. Welcome to Ithanéquinath. May immortality be kind.'

CHAPTER EIGHTEEN

Ithanéquinath

'But will you not eat and drink with us? Come, I offer you a toast to the happiness that never ends. To the land of joy where pain and sorrow never come. To long release from all the griefs of living. We are glad to see you here among us, yet another such as we, whose heart may learn to heal its wounds as the fire of the sun is stilled for ever by this friendly darkness!'

And he held out a cup of wine to Ewan.

Ewan shook his head. 'No, I thank you,' he said. 'But I may not drink or touch your food, on pain of never returning to my own century. I come on a different errand, through the gate of time there.' And he pointed to the archway through which he had come. It stood there, a simple arch alone in the wood, encrusted with ivy as if the building to which it had once belonged had long ago fallen into ruin around it. In this world it contained no door between its columns, but had been blocked with rough stone, so that it looked like a blind gable-end.

'Through Time's Gate, *Menadhura*,' whispered the master with awe. 'But how is that? I thought the key had been lost – a century ago, as men count the days.'

'It was lost and has been found,' said Ewan.

'Well, it is a strange way to enter Ithanéquinath,' said the other. 'But no matter. Now you are here, what need to return? This is a land where joy never ceases, and where the centuries flick by like passing minutes. There is no sleep to slake our thirst for happiness. And none ever dies, though he may grow older if he wishes – until he is tired at last of pleasure, and longs to become one with the green forest and the blue sea.'

'Ithanéquinath,' said Ewan, gazing about him at the scene of quiet contentment spread out beneath the bright lantern-fruit of the trees. 'It is a tempting place to dream of.'

'It is no dream,' said Almelkalar softly. 'As you see. For if a man

124

dies before his time – or if, being old, he is yet too afraid to face the mysteries of that state that men call death – then he comes here to live for ever, or until the memory of pain and the desire of life are healed within him. For life and pain are bound together as the veins of the body are melded to the heart.

'So why not drink and eat? Who would wish to return to the world once they have seen the bliss of Ithanéquinath? Its name means, in the Old Tongue, "The land that is neither here nor there"; for here you are neither one with the buzzing whirring stream of sensation that is life, nor one with the depths of reality that lie within it. For a man who dies unprepared, with longing still in his heart, disturbs the equilibrium of things, and must enter this place of preparation till he reaches a deeper wisdom.'

A shadow of something like regret and pain passed then swiftly across Almelkalar's face. Struck by a sudden thought, Ewan asked: 'Then you yourself . . .?'

The old man bowed his white head. 'Yes, I myself.'

Almelkalar's sudden sadness was, Ewan knew, a warning. Nonetheless, the longer he stayed in this strange place, the worse his hunger became. The crust of earthly bread he had eaten but a minute before had done nothing to still the pangs of hunger that now began to gnaw away at his stomach. Oh to taste some of that delicious food that loaded the woodland table! And to slake his thirst! The tongue was dry in his mouth, and his throat rasped with pain as he struggled to continue.

'My errand,' he said desperately. 'I must not forget my errand. And indeed,' he added, taking courage from the old master's momentary doubt, 'it seems that the gods themselves bless my quest. For the very person I came here to seek ran straight into my arms before I had spent one minute in the place. Here and now,' he said, holding up Talisman's hand that still clutched his in its warm grasp. 'It is Talisman I come for.'

A look of agony came into the old man's eyes. He clutched at his heart as if it pained him. His voice was almost angry as he replied: 'You come here, bringing memories of fear and torment into the peaceful land of treelight. Why, Talisman, she . . . is the ancient victim of the wizard's spell. The little girl whose blood was shed to shut out the darkness of Kendark. What have you come for, trickster? To bring her more pain?'

125

'No, no,' said Ewan softly. 'Merely to take her back to a long life in the world. To undo the evil that was done so many years ago. To a life of . . . I swear to you, I shall do all in my power to make her happy.'

'Happy?' cried Almelkalar, as if it hurt his lips to speak the word. 'What happiness is there in the world – or out of it, save here? No, no, you shall not take Talisman away from us!' And he bent towards the little girl to take her hand.

'Talisman,' said Ewan, 'what do you say? For it is your decision.' He sat down on one of the rough chairs by the table, so that his eyes were on a level with hers. 'Listen, I shall explain things to you.'

'Would that I could prevent you,' said the old man bitterly. 'No violence may be done by treelight. But do not suppose you will get the better of this argument.'

'Come, Talisman,' said Ewan gently. 'Do you remember who you are?'

'Why yes,' said she, wide-eyed. 'A country far away – they call it Feydom, I think. And my father's little cottage by the sea. And my mother and sisters. White wings in the sky, black wings on the sea. And men – ah, men with spears . . .' She hid her eyes in fright.

Almelkalar made an impatient, hostile movement. 'You see what you have done? Your presence here reminds her of what is better not recalled. Come Talisman, leave this cruel man.'

The girl was sobbing now. 'Oh yes, I remember so much. The darkness of the tomb under the earth. The glitter of the sword. And oh . . .!'

She screamed. A single piercing scream.

The green-clad figures round the table shuddered away, and its wooden leaves, caught by someone's hasty movement, turned upside down on their trestles and spilled their contents over the grass. The people of the treelight shrank into the shadows of the glade and stayed there, gazing at the little trio by the table with the anxious shyness of wild animals. The songs and talk were silenced now, and the trees themselves seemed breathless with apprehension, listening, watching.

'Talisman my dear,' said Ewan, 'that is all past and gone. There will be no more terror. I have come to take you back to the world you left so long ago.'

The old man reached out his hand again for the girl's. But despite her fear she was clinging tight to Ewan's fingers.

'Talisman,' said Almelkalar, 'don't listen to him. You think you have been here only a hundred days. But a hundred days is as many years in the world. Your parents, your sisters are all dead, and their own children too. Even their grandchildren are near the grave. You will find no friends in the world, no relatives. You will be solitary and alone, a child cast out from her own time into another age.'

'No, that is not so,' said Ewan. 'I shall be your father. And Catchfire, princess of Ashenfell, she shall be your mother. I am the King of Kendark, and I offer you – whatever is in the power of the world to give. The sun, the bright spring flowers, change, life, and movement. The beautiful changeable earth with its summer and autumn, its heat and cold, its contending day and night. You will grow up, my dear, into a beautiful young woman, tall and straight. You will marry and have children of your own. You will grow older, sometimes be sad, sometimes be happy, knowing both sides of the coin – for there are two sides to know. You will age and look back on your life, and see your own grandchildren on your knee. There will be joy and sorrow, no doubt. Perhaps pain. But that is the way of life, and it is good to be a woman, and dance to the music of the years.'

'Don't listen to him, Talisman. He admits himself that all is not joyful in the world – disease, famine, wars and massacres, cruelty and disappointment, fear and despair.'

'I cannot answer those questions,' said Ewan. 'But that is how the world is made. And if one wishes to live and act, to seek and perhaps even to find, that is the world in which one's actions must move.'

Talisman had opened her lips and was saying: 'I want . . . I want . . .' with a sort of wonder at her own words.

'She is too young,' said Almelkalar with a kind of quiet rage. 'She remembers the past too well. And the power of life has still not been quenched in her heart. *Aî céreti*: she still desires.'

'Yes,' said Talisman, turning her deep brown gaze upon him. 'I still have all that living to do. I want to see the sun. And grow up to be a woman and have children of my own. And somehow I feel that this man is good and kind – and was intended to meet me here,

127

to lead me out of the dark. Why, somehow, when I first set eyes on him, I knew, I knew this was meant for me.'

'You have lost, Almelkalar,' said Ewan, almost with regret. His stomach was writhing in an anguish of hunger; he longed to slake his thirst. And he felt a terrible betraying pity for the old man. His grief was real, his horror at the world – in which so much evil happened – was perhaps good and right. Yet he himself still longed for it.

'Come,' said Almelkalar in one last desperate throw. 'You shall be king of this country after me, when I have chosen the inward path and say farewell at last to the treelight. You shall have joy and music, laughter and dancing. You shall be monarch of the world beyond the world. The eternal summer shall be yours as long as you care to taste it. And the ghosts of the dead shall bow the knee before you.'

'I am deeply sorry,' said Ewan, tears in his eyes, but gritting his teeth against them. 'I have tasks that await me in the world outside. There are people who depend on me, and I on them. And how shall I face the world that is to come if I have not lived and chosen, chosen and lived? And sought perhaps for a meaning to life.'

'There is no meaning to life,' said the Master in a voice of despair. 'Or, at least, you will find none there. Heaven is silent. The gods do not speak to man as once they did.'

'No matter,' said Ewan. 'For how may a man understand what a meaning is, unless he has learnt, by finding his meanings for himself, what it is to be and to mean? Or see the unseen if he does not know what it is *not* to know? I am sorry, Almelkalar. But I have promises to keep. There are those who love me and wait for me in the world of seasons. And who love and wait for you, Talisman. It is time to return.'

For the treelights dimmed as he spoke, and then swam up out of the darkness again, as if with restored vigour. One fell from its branch at Ewan's feet, and he could see it was wizened and soft, like a rotten fruit. And another swelled on the same branch and grew into a golden melon of light as he stood watching. He knew that, beyond time's gate, the sun had set and risen once more. It was already tomorrow, and they must be gone.

Almelkalar raised his hand sadly, but in a wordless blessing, as Ewan and Talisman turned their backs on the lighted grove. And the throng of ghosts and silent children parted with closed lips to let them pass, and hid their eyes. Ewan and Talisman stepped through the bricked-up doorway, which melted like a film before their feet and closed behind them in a silken whisper of darkness.

Bright day, and a bitter wind.

CHAPTER NINETEEN

The Star-Twins

Magic, as Catchfire had said long ago at Midnight, is always logical. The Spell at Midriver rested upon certain conditions, all of which had to be fulfilled for it to stay in being. The first was that the Necromancer's corpse lay still in its tomb. The second, that the ritual sword still pierced his heart. The third, that the necessary spells had been said. The fourth, that a child's blood was shed upon the tomb. Well, the spells had been said indeed; and nothing could unsay them now. Nor could the sword or the tomb be disturbed so long as Erebor guarded them. There was only one way left – to restore the murdered child to life. And that was impossible. And that was what Thousandring had known how to perform.

As Talisman stepped back into the world of time, she stumbled and fell to her knees. Her pale-green skirt, the colour of leaves in spring, swirled around her in the grass. She clutched both hands to her throat, her eyes drawn wide against a terrible darkness of fear or pain. She screamed, the shrill melodious cry of an animal knowing death.

And she fell, weeping bitterly, upon the ground.

Ewan knelt down, putting his arms around her and stroking her head to comfort her. 'There, there, it's all over, nothing horrible will ever happen again. We shall look after you, Catchfire and I. You need have no fear' (for, he thought to himself, it is the moment of sacrifice a hundred years ago – it is *that* she remembers). 'It is all so long ago now, and you're safe, quite safe with me.'

She gazed around her wildly. 'I thought they were here again. The torches, the sword at my throat.'

'No, no, the sun and the peaceful wind. The empty sky and the mountains. Those evil men are all dead these seventy years.'

Slowly, as he consoled her, Talisman's frightened sobs

quietened. Finally she stood up and, with one corner of her skirt, wiped the last tears from her eyes. Then brushed its green hem clean of the grass. 'I'm brave now,' she said. And, with a touch of returning cheekiness: 'Well, King of Kendark, is this your palace?'

'Hardly a palace,' admitted Ewan. 'But still, it belongs to me right enough. A little human food, I think. Would you care for some breakfast?'

And he hammered on the resounding wooden gate with the pommel of his sword.

Breakfast was more like dinner. For Ewan was ravenously hungry after his enforced starvation in the Land of Peace. As for Talisman, if the food of men gave no satisfaction in that other world, neither did the food of Ithanéquinath in this one. And, as she put it herself, eyes widening at the thought:

'Imagine! I haven't eaten for a hundred years!'

Ewan served her a third helping of mutton stew with his own hand.

At last Talisman said, leaning back with a sigh, and swinging her feet under the chair, 'Well, what do we do now? Is it all going to go on being as exciting as this?'

'Don't you think', said Ewan, looking at her quizzically, 'that you had enough excitement the last time you were in the world?'

'Ooh well,' Talisman said, though with a little shudder, 'that wasn't the right sort of excitement, was it?'

'No, I suppose it wasn't.'

'And you did promise me the right sort, didn't you?'

'Well, I thought, first a little rest. I'll get one of the maids to look after you. Heartstill would be best, she's as motherly as a hen with only one chick. She'll show you the ins and outs of the castle, and entertain you properly till I get back with Catchfire.'

'Well, I'm sure,' said Talisman with a little pout, 'old Heartstill is a *dear*. But what are *you* going to do?'

'Well, I,' said Ewan, caught off his guard, 'am going off to meet Catchfire. It's rather a long way, I'm afraid, right the other side of Kendark at least. But you know, it had never occurred to me before, but *if* the Spell of Midriver is well and truly broken, then I think I have a brilliant idea.'

'Oh, do tell me.'

'No,' said Ewan, looking at her carefully, and wishing he hadn't

131

spoken his thoughts aloud, 'I don't think I'd better do that. After all, I'm not at all sure it'll work.'

'Why not? It sounds interesting.'

'Well, it's rather a creepy place, I'm afraid. And I think you might be rather frightened. And it's certainly dangerous.'

'Oh, good.'

Ewan was beginning to wish that he'd bitten his tongue off rather than even hint at his plans. 'Look here, Talisman,' he said in his most practical voice, 'you really ought to take a little rest first, you know. Isn't it rather a shock, coming out of the Land of Peace, straight into this one? And with *your* memories? Why don't you just run around the castle for a while, stuff yourself full of good human food . . .'

'I don't want to be *fat*,' said Talisman.

'. . . and just get used to the real world again? Besides, the place I thought of going . . . I . . .' But Ewan had already made his big mistake, even voicing his thoughts in veiled terms. How could he explain to Talisman that the place he was going was the very place where her memories of terror belonged, and where they would be at once most piercingly aroused? He did not dare remind her of her fears. But by failing to be frank he had made her look forward to excitement. What was he to do?

'I'll send to Riversmeet for toys,' he suggested. 'They make fascinating things down there – dolls all of wood, with copper joints. You can make them walk and wave their arms, and their mouths move. I'll send Pluckspur this very day. You'll *love* the . . .'

'No, no, I want to come with you. I've grown out of dolls. I'm nine, you know. Actually, I'm a hundred and ten, but perhaps that doesn't count. Besides, you promised', she added ingeniously, 'that you would look after me. And I want to meet my new mother.'

Ewan froze in his chair. He felt guilty, protective and frightened for her, all three emotions together.

'I don't trust anyone else but you,' said Talisman, calculating little madam that she was. 'You just can't break your promise and leave me with other people *now*.'

'It'll be dangerous,' said Ewan, weakening.

'But I've been so bored. For so long.'

'Oh well,' said Ewan, trying to be firm but failing. '*On one con-*

dition, do you hear me, Talisman? That I learn before the day is out that the Spell really, really has been broken.'

But this line of defence was soon to fail him too. A little later, he and Talisman were out on the battlements surveying the mountains, while Ewan told her how the Necromancer had been defeated, when a tiny black speck could be seen in the western sky, approaching at immense speed. It was the dragon.

Coal-black as ever, but glowing now like a brazier with joy, hovering above them like a thundercloud, he spoke this enigmatic message:

'*Radiôs sweloio vulons danti; ôs warunoio taiam kusti.* The branches of the sun give forth their leaves; the mouth of heaven kisses the earth.'

Talisman, dwarfed in the dragon's huge black shadow, gaped upwards at him in mingled fear and awe. Yes, thought Ewan, giving her a sidelong glance, surely this is frightening enough to make her think twice.

'Do dragons love riddles too?' he cried to Whirlwind. 'But your meaning is clear. It is raining in Feydom.'

The dragon inclined his head. 'You have done – not badly for a mere human being,' he admitted with a touch of unwillingness. 'But who is this? Witfix's sacrificial victim, I think? Introduce me, mousekin.'

Talisman curtsied prettily, and told Whirlwind with bated breath that he was very big and very beautiful. And, then with a rush, that she had always wanted to meet a real dragon, and were there others about just like him?

'Nobody', said the dragon with a touch of pique, 'is just like me. I have scales of jasper and hematite, and talons of obsidian. Do you see?' He circled in the air slowly, and he and the little girl gazed at each other with frank admiration. 'She does not seem too much afraid,' he remarked to Ewan.

No, and that's just the trouble, thought Ewan ruefully. Aloud he said: 'She likes excitement, I'm afraid. And you, my lord, are an exciting experience.'

'*Kweti!*' said the dragon with some self-satisfaction. 'However, I cannot linger here in idle conversation. There is work to be done in Feydom. Reluctantly, I must bid you: *kalya 'ti kratya!*'

And he soared upwards with a sudden blow of the wings, so that

133

the cold air lurched sideways and nearly knocked Talisman off her
feet. Then he circled again, slanting his head down towards them
in a last farewell. 'Look after the little maid for me!' he cried, in his
lizard's rasping voice.

And he was gone, veering off like a great black bat through the
air towards the west. Dimly, behind him, a single word dropped
through the air:

'*Drakamítoi!*'

'What – what did he say?' asked Talisman, wrinkling up her
nose in puzzlement.

'I – I think it means "dragon-friends",' said Ewan reluctantly.
For how, after this, was he to stop Talisman from coming with
him? Flattered by the dragon's appreciation, thrilled by her own
fear, delighted at having overcome it, Talisman was ready for anything. Sighing, he glanced towards the foot of Eversnow, where a
pencil-stroke of black against the pure white of the mountainside
marked the tunnel's entrance. Well, he thought to himself, it looks
as if I shall have to take her with me. I only hope she doesn't
remember Midriver too clearly – and that my hunch about the
second door is right.

It was now the fourth morning since Catchfire had left for the
castle of Spylaw.

And what indeed of Catchfire?

Just a little earlier that same day, while Ewan and Talisman were
breakfasting in the tower of Midnight, there were Catchfire and
Threadseam riding post-haste through the lashing rain on their way
to the city of Midknow. They cut across country first, so as to
avoid the route by which Fetch might return. They would be ill-
advised to meet him on the road lest he shoot them down on the
spot before the witch-girl's magic had time to work. So, whereas
Fetch and his men had no doubt entered the city by its eastern
gate, the two girls rode in from the north.

Into a city of weary apprehension.

For, while there was some pretence at bustle at the gates – horses
being saddled, sergeants-at-arms handing out pikes and swords,
and a regiment of townsfolk being drilled in the use of arms in the
little square behind the outer gate – both horses and men looked
pitifully thin and weak. And their numbers were tiny – a mere

handful of thirty youngsters – all those strong enough to bear arms that could be found in this quarter of the city. An atmosphere of dread hung over the narrow streets, and the folk that watched from the windows were hollow-eyed and listless. The shops all had their shutters down – for there was nothing left to sell. And as Catchfire and her maid advanced further into the city, climbing its narrow winding alleys towards the palace, on three separate occasions they had to press themselves against the walls to let a funeral procession go by. It was a city of fear, full of the dread of present famine and imminent invasion.

In those far-off times, palaces were almost as freely open to the public as art galleries are today. Catchfire had drawn her hood down to her eyes, and muffled her face in her scarf, so that she might not be recognised. But there was no difficulty in entering King Dermot's palace, for there was always a throng of people going and coming, some on royal business, others with pleas and petitions for the King's ministers or for himself. So no one questioned the two girls as they mounted the steps between the carved lion and lamb that guarded each side of the balustrade.

And, once inside, Catchfire knew her way. She led Threadseam (muffled in her scarf too, lest Fetch's men should still be about) through a narrow corridor to the servants' quarters, then up a spiral stair to the royal suite four floors above. The princess's chamber.

Here, at last, guards challenged them. But as the two men stepped forward to ask their business Catchfire spoke to them softly, twisting her locket between her fingers:

'You cannot see me.'

'We cannot see you.'

'You think we are not here.'

'We think you are not here.'

'And that', said Catchfire with satisfaction, as she pushed open the door that gave entry to the princess's rooms, 'is the only proper way to make oneself invisible.'

To the bedroom of the Princess Starfall.

A turret-room that gazed out over the rainwashed plain and the unseen mountains far to the east. White curtains of rain outside the windows, white curtains of muslin within. For the princess's room was the hue of frost-bound snow, from its painted door to the curtains on the bed, from the tapestries on the walls to the sheepskin rugs on the floor. Only the slender outlines of flowers, daffodils and crocuses embroidered into the white silk, faintly gilded the room with colour; and the yellow glimmer of the candle burning always at her bedside, even by the light of day.

Catchfire bent tenderly over the pillow. The princess did not stir, though her eyes moved and gazed at Catchfire – but as if unseeing; as if there were no one behind the eyes who could look through them. And Starfall's skin was whiter, more transparent than her snowy counterpane. She lay there unmoving on her bed like a statue shaped out of glass. And, indeed, you could see the gold embroidery on the pillow under her head, misty and distorted like flowers seen through a crystal goblet. Only her eyes, now Catchfire looked into them with her own dark blue gaze, seemed to catch and reflect some of that gentian colour. And the flame of the candle could be seen mirrored deep within the crystal of her cheeks, as if it burned, not at her bedside, but in the princess's own slumbering mind. It was a strange sensation Catchfire felt, as if the figure on the bed were herself, as if she, Catchfire, were the princess's soul, returned in a dream to visit her sleeping body. She beckoned to her maid.

'Do you see, Threadseam?'

The little serving-maid approached the bed, then put one hand to her mouth, her eyes wide with awe. 'But . . . is she real? She looks like your reflection in the glass – or your own image fashioned out of crystal.'

'She is myself,' whispered Catchfire, 'and I am she. As I drew nearer Midknow, all the dusty way from Snarewood, she has been growing paler, less solid, more like an image of glass. She is my other self. And now both selves are here, to be joined in one.'

She drew back for a moment from the bed and put her finger to her lips. 'Hush, Threadseam. Say not a word. For the spell must act in silence.'

And, gazing fixedly at the transparent figure in the bed, she began to whisper softly in the language of witchcraft:

> *Quae tris glaciata fuisti . . .*
>
> *. . . Vitrum in glaciem*

Glaciem in aquam
Aquam in aera
Aera in animam

Then she bent over Starfall's motionless face again, and gently kissed her on the lips.

The crystal princess drew her white arms out from the sheets then, and with feathery lightness clasped Catchfire round the neck; she returned the kiss. And, as she did so, the glassy transparency of her body melted into a white mist, like the vapour that steams from a frosty field when the sun rises. Catchfire's slim figure began to shimmer and waver, as trees do above a hot field in the blaze of midsummer. For a moment the room was full of a cloud of dancing frost crystals, sparkling and shifting in the air. The light flickered and stabbed at Threadseam's eyes. She was dazzled, and shut them tight.

And when she opened them again, the bed was empty. There was only Catchfire there – but standing three paces away from where she had been, and facing in a different direction, laughing silently at her, her white teeth smiling, and somehow pinker in the cheeks than before, and with a warmer light glowing in her dark blue eyes. The glass princess was nowhere to be seen.

'But where?' breathed Threadseam.

'Me!' cried Catchfire, pirouetting with joy. 'Myself! We are one again! Complete!' And she did a little dance of delight up and down the room.

Threadseam fell to her knees, making the sign against evil. But Catchfire took her by the hand, and drew her up from the white carpet – and laughed at her. 'It's funny,' she said, 'magic usually is *tiring*. And I've done so much magic this morning. But I feel – rested, like after a good night's sleep. How do you explain that, then, Threadseam?'

'How do you explain anything? I . . . I don't understand. And you frighten me. If you can do that to *her* . . .'

'Now, Threadseam, no need to be scared. See.' And she pointed about the room at the hangings on the bed, at the curtains on the window. The frosty pallor of the hangings, the very image of Starfall's own transparent whiteness, was turning colour slowly, blushing to a gentle pink as if their life too had been restored to them.

137

'Starfall was simply', said Catchfire, 'a lost part of myself. You shall come with me to the King, and hear me explain it all to *him*.'

And she went to the princess's closet, and took out one of Starfall's dresses: gentian blue, the colour of her eyes, falling full to the ankles, and with a little chain of gold for a belt.

She checked first that the gold links were delicate enough; so that, when she wanted to, she could snap them between her fingers.

CHAPTER TWENTY

The Spell of Sundering

Though it was still close to midday, King Dermot's audience-chamber seemed sunk in twilight. It was a pale and rain-soaked sky that shone through the window, a mere sliver of grey-ness between the sable hangings that shrouded the curtains, the canopy over the royal throne, the heavy tapestries on the walls. For the Court was in permanent mourning for Starfall's sickness. The guards at the throne and by the doors were motionless as statues; only the three men in the centre of the room were in movement, the King flapping his hands ineffectually, Fetch pacing the room in angry impatience, Tatterbeg gesturing sternly as he spoke. But they too froze to the spot as Catchfire and Threadseam entered by the inner door. For a moment nothing stirred. A tableau of shock and bewilderment.

Then Fetch put his hand to his scabbard in a sudden ferocious impulse. But his sword was not within it. For all weapons are left beyond the door to the King's apartments.

'Ca ——!' began Tatterbeg, astounded. Then recollected himself. 'Starfall!'

'The impostor!' cried Fetch. But – how could she have escaped from Spylaw? He too paused in doubt.

The King's knuckles were sharp and white on the arms of his gilded throne. He had gone so pale that his lips were almost the colour of his blue robes. He opened his mouth to speak, but the breath was stuck tight in his throat and it was several seconds before he could make his voice work. 'Starfall?' he said. 'Starfall?'

Then the colour leapt back into his face. He hauled himself awk-wardly to his feet and came stumbling down the steps of the throne, so that Catchfire had almost to hold him up as he reached her, repeating his daughter's name over and over again. In a tone of disbelief, first. Then plaintively, mourning for his own past grief.

'Downright!' he cried to the nearest soldier. 'What are you

139

thinking of, man? Tear down those dismal black hangings from the walls!' Then his face crumpled, and the tears began to pour down his cheeks. Both he and Catchfire were weeping now and holding on to each other.

'This scene is very touching', said Fetch softly, 'but before Your Grace gives way to his very natural delight, hadn't he better check in the princess's own bedroom? And question the guards? After all, I told Your Grace about the impostor.'

'Your tone, Lord Fetch,' said Tatterbeg, equally softly, 'does little credit to you.'

But the King was laughing with joy and incredulity, though the tears still streamed down his face and ran into his beard. 'Yes, yes,' he cried, 'go and check, Stayfast. Though I know what you will find already! And Goodspeed, run to the mayor of the palace, and get him to ring the bells. Why, this is the happiest day that ever dawned in Feydom. Make those bells shout till they crack the palace roof! And call the people to thanksgiving at the temple of Sterros, king of the sky!

'Oh, my little wood-pigeon,' he said reproachfully to Catchfire, 'is it really you? How worried I was for you!'

In the long months of Starfall's enchanted sickness, the King's black beard had turned to a snowy white. Catchfire noted this with a stab of pity.

'Dear father. Of course it's me. Completely me.'

'But are you well, my linnet? You look – ah, the picture of health. But do you think . . .? You mustn't overtax your strength, you know.'

'Never better, father,' said Catchfire, laughing. 'Moreover I know . . . something of what has been going on during my nine months' "absence" from this palace.'

'Ah yes,' said the King, beginning to weep again. 'Why, we shall have a double celebration. Today a thanksgiving, tomorrow a wedding.'

Catchfire opened her mouth to speak. But at that moment the soldier returned at a run from the princess's suite. 'Your Grace,' he panted, falling to his knees before Dermot, 'it is all quite true. The guards saw no one enter, and the princess is no longer in her bed. Your Highness,' he said, kissing Catchfire's hand, 'may I dare to say how glad we are to see you back amongst us.'

Catchfire went among the guards, taking each one by the hand. Then she turned again to the King, who was still shaking his head in wonder and wiping his eyes.

'This matter of a wedding,' she began.

Fetch kneeled to the King in his turn. As an afterthought, he too kissed Catchfire's hand. For, whether she was the princess or not, it was the politic thing to do. 'Your Grace,' he said, 'I claim my destined bride. As Champion of Feydom, restorer of the Spell of the Gates . . .'

'Not so fast,' said Catchfire, raising her voice so commandingly that it seemed as if all the illumination in that rain-lit room was concentrated in her. 'I suppose *I* have some say in this matter, father?'

'Why yes, of course, little wood-pigeon,' stammered Dermot. He had never seen his daughter like this before – so regal, so determined. 'But on the other hand . . . the advantages of this match . . . Lord Fetch's noble ancestry . . . his fiefs and titles . . .'

'Father,' said Catchfire firmly, 'don't let yourself be taken in by appearances. I am the person this wedding concerns most closely, I'm sure you'll agree? And I say . . .'

She took one pace nearer to Fetch, and gripped in both hands the chain that encircled her waist. 'This promise was none of mine. And I say this wedding shall not take place. By the Spell of Sundering I swear *it shall never be. Vatur!'*

And she snapped the slender golden chain apart in her fingers, and handed it to her father.

Well, Fetch argued and shouted. Then he tried what pleading would do. Then he stamped and swore. Finally, turning upon the King, he threatened him:

'You will live to rue this day, I promise you. I command one half of your army. My family rules one half of your domains. Do not think you can lightly break your word to *me*.'

And with this he strode from the room like a black and white peacock.

'Good riddance,' said Catchfire smiling. 'And now, father, we have much talking to do, and little time to do it in. Somewhere private, I think.'

As they ascended the stairs to the princess's suite, Tatterbeg paused and drew Catchfire aside.

'It's as well you managed it yourself,' he whispered. 'I've been
here three days, but he wouldn't make up his mind. It was "Oh,
can't offend Fetch" and "Oh, I'll have to consult Hoodwill" and
"Oh, let's just wait and see, shall we?" Really, your father – he's
the most impossible man!'

'I know,' she nodded.

In the princess's own private drawing-room, that looked out over
her little rooftop garden fifty feet above the city's gables, Catchfire
related the whole story. How she and Starfall had been born at a
single moment sixteen years ago, as the star Cera shed its last ray
into the dawn. How Starfall's twin had been brought up by
peasants in the forest of Capdale, then adopted by Matchcurse,
witch of Ashenfell. How, in that brief moment when the Spell of
the Gates had been suspended, nine months before, Matchcurse
had drawn Starfall's soul out of her body – had drawn it on the
wind into Kendark, up the river, across the forest – and had
thought it washed apart by the rain. But Starfall's soul had flown to
unite with that of her sister Catchfire.

'For we are *Sterroyúmenai* – Star-Twins. Two babies born from a
single spark – the last throb of Cera's light as she faded into the
dawn, caught between the dark and light of earth, between the
glitter and eclipse of a star. Such children can learn to read each
other's minds and, throughout our childhood, we both of us caught
momentary glimpses of the other's life, the other's thoughts – like
being in two places at the same time, as that single particle of
Cera's light had been. I am Catchfire and Starfall, the fire caught
falling from a star – and hence my double name.'

The King sat silent for a long time when Catchfire finished her
tale. Then he shifted uneasily in his chair. 'Well, my little linnet, I
don't know what to say. I can hardly tell whether I believe you or
not. I should rather think this is some strange dream you have been
undergoing these last long months. But what matter? A few days'
rest and peace! We'll set the fountain going once more in your
garden here, feed you up a bit after your ordeal. Maybe, then, we'll
all be able to think a little more clearly. About Fetch, for instance.'

Catchfire pointed to the broken chain in the King's hand. 'That
promise is dead,' she said. 'Malediction on him who revives it.
Besides, I need no rest: I have never felt better in my life. And
there is much to do.'

The King listened, shaking his head, as she told him her plans. He hardly knew what to make of this new daughter who had been so suddenly restored to him from the dead: she was so certain of herself, so self-assured. And she had things so well worked out. He himself had never been good at making decisions. He had always left the running of his kingdom in his wizard's hands. For Hoodwill, he felt sure, was much better at ruling than he was himself. So he was left quite at a loss now. He didn't much like what Catchfire proposed. But on the other hand he couldn't think up any arguments to counter hers.

'Oh, I don't know,' he said at last. 'Why do you have to bother your pretty little head with all this . . . statemanship? *I* never have. Much better to drift along and leave everything in Hoodwill's capable grasp. He has the experience, you know. And I'm sure it'll all turn out right in the end. It always does.'

'Father,' said Catchfire, 'don't you realise your kingdom has been invaded? You will have to *do* something.'

'Well, I'm sure Hoodwill has things well under control. And I'm riding off to the war anyway, as soon as I can. Hm. Tomorrow maybe. Or better the day after. Just to be there, you know. Fetch will do all the fighting.

'Besides, what on earth is all this about marrying the King of Kendark – Ewan, or whatever his name is? The monarch of the land of darkness! Hoodwill says . . .'

'Father,' said Catchfire patiently, 'haven't you heard a single word I've been saying? It is the only way to save Feydom from the enemy. Only the magic of the Forbidden Kingdom can help you now. You had much better stop listening to Hoodwill, and try making up your own mind for a change.'

The King held his head in his hands. 'Well, well, we'll see. We'll sleep on it. I'll go along to the battle and see how things turn out. What do *you* think?' he asked, turning to Tatterbeg. 'Oh no, I forgot, you're on her side, of course.'

Well, thought Catchfire to herself, what do I do now? Use my magic locket to charm him? But exercising witchcraft on those you love is just a bit unfair, isn't it? No, first let's try another way.

'Dear father,' she said aloud, 'I must ride with you. Before we go, I shall cast the Spell of Healing on your lands. For the plague

must be checked. And I must be there at the final battle. For yo
will need my sorcery.'

And then, as the King looked at her incredulously, she rose
her feet. 'Don't you believe me? Look.'

Crossing to the window, she stood there for a moment to cor
centrate. Then lifted her voice, as in a song, chanting out the word
of a charm. As the spell died, she pointed one finger at the centr
of the roof-garden. The little fountain, dry in the midst of th
empty flower-beds, suddenly rose ten feet in the air, shining an
trilling like a silver bush full of finches.

'I hope you don't mind too much, father. After all, childre
never turn out quite as they're expected to.'

Dermot stared at the sight, his jaw dropping. Then he looke
slightly scared. 'All right, my darling, anything you tell me. I'
follow your advice . . .

'Though what Hoodwill will say . . .'

A discreet knock at the door. A servant stood there bowing
'Your Grace,' he said. 'A messenger from the Dark Kingdom. He
he demands to see the Princess.'

CHAPTER TWENTY-ONE

Interlude: Rain

It rained and rained for five days without pausing. Now that at last the reviving water from the sky had come, it seemed it would never stop. The furrows swelled into streams, the roads ran like rivers, and the rivers like inlets of the sea. There could be no setting out in such weather. For the wheels of the provision wagons would stick in the mire, and the horses themselves could hardly make their way along roads knee-deep in mud.

The only consolation was that it would be equally hard for the enemy. The forces of Kennaught too were bogged down, unable to move, caught on the southern side of the River Hale. As for crossing that river, that was quite out of the question. For the waters of the Hale were flowing again, past Midriver, past Otterbridge and west from Bourne towards the sea of Eventide. And they were in spate. It was said that all bridges between Bourne and the coast had been swept away. To ford such violent floodwater was hopeless. And the army of Kennaught lay now, scattered across the southern provinces of Feydom, unable to move either forward or back.

Catchfire, however, did not waste time. Ignoring her father's protests, she climbed to the top of Starhigh, the wizard's tower. There she turned his empty mirror to the wall, for she was half afraid it might suck her shadow too into its sinister gleaming depths. Five hundred feet above the city's roofs, she stood looking out across the drenching rains that swayed and steamed over the fields like a myriad pouring faucets. And she performed the Spell of Healing, to ward off plague from the realm.

The sixth day dawned bright and clear, and the spring sun began to warm the sodden land. Another two days, and the roads became passable again. But now they must hurry, for if the army of Feydom could be on its way then so could that of Kennaught. On the ninth morning, therefore, a little troop of soldiers set out from

Midknow for the east – a hundred horsemen and two hundred infantry called in from all the surrounding region. At their head rode Catchfire, King Dermot, Ewan . . . and Talisman on a little white pony.

As they set off into the morning sunshine, surrounded by a bronze glitter of spears and shields, Talisman's cheeks were flushed with pleasure. 'This *is* fun!' she said.

For Ewan's guess had been right. On the afternoon of the dragon's message – once he had learned that the rain had returned to Feydom, and that the Spell was broken – he had taken Pluckspur and Talisman with him and entered for a second time the dark tunnel that ran into the side of Eversnow. A hundred and one steps to the stone slab. Once again it faded into mist before the pointing blade of Giftwish; and once again they stepped into Erebor's gloomy den.

The moment they were in, Ewan turned on his heel and sought the door with the point of his sword a second time. For he felt a nagging fear that something might still be wrong – despite the breaking of the Spell, was it not just possible that the door would stay tight shut as it had done before? And that . . .?

But no. With a sigh of relief he saw that all was well indeed: the slab melted again before Giftwish; the way back was clear and open; their retreat was secure, if they needed it.

And now for his guess! What had the door had inscribed across its lintel? *Ath trismiam yugoio*: to the three-in-one of joining. And indeed here was the second door, a mirror image of the first, but standing ten yards up the passage from it. Giftwish tugged obediently upwards once again; the stone slab faded as the first had done; and they stepped across its invisible threshold into a third stone corridor drilled into the heart of the rock.

This time no unpleasant surprises lay in wait for them. For yes! Ewan's intuition had served him well. Long, long ago, while the Two Kingdoms were still one, both ruled from Midriver by the line of Varos, the High Wizards of the land had carved out of the granite these magic passages that somehow, twisting and turning in the darkness, slipped in and out of some otherworldly dimension of space, and formed a link between the land's three capitals. So that, with the bronze key in their hand, the Kings of Kendark and

Feydom could step across the barrier of 600 miles as easily as one can tread across a threshold, and pass in the twinkling of an eye from Midnight in the east to Midknow in the west.

The tunnel came out at the foot of Starhigh, the wizard's tower that stood at the heart of Midknow.

And that was why, when Catchfire and Dermot called the ambassador of Kendark to the princess's roof-garden – and when the ambassador came – they found to their amazement that it was Ewan himself, with Pluckspur on his left, and Talisman clutching his right hand, pleased as punch with herself and with her new parents.

Catchfire and Ewan hugged each other, and walked out into the roof-garden in the pouring rain to talk to one another for a long time.

'Oh, Ewan, Ewan! I never thought to see you again in this world!'

'Now why ever was that?' asked Ewan in surprise. 'For it really turned out to be quite easy – at least, it seems easy now!'

'Ah, but you see, we gazed in the crystal ball to look for you. Only last night. And you were nowhere to be seen.' And Catchfire explained how this was a sure sign that the sought-for person was not to be found – that he was no longer living, no longer in this world.

Ewan felt the hair rise at the nape of his neck; a chill ran through him. It was strange: he had hardly thought of it at the time. But of course it all made sense: the explanation was obvious enough. 'Last night, you say? No longer in the world? Yes, yes, that is easily explained.'

'Is it? I don't understand. I was afraid for you, Ewan, terribly afraid. Why couldn't I see you?' cried Catchfire, her eyes dark with the memory of those hours when she had thought him dead.

'Well, I can hardly believe it myself. Do you realise who that little girl is? Talisman? She is the victim of the sacrifice a hundred years ago. Her throat was cut by the wizard Witfix over the Necromancer's tomb when he sealed the Spell, with her blood soaking into the dark red clay. No wonder you searched in the crystal ball and could not find me. For indeed at that moment I was in the land of the dead – I had gone to fetch Talisman.'

And he related it all: the skydragon Whirlwind, their journey to

147

Rooftree Forest, the secret told him by the Oakwitch, and his entry to Ithanéquinath. He and Catchfire stood there oblivious of the rain wetting their hair, running down their faces, drenching their clothes, as Ewan told his tale.

But Talisman was getting impatient.

'You'll get yourselves soaking wet,' she shrilled reprovingly, peeping out through the door into the garden. 'And you'll catch the ague, and then what shall I do for parents? Or rather, for a sister and brother,' she added. For it was true: they were only seven years older than she was herself.

Ewan and Catchfire laughed, and walked back into the shelter of the drawing-room.

There was not much resistance from Dermot after that. For to tell the truth his daughter had always been able to twist him round her little finger, even before. But now she had such a regal way with her, how could he deny her anything? Besides, he was very much taken with Talisman. Yes, in return for Ewan's help against the invader, he would be betrothed to Starfall and become heir to the Kingdom of Feydom.

'That is, provided Hoodwill has no objection,' added the King, shaking his head sadly. 'For what he will say to all this, I really don't know. I hope you think you can persuade him.

'Anyway,' he said, 'we'll just leave it in *his* hands, shall we? I mean, we don't have to decide now, do we?'

'Yes, we do, father,' said Catchfire, her eyes flashing.

So Dermot agreed. But it was obvious that, if he were given half a chance, he would change his mind at the drop of a word from the wizard. He would have to be watched. And so would Hoodwill.

Then Ewan was reunited with his mother, who was indeed safe and sound in Midknow, just as Dermot's envoy had assured them, it seemed like months before. She was moved, however, to a more comfortable room in the royal suite, where she had a fine view over the northern plains towards her own little home of Moorskiff.

'There you are,' she told Ewan proudly. 'Everything has turned out *so* well, and I hear you're quite an important person in Kendark these days. Didn't I always tell you there was nothing to worry about?'

'Well, you were right, mother,' said Ewan. 'As you always are.'

'Your poor dear father would be so proud!' And then confidingly: 'But isn't His Majesty a charming man? Not very practical, of course, but every inch a king!'

As for the Mole Erebor, Ewan and Catchfire debated whether they should call up the she-dragon to destroy it. For it might go hunting human flesh again at any time. But Catchfire said:

'As long as Erebor is there in its den, at least Hoodwill can't play any tricks. Now that you've opened the Gates, Ewan, from outside, as it were, Erebor acts as a lock to ensure that they stay open. Just as it acted as a lock before, to ensure that they stayed shut. I think we had better leave the monster alone for the moment,'

'Yes,' agreed Ewan reluctantly. 'At least till we've settled things with Hoodwill. Persuaded him that the Gates must remain open.'

'If persuasion is possible,' said Catchfire grimly.

And now, as Ewan, Catchfire and Talisman set out upon the road to Hemdark, let us leave them for a moment to see how things stand in the war against Kennaught. Well, the best way to spy out the land – if Whirlwind will be so kind – is to fly on dragonback again. For we need a vantage-point high in the windy air above the plains, so that we may survey the path of the invasion, and see how things fare with Dermot's ragged, starving army.

Between Bourne in the east and Sealholt in the west, there is no bridge left standing. And this is just as well, for the King of Kennaught has gathered a huge army. Seven thousand men lie waiting south of Rooftree Forest, waiting for the roads to become passable again. And to their left, almost the whole of Feydom south of the river is in their hands. Nine thousand more troops lie scattered about the countryside. There is hardly a town between Sealholt and Threshold that has not fallen into their hands. For the people of Feydom are almost too weak to fight; and in places the ground is of clay, and has shrunk and split open in last summer's terrible drought; so that the city walls are breached, and their towers tumbled to the ground. Nor can the Feylanders repair them, being too faint with starvation. There is no food to be found in the towns and villages, so that an army cannot move unless (like that of Kennaught) it brings its own supplies with it. Except on the borders of Hemdark, where the crops still grew last year.

Wait till the Kennaughters repair the bridges! Then north to

Midknow! And the land will be theirs!

And, as the rainclouds pass, they are on the march again. You can see the campfires being damped down south of Rooftree, and the horses being saddled. The tents are folded away and packed into the baggage train. The soldiers form into ranks. Seven thousand men, in a long broad column of crimson livery, march out along the road to Bourne. There stands the one surviving bridge across the Hale. And from there they may strike north-west towards Midknow, the heart of Feydom. Their spear points are thick as corn spikes in the morning sunlight, and even from high in the air above them you can hear the rumble of the wagon wheels. Their battalions snake through the land like a crimson dragon, horses, baggage train and all, four miles long, with a cavalcade of black-plumed cavalry riding up ahead and a rearguard of warriors in yellow, who ride bareback and wear bright paint on their faces like the men of the Frore.

Not that they fear attack. For who, in this blighted land, has the strength or the will to oppose them?

As for King Dermot's army, it is a mere fifteen hundred men. Of these, a half had been occupied in Hemdark and on its borders. This was Fetch's army, and he drew it south towards Bourne, to defend the bridge across the Hale. Then there are the men of Bourne itself, including stragglers and refugees who have been trickling in from the south, running from the invaders.

Meanwhile Ewan and his friends marched to Snarewood. There Catchfire stood in the stirrups, her slim arms in the air. And she spoke the spell of illusion's ending, the same that Hoodwill had uttered against her but two weeks before:

> *Dik-tvam, maïa! Prován tínam mórcam wéram!*

And the wood turned slowly to stone.

It was just a little round wood like a beehive, almost leafless, except that here and there around its rim a cone-topped pine-tree jutted out dark and green. At the centre, a honeycomb of boughs, a huddle of modest, hump-backed trees with, in their midst, a gigantic oak that marked where the geometric centre of the wood should be. As they had noticed before, it all seemed abnormally circular, like a plantation rather than a natural growth. Yet this was not the reason. It was a perfect circle because it was an illusion powered from its centre by the invisible tower of the keep. As if a darkness, a swirling force of deception spun from that central round tower, bending the very light in the air like water gyrating in a whirlpool.

But now the whole wood flinched and flickered in the windy air, like a candle guttering in its saucer. It swithered between castle and wood as if it could not decide which it should properly be. And they could see that it was indeed a phantasm. For as it pulsed to and fro between angular towers and rounded tree-tops, each a faithful distortion of the other, it could be seen that the trees were like shadows cast from within upon an invisible sphere of air, and rounded by its curvature. As the force of the ancient enchantment dimmed and diminished, quailing inwards upon itself, the encircling outer wall emerged from the grip of the illusion. The sharp-pointed pine-trees all turned to turrets capped with dark green tiles, shining in the sun. The thin grey fretwork of the boughs filled out into battlements of stone. And there, it seemed for a moment, was an innocent little wood surrounded – absurdly – by a rampart, by machicolations, by defensive towers.

Then the whole mirage shimmered up in a dazzle like a flame dying, and was snuffed out. All that remained was a sullen castle, scowling and squat among the fields, a little grey and peevish at having its disguise spirited away so suddenly. Only one curious detail was left as a reminder that it once had been a wood. A roughness on the walls like a rind of petrified bark. Or was it the stone itself, pitted, flaking in the wind?

So the mask of Snarewood was torn away, and it became the castle of two weeks ago.

Catchfire raised her arms again, blazing in the spring sunlight like an X of scarlet:

'*Eti men, ithil gel! Aïnec meril tâ!* And remain, and freeze thus! And melt no more!'

The Marchmen were still safe in prison. They were released, and the garrison was emptied of its men. 'Go and seek the King at Bourne,' said Ewan. 'For Feydom has need of you.'

Then on with a tiny escort to Tetherdown. Slashbuckle greeted them with joy. For the horsemen of Frore had arrived. But . . .

'No,' said Ewan. 'I need you all at Bourne. For Hoodwill is over-thrown, or he will be before long. Leave enough soldiers here for the defence of Hemdark. But you are liegemen of Kendark from now on – or else free men. As you wish.'

'Sire,' said Slashbuckle, smiling, 'since you give us the choice, we will be free and your subjects too.'

There Caperstaff and the archers of Capdale joined them. And they marched on south along the river.

Three days later, under a thin drizzle, they crossed the bridge and entered by the northern gate of Bourne. To the south, in a vast half-moon around the city, the enemy held the heights, spears standing out against the sky like a forest of giant thorns. It was as if some god with a red paint-brush had drawn a thick line across the profile of the hills, to split off the green of the grass from the blue of the sky, a line thirty soldiers deep, and the colour of congealing blood.

CHAPTER TWENTY-TWO

The Battle of Bourne

'I am not looking forward to this meeting,' said Ewan. 'The command of the army has been given to me. But I doubt if Hoodwill and Fetch will accept that. Will they even agree to fight alongside of us?'

'Well, we shall see,' said Catchfire. 'But we shall go well guarded. And I should keep my hand on my sword, if I were you.'

But, when they met that evening to discuss their plan of campaign, all was suspiciously easy. Hoodwill and Fetch shook Ewan's hand and welcomed him; apologised for the 'unfortunate misunderstanding' at Snarewood; expressed gratitude for his help; and settled down to hear his proposals without a hint of protest. Catchfire glanced at King Dermot out of the corner of her eye. He had been there before them (for he had taken the direct route to Bourne). Had he managed to persuade them? If so, it was the first time in his life that he had overruled his advisors.

'And what about the Gates, Hoodwill?' she asked. 'They are open now. Are you content that they should remain open?'

'Well, well,' said Hoodwill evasively, 'it seems that till this battle is over, we shall need some of your dark sorcery. Afterwards, of course, the situation may well change. We shall have to see. Of course,' he said with a thin smile, 'I am always open to persuasion.'

'One cannot speak fairer than that,' echoed Fetch. But the glance he shot at the wizard made Catchfire feel that he did not agree with him – that he had, perhaps, other plans. We must be careful, she thought to herself. This story is far from over yet.

'But tell me, as one magician to another,' went on Hoodwill, 'how did you manage to do it? You can't have got past Erebor . . .'

There was almost a note of pride in his voice, thought Catchfire. Strange. A thing worth storing in her memory to think about later. She answered, 'No, we didn't,' then checked herself, grateful that

Talisman was safe in bed at Bourne, and not here to blurt out the truth herself. 'I'm afraid,' she said carefully, 'that will have to remain our secret.'

'What a pity,' said Hoodwill pleasantly. 'New forms of magic are always so *interesting*. I must admit I am very curious to know more about it.'

She would lock Talisman's room with a spell, thought Catchfire. There was an undertone of irony in Hoodwill's voice that made her wonder if he had guessed more than he pretended.

But Ewan broke in upon her thoughts. 'This is all very well,' he said. 'But we have pressing business to discuss. If you are agreeable . . .'

Fetch and Hoodwill bowed politely.

'. . . let us turn to tomorrow's battle. Now here is what I propose.'

And he outlined his plans for the morrow. Fetch and Hoodwill listened in silence, only occasionally asking a question, or nodding their heads in assent. 'The enemy', said Ewan, 'have seven thousand men, nearly three times our number in the field. Besides, they have the advantage of higher ground. To tell the truth, our position would be hopeless – except that I plan a little surprise for them. Once they are on the move against us, their wings and rear will be vulnerable to attack. And when they have committed all their troops against our little army, then my reinforcements will come into action.'

'Your reinforcements?' said Fetch. 'And where might they be hiding?'

'In the margins of Rooftree Forest,' Ewan said. 'Off to the enemy's right.'

'Are they a large enough force? How many men exactly?'

'Well, that, I shall not say. But I can assure you they will prove sufficient.'

'But do the enemy know about them?' said Fetch. 'For in matters like these, surprise is all-important.'

'Oh, I think the secret has been well kept.'

'One thing worries me,' said Fetch. 'How do you propose to get into position before the enemy attack us? *We*, after all, are encamped on the plain below the hills. They will see us moving, and will take advantage of that to destroy us.'

'That is no problem,' said Ewan. 'We shall move under cover of darkness, the moment this conference is over. Besides,' he added enigmatically, 'it will be misty tonight.' And he touched the ring upon his left hand.

The leaders of the army separated, to set about marshalling their troops. Fetch's eye caught Catchfire's, and he drew himself up, flicking a speck of dust from the white lace at his cuff, preening himself like a cock strutting in a barnyard.

'I am *delighted*, Highness,' he said, 'by the aptness of your choice.' And his blue eyes looked as vicious as a pair of daggers as he added: 'I did not know that princesses had such a taste for peasants.'

He turned on his heel and left the room. Yes indeed, thought Catchfire, we shall have to be very watchful. Pensively, she too turned to leave, but reached the door of the tent at the same moment as Hoodwill.

'By the way,' said the wizard with deliberate casualness, standing aside to let her pass first, 'why ever did you bring that little girl with you? Talisman, isn't she called?'

'She has to come back to Kendark with us, you see,' said Catchfire evasively. And she felt more worried than ever.

Hoodwill was about to follow up this question with another, but she stepped in hastily to change the subject. 'Come to that,' she said, adopting her very sweetest voice, 'I have a question for you too. What do you know about Erebor? You do realise, don't you, that it can't have come from Kendark while the Gates were shut. And really, it was very useful to you, wasn't it? While the Spell still lasted, I mean.'

Hoodwill smiled at her coldly. 'Whatever are you suggesting?' he wondered. 'That *I* have something to do with it? The Gates were *not* shut. The monster *is* from Kendark. And that is that.'

'That isn't true,' said Catchfire, 'and you know it. And it's rather a nasty creature, isn't it? Why, Slashbuckle told us all about Erebor. He'd seen the thing happen!' She shuddered. 'It sucks out the bones of men from below the ground. Ugh! I don't like to think of it. Your own messenger too.'

Hoodwill for some reason suddenly became angry. His grey eyes flickered with a sharp cold light, and he almost spat: 'It is a creature of night, a spawn of the kingdom of evil, a shadow. What are you accusing me of? I – I have no darkness in me! It has nothing to do with the Wizard of Light!'

He pushed his way out of the tent ahead of her, into the darkness of the night.

Ah, thought Catchfire gazing after him, a great light of under-standing dawning in her. According to Hoodwill, a man is not re-sponsible for his own shadow, isn't he!

By dawn on the following morning, Ewan's army was in position. He had chosen rising ground half-way between the city and the hills that overlooked it to the south and were occupied by the Kennaught men. It would seem to the enemy a poor position to fight in, for they had the advantage of the slope, and their impetus would carry them with crushing force into the Feylander ranks. And, indeed, this was part of Ewan's plan. A frantic charge by the Kennaughters, a rush to overwhelm Feydom at the first onslaught – and they would be in confusion, ready for the ambush to be sprung. Besides, his wizards would be able to hold off the enemy, at least for a longish breathing space. No, Ewan did not falter as he gazed out into the mist – rising now from the ground and fading into the grey light of dawn – and caught his first sight of the enemy ranks massing on the hilltop eight hundred yards away.

For they too were ready. They could hardly overlook the clatter of weapons and jingle of harnesses that sounded through the fogbound night below them, as Ewan moved his men into position. They had hastily crawled from their tents and formed into battalions on the hillcrest, ready for the grey wind of dawn to carry the mist away. And now seven thousand men faced Ewan's troops from the summit of the hill.

The cavalry first. One good charge.

From somewhere within the dark crimson mass of the Kennaughters, a trumpet sounded. Then ten more all together, neighing like war-horses. Then the ground began to tremble.

It was all that could be perceived at first; just a trembling of the ground that could be felt rather than heard. And it seemed as if the black plumes on the helmets of the horsemen ahead of them were shaking a little more wildly in the breeze. But gradually they drew closer; the plumes bobbed and rippled; the horses and their riders were growing bigger as they filled out more of the grassy space between the two armies.

Ewan's men fitted their pikes into the ground at an angle of thirty degrees, each man digging his own little hollow in the grass to hold fast the butt of the pike. They stood in four ranks, ready to lean against the pole and steady it with their own weight as the brutal shock of each ten-stone rider, each hundred-stone charger, hit them. Four lines of pikes like the spines of a hedgehog, curled and sprung against the foe.

But to tell the truth this was but a practice run. Caperstaff (who last night had taken on board an immense quantity of mead and beef stew – 'to make sure I have enough strength for my own magic,' he had said) had been busy already raising his staff and singing out a charm:

'Give me a gift, true light, of truest light . . .' (Only the words, of course, were not in the modern tongue, but in Sorcerish, language of spells.)

So when, all along the left wing of the army – where Ewan and the men of Kendark stood – the charge struck home . . .

There was a singing of glass in the air, a series of cracks like a gladeful of boughs breaking; and the long line of horsemen bearing down upon them seemed to spring into the air and hover there for a moment, like crimson bats on the wing.

It is all very hard to describe. You must understand that the cavalry of Kennaught were advancing at a frantic pace, but all seen from the front, so that they looked to each man of the army facing them like two-headed horses ten feet high, and seemed to be capering rather than galloping, expanding rather than approaching. The upper head was a long-jowled helmet with a plume for a mane. The lower one was the horse's head, clad too in bronze, and leaning at an angle as its master spurred it forward. And only its two front legs could be seen, bowing and flexing, bowing and flexing, as it danced itself bigger every minute.

A two-headed, two-legged centaur, prancing – growing like fear as it charges out of the dawn.

Then leaping in the air and falling into space. Hands out. Sabre curving away into its own independent orbit. A tableau like time at a halt, a man with his arms and legs kicking, helpless as a swastika without its flag, swimming like a wingless fly in the zigzag air.

A crashing and tinkling as the glass gives way.

For Caperstaff had raised, in the path of the charging cavalry, a wall of wizard-glass – invisible but solid, twenty feet high in the air. And into this barrier the first line of the Kennaught assault had crashed.

But a spell will serve only once. And Caperstaff was busy with his wizard's wand again:

> *Donum dona,*
> *Aqua vera,*
> *Veram aquam . . .*

For already the second and third lines of riders were upon them. Many horses had gone down, tripping over the struggling bodies of men and steeds below them, stunned by the wall of glass. But the second line of cavalry hit them with a violent shock.

'*Now!*' cried Ewan into the tumult: 'Hold them. The time is *now!*'

A tangle of pikes and horses. Screams and prayers. Bright blood staining the grass. But now is no time for such thoughts. This battle must be won. Or we die.

Caperstaff's second spell sank into the ground, in a manner of speaking. That is, literally. An appeal, not this time to the air to turn to glass, but to the wellsprings of the hillside to gush forth into the earth. The ground over which the fourth wave of cavalry came was transformed on the instant into a deep quagmire, in which horses sank, struggling and whinnying, while their riders cringed under a hail of arrows from the Capdale archers. Four-foot shafts tipped each with bronze and shot at a rate of one every six seconds from bows of six-foot yew.

Over to the Kendarkers' right, however, things were not going so well. Hoodwill too had begun by raising his staff in the air and calling up a wall of wizard-glass. Now, since wizard-glass is made of air and is totally invisible, it is impossible to see, until one touches it, whether it is there or not. And Hoodwill's spell had failed.

For the first onslaught of the Kennaught cavalry against the centre, commanded by the King and by Hoodwill, went home. The pikemen reeled under its shock, but held firm. Firm too they held as the second and third waves of horsemen crashed against them. Nonetheless, the impact was terrible: a sheer brute weight of flesh and bone, battering against Feydom's narrow hedgehog line of pikes. They could not hold out for long against such force, and

Hoodwill, deathly pale at the failure of his first spell, raised his staff in the air a second time, appealing in his turn to the waters of the hillside – a swamp to check the onrush of the cavalry.

But again, nothing happened. The green turf of the hillside stayed as dry, as solid underfoot, as it had ever been. And the infantry of Kennaught were now advancing down the slope to join battle with the Feylander centre on level terms. Ewan gave rapid orders to his bowmen to turn their hail of arrows on these men, so as to protect the reeling centre with cross-fire.

But what was happening over to the right, in the wing of the army commanded by Fetch, and consisting entirely of men from Fetch's own lands? Ewan had been relieved at first to note that Kennaught had not moved against the right wing. A dangerous tactic on their part, he had thought. But he was now to learn the dismaying reason for it.

For through the shouts of battle, the screams and yells that rose from the Feylander centre, a new cry began to pierce, louder even than the noise of combat:

'Treason! Treason!'

Ewan stood up in his stirrups, and peered over to the far right of the battlefield. It was half a mile away across the shoulder of the hill, and he could make out nothing at such a distance – it was, in any case, partly concealed from him by the switchback terrain. Hastily he sent his ensign Pluckspur galloping off to the right to discover what was going on. He sat in the saddle, biting his nails with impatience and wondering when his allies from the forest would choose to strike. Surely they must have seen by now that the battle had been joined on the foothills below them. And he peered away off to the left where the edge of Rooftree Forest lay, like a green wig of conifers set upon the mountain's head. No, there was no sign of movement yet among the trees. Instead he could see a huge force of crimson-clad Kennaughters massing on the higher slopes between the battling armies and the forest. He felt increasingly worried. Had the enemy somehow heard that there were reinforcements expected from that quarter? Indeed, they must have done. For they had sent out a vast shield of pikemen to guard against that threat.

Pluckspur returned, his horse sliding to a halt at Ewan's side. 'Fetch's army, lord,' he gasped. His face, always pink, was even pinker now with haste. 'They have attacked their own countrymen. They have turned upon the Feydom centre, and are mowing it down like corn under the scythe. And Fetch's rearguard has turned upon ours – turned on the Froremen. It is treason, sire, treason!'

'Nightshade!' swore Ewan violently. But he hesitated only for an instant. 'The dragon,' he said to Catchfire. 'Now!'

For this was terrible news. Fetch controlled half the Feylander army. He had, too, the advantage of surprise, and of confusion in the King's own ranks. Attacked at once on two sides, taken unawares, hardly knowing who, now, was friend or foe, how could Dermot's centre stand for long against this double assault? As for his own Froremen, he had no such doubts: there were only three hundred of them here, but they were the toughest fighters in the Two Kingdoms. They would hold their own.

But time was now of the essence. Again he strained his eyes towards the forest from which, surely, any minute now, help must come. Yes, it was clear now: Fetch had planned this treachery; he was in league with the King of Kennaught, and that was why, up to Ewan's left, the Kennaughters had positioned a great force to hold off Ewan's allies from the forest.

Ewan turned to Caperstaff, sitting his horse calmly, holding his wizard's staff aloft in the air with both hands, as if all the weight of the waters of the hillside pressed upon it. Caperstaff was smiling gently, and there was a misty look in his eyes as if he were dreaming of last night's dinner.

'The magical moat!' cried Ewan. 'Can you set it off to the right? To protect the centre as well?'

Caperstaff's absent smile vanished instantly. 'No,' he said softly. 'My strength is only so much. And we shall need this morass all around us soon.'

He nodded (for both his hands were busy with his staff) to the left and rear of the army.

It was true. To the left and right of the battlefront, the enemy's rearguard had been slipping round the sides of the mountain to surround them. Ewan could see the Kennaught horsemen now – a thousand, two thousand of them? – unfurling in an endless line of jolting hooves, turning round the slopes to the south and north, in a vast manoeuvre of encirclement. Soon they would come at Kendark from behind, and Caperstaff would need all his magic then.

160

Ewan swore softly again. Hurry! he whispered to himself. If only he could send a message to his allies in the forest!

Meanwhile, Catchfire had got down from her horse. Sheltered among the riders of Ewan's royal guard, she crouched on the dry earth and pulled, from the leather scabbard at her waist, not a sword as you might expect, but a long wooden firestick. She knelt in her bronze-plated armour over a hollow in the grass, tipped dry branches into it, and aimed the pointed stick. She lifted and shot home its handle three times, like someone priming a hand-pump. Three sparks shot from the firestick's tip. Smoke rose.

Returning to her saddle-bow, Catchfire lifted off a sack full of rowan twigs. These she scattered on the fire, then, bending, held out her hand to the flames. The little ring encircling her finger glittered with its ruby light. And slowly, as if golden drifts of sand were blowing from a golden carving, coils and ripples appeared through its smooth surface. The shape of a wingless dragon.

Waves of sound from the battle beat upon Catchfire's ears, but the left wing was a haven of comparative peace, calm behind its dykes of magic swampland. Ewan was whirling in his saddle, shouting. But she took no notice. She took off her ring and held it to her eyes. Through it she could see a tuft of moorland grass on the hillside in front of her. Then the green faded, and darkness replaced it. She was seeing down into the lightless depths of the mountain. Heat and a faint whiff of burning rose through the narrow circle of the ring, as if it were a tiny borehole sunk into the earth's core. An eye swam up through the gloom – cold, yellow, reptilian. A voice spoke. A voice like the snapping of teeth.

'*Ám-gwena*, friend,' it grated. 'Do you need me?'

'Yes, lady,' said Catchfire. 'The time we spoke of is here. It is the battle. Fetch has turned upon his own countrymen. He destroys them as we speak. And we are close to defeat.'

'*Tína vau mína*,' came the voice in tones of grinding coldness. 'Your will is mine. Be patient. And trust me.'

The yellow eye went out like a light. Catchfire slipped the ring back on her finger, and swung into the saddle, scanning the scene around her.

Ewan's little army was completely surrounded. The Kennaught cavalry was a hedge of crimson, massing to ride up the slopes behind them. Struggling with his staff as with a reed swaying in a torrent, Caperstaff spoke again the words of the water spell:

'*Donum dona* . . .' His voice was a faint murmur against the roaring chaos to their right.

As for Ewan, he cried to his pikemen to guard the left and rear. They would stand firm, he told them. 'You hold the fate of Kendark on the tips of your pikes. Now is the moment! Help is on the way!'

If only it was. For Caperstaff's magic still held good. But what of Dermot? As the cavalry breasted the hill, he would be caught between three fires instead of two. And the havoc in his ranks was frightening now.

Ewan tapped his teeth with his fingernails, waiting, counting the minutes. Unless the dragon – and his allies in the forest – acted soon, Fetch's plan might be close to succeeding. For up the green slopes below them the horsemen of Kennaught moved to the attack.

Droplets of sweat were running down Caperstaff's plump face. Catchfire clicked her tongue and urged her horse forward several paces. Reaching over her head, she grabbed with both her hands at the wizard's staff, helping him to brace it as it swayed and wavered, buffeted by the high wind of reality. As she breathed out the words of the water spell in her turn, the tall staff steadied in the air and, below them, the hillside began to sweat great puddles of mud and brackish water. A spring burst out from the rocks, and seethed down among the clumps of heather, turning the ground slippery. A cheer went up from the troops. They were encircled by marsh now on all three sides. And Caperstaff, taking care not to move his hands from his staff, wiped the perspiration from his forehead with his sleeve.

'*Dwenom wergom!* Good work! Shall I leave it in a witch's hands?' he joked.

'No, no,' smiled Catchfire. 'Both left hand and right, both man and woman. The strength of six.'

A mile away to the left, where the great greencapped mountain of Rooftree stood above the battlefield like an upturned bowl all furred and rusty green with pine-trees, they could see . . . was it true? Ewan shouted for joy!

162

CHAPTER TWENTY-THREE

Battle's End

The smooth rounded slopes of the mountain rose to their left, capped with a mane of conifers, green and honey-brown with the year's new candles, motionless in the breathless cool of this spring morning. But through them now ran a movement like a parting through hair, a line of quivering scored from the mountain's summit to its foot, as if a narrow swathe of pines in the centre of this still forest had suddenly turned liquid, and was dancing and glittering like a stream held between stationary banks of foliage. A shock-wave passing underground, so that the trees in a narrow strip above it tossed and waved their green-plumed heads.

Stillness again. The forest was stiff as frost. Ewan, peering at the foothills between the trees' fringe and the battle, could detect no movement. But surely, what he had just seen . . .

Yes! There was a sudden shriller note to the roar of the battle on his right. A tongue of flame and a spurt of smoke shot suddenly upwards from the thick of the press; and, leaping out of the depths of the hillside, as if rock was to it no more solid than water, leaping like a giant salmon from a pool, and flashing, coiling in the air in a green-blue glitter of scales, the earthdragon erupted from the solid earth beneath the soldiers' feet. As she leapt, she snatched up a man in her ten-foot jaws, like a fish leaping for a fly, and tossed him aside into the ruck. Fetch's black-and-white banner tilted, swayed and went under, vanishing like the mast of a capsizing boat. And the she-dragon surfaced for a second time, with Fetch's body limp between her teeth. She spat him over the heads of the battling soldiers in a belch of fire-laden crimson. And he lay there alone on the grass between the two armies, his tunic singed, his neck broken.

For this was Whirlwind's mate, Taivimbra the earth-dragon, wingless, shining like the rocks' own crystal heart, who swam through the dense black earth as swiftly as her husband swam through the sky.

Half Fetch's soldiers, their commander gone, turned to run; others flung down their arms and shouted for quarter. The combatants seethed like floodwater caught against a dam, vainly surging to and fro for an exit. And the King's troops were as terrified as Fetch's. They threw away their spears or sank to the ground in dread at the sight of the huge earth-dragon.

But Kennaught, breasting the hill to their rear, still came on, imagining victory within their grasp.

At this moment a din of shrill alarm and wonder rose away to the left on the plain below the forest. On this side, as you know, a whole division of Kennaught had been stationed, ready to repel Ewan's reinforcements. But now their spears bowed and wavered like corn in the rain as they saw what reinforcements these were.

For it was as if the forest itself had begun to march.

Like dark-green paint flowing down the mountainside and over the foothills below it, a flood of tossing branches and pine-fronds, a tide of trees advanced down the slope, each monstrous trunk sixty feet high above the earth. And they covered the ground at immense speed; for it seemed that each tree had grown a pair of enormous legs the size of young oaks – and all these monstrous legs were running, faster than a troop of cavalry, faster than a band of war chariots.

A man can cover a mile, perhaps, in less than six minutes. But these two-legged trees were ten times higher than a man – and running at ten times human speed. In only half a minute they had closed the gap between themselves and the army of Kennaught to a mere three hundred yards. Many Kennaughters at the rear of the phalanx broke and ran at the sight. But the mass of them, though quailing, held their ground, and a ragged volley of arrows went up, ill-aimed, spattering the ground between trees and men. Those few shafts which found a target were brushed away as carelessly as if they were a flurry of snowflakes.

But the charge of the oakmonsters (for they it was, come to Ewan's aid in repayment for their lives) slackened and drew to a halt. They stood undecided, swaying as if in a wind, barely a hundred yards away from the Kennaught lines. The Kennaught commander plucked up his spirits at this, and opened his mouth to call for another volley of arrows.

That order never came. For now the oakmonsters each raised fifty feet in the air the great green fir-tree he carried for a spear. They plunged them deep into the earth, as if they were staking out a field. And as they did so, a chorus of pain and horror was wrung from the men facing them. They cowered away like a red wave curling from a dam, and those who had thrown down their bows in time turned and fled. But for the rest it was too late. The feet of each crimson soldier snagged in the earth as on a tangle of roots, and they flung out their arms in a gesture of appeal, turned rigid in the air in the last desperate movement of their lives. For every man who still held weapons in his hand was pierced through, as if by his own violence bursting out from inside him. There was a sound of bones snapping, and a dry crackle of twigs and branches expanding, spluttering open like fans. For a moment it looked as if antlers were growing on their heads, as if skeletal wings were sprouting from their shoulders, as their spines fused to the fixity of tree-trunks and an explosion of branches stabbed outwards through their skins into the air. Each branch was dry and brittle, sharp as a splintered spear.

As for the commander, he had opened his mouth to rasp out the order, but instead of words a dead branch jutted up through his throat and split his teeth apart, a broken jagged branch the shape of a scream. He choked on his own wooden tongue.

And there was nothing left standing on the slopes of the hillside but a dry and leafless forest, an army of trees all dead, motionless for ever in a frozen exclamation of wood. To this day they call the place *Kwitadrúon*, the Vengeance of the Trees, the Dead Wold of Bourne that grows no leaves, no fruit, but where only rusting weapons and mouldering armour hang from the boughs.

The oakmonsters roared then, mouths wide as caves full of icicles. And, plucking their fir-spears out of the ground, began to move round the edge of the enchanted wood. Towards the centre of the crimson army. Slow, this time, and purposeful as an avalanche.

Ewan turned to his trumpeters. 'Now!' he cried. 'Sound the question!'

It is the custom in the Two Kingdoms for the trumpets to ask with a shrill fanfare if the enemy surrenders. And he too, if he concedes the battle, speaks that message on his trumpets.

As the King of Kennaught did now.

The Battle of Bourne was over.

The cheers of Kendarkers and Marchmen deafened the morning air, and sparks of sunlight broke like waves around Catchfire as they brandished their spears. '*Seca!*' roared the men of the Front and the March. 'Victory!' chanted Kendark. She rose in her saddle to peer into the dense throng to her right. Was the King her father safe? His banner was there still, certainly. And that should surely mean . . .?

She saw indeed to her relief that the damage to the King's army had not been too grave after all. The archers of Longyew had kept off the worst of the Kennaught attack, Knifeskin's Froremen had cut Fetch's cavalry to pieces, surprised though they had been, and outnumbered by two to one. And now, between the King's army and the traitors of Spylaw, the dragon was coiled, no longer blowing fire from her jaws, but with two little curls of smoke ascending from her nostrils – a hundred feet long she lay, in a glitter of turquoise and azurite, watching over Fetch's henchmen with all the disdain of a sheepdog herding a flock of frightened sheep.

Yes, the King was unharmed. She could see him clearly now, edging on horseback through the press, to ride forward up the hillside and meet the defeated enemy, the King of Kennaught, picking his way past the bodies of dead and wounded men to parley and dictate their terms.

But the King was alone with his bodyguard. Where then was the wizard Hoodwill?

Catchfire felt a shock of anxiety. Hoodwill was not to be trusted. His place was beside the King, yet he was not to be seen. Had he some devious plan of his own, even at this late hour? She whirled in her saddle, and stood in the stirrups, scanning the throng ahead, to her right, behind her. It was then she saw, out of the corner of her eye, a moving flicker of light.

A wizard's conical white hat, dagger-bright in the morning sun. Three figures on horseback descending the hillside at full speed on their way back to Bourne. Hoodwill. Half a mile away already, galloping, widening the gap between them every second.

It was as if her breath had been taken away. A sudden certainty of fear. For where was the wizard's apprentice, Mazewit? Ah, what a fool she was ! Where had he been all morning? For no magic had been done on the right of the army, except Hoodwill's, and that had failed. She had left Talisman well protected with spells and instructions. Surely she would be safe? And yet why had Mazewit been absent from the battle? She cursed herself for her lack of foresight.

Grasping Ewan by the arm as he was about to press forward too onto the open ground between the armies, she said to him forcefully:

'Ewan, no! Let Caperstaff speak for you. He knows your mind; he can dictate your terms. For look! We are needed more urgently. Hoodwill! Talisman! The Spell! Now, this instant, or it will be too late!'

And calling out to the three soldiers nearest her – 'Tatterbeg, Pluckspur, Bodefair! Follow me!' – she clapped the spurs to her horse's flanks. There was not a moment to be lost.

Talisman had pouted and stamped her foot when she heard she was not to be taken to see the battle.

'But I shall be so bored,' she told Catchfire. 'After all, I've had such a quiet life for the last hundred years. I've never seen a real live battle. Can't I go and watch it from that little hill over there?' And she pointed through the window to a little grassy knoll that stood half way between the city walls and the hill-crest where the Kennaught army lay in wait.

Catchfire shook her head. 'Far too dangerous. We can't afford to lose you, you know. No, you must stay right here in the Mayor's tower. It has a very good view,' she added diplomatically; 'you'll be able to see everything just as well. And be quite safe.'

'I don't want to be safe,' said Talisman sulkily. 'I've had quite enough of nothing happening.'

'I'll give you a picture-book to look at. A very special picture-book. See.'

And Catchfire showed the big leather-bound volume she'd been holding all this while behind her back. 'Look, all the pictures are coloured. Here are the dwarfs and the wicked witch. And the swan-princess. And the goose-girl and her treacherous maidservant.' (For the tales of Earth are immensely old, and the children of that distant time knew them as perfectly as we do now.) 'And here, at the end, is the history of Feydom. Varos the bear-king, founder of the realm. And his battle with the giant Crackmarrow. And Vasos his son, who stole the wings from an eagle, and learned to fly. And

167

Albanac, who quarrelled with Sermaros the sea-god, and drew the waters of the ocean in a net to Midknow – and when the net broke, drowned his own people, so that he died of grief.'

'I've seen picture-books before.'

'Yes, but not one like this. Can you say *agete, movete*? They're wizards' words!'

Talisman repeated them, frowning a little.

And behold! They were looking at the picture of Albanac holding the net in his hands, a trawlful of fish, with a boat caught capsizing at one corner, and a dolphin jumping out through the meshes. And the net began to move, tossing up and down like a bayful of storm-blown water, glittering blue and white in the sunlight that came through Talisman's window. And Albanac struggled to hold it, the muscles standing out on his bare arms, his face going red with effort. The net burst open, and a flood of leaping fishes and octopuses wriggled down the page and ran away into its margins. And the boat was left stranded, high and dry on the empty rock at Albanac's feet.

'Ooh,' said Talisman. She turned the page to the picture of Feydom lying under the floods.

'*Agete, movete,*' prompted Catchfire.

'*Agete, movete,*' said Talisman obediently. And the storm-water swayed and billowed. And little people in boats and on the roofs of houses could be seen waving their arms like mannikins no taller than a fingernail.

'There you are,' said Catchfire, satisfied. 'You see, you'll be quite happy. Now, promise me you won't open the door. You won't let anyone in. You won't leave this room till the battle is ended.'

Talisman hesitated. 'Oh, all right,' she said at last. 'I promise.'

Catchfire kissed her.

But for greater safety, she barred the door with a spell. And told two men of Kendark to stand guard. 'No one must come in. And Talisman must not come out.'

Left alone, Talisman pored over her book for some time. It was certainly nice to say the two strange words that Lady Catchfire had taught her – she must be a witch – and see all the little figures on the pages leap alive, move, even speak, and disappear. But when in this way she had wiped a couple of dozen pages clean of pictures she began to be bored. She peered out of the window, across up the hill to the battle. But all she could see was a sort of meaningless surging and eddying, no better than the toss of the waves in the picture of Albanac. Dust rising, and a dim continuous roaring like the sea heard far off. As pointless and obsessive as a whirlpool, no purpose in it. Sighing, she turned back to her picture-book.

But somehow she was not so interested now. She found she was saying the words *agete, movete* with less conviction. As if she didn't really want them to work at all.

And the moment she didn't want them to work, they didn't. There were merely painted pictures in a dull old book, odd-shaped daubs and curlicues of ink.

For after all, thought Talisman, these pictures – even moving – aren't real. No more real, perhaps, than Ithanéquinath. She yawned, and moved across to the window.

She was leaning out like that, elbows on the stone sill, head in her hands, gazing away southwards to the battle, when Mazewit appeared in the street below her, almost too slight for his wizard's robes, too young for his tall pointed hat.

The guards greeted him in respectful tones, but firmly. He replied softly, pointing at each one in turn. They were guards no longer, but two statues of flesh and bone and stiff leather armour, staring blankly into the cool spring sunshine.

CHAPTER TWENTY-FOUR

Talisman

Talisman! Talisman! said Catchfire over and over to herself, as she rode like a gust of wind downhill after Hoodwill, skirting grassy hummocks, springing over hollows in the ground, spurring her horse towards the gates of Bourne a mile and a half away. For it's not so much the Spell now. We have fought and won, and Kennaught is defeated and utterly frightened, and anyway, we'll find another way to open the Gates – I don't know how, but we'll find it. No, that isn't the problem, it's Talisman's life and all that she wants to do now she's here in the world again and the children she might have and the life she wants to lead and . . . Hurry, hurry!

Mind you, it might not be so easy, either, if Talisman is killed. The oakpeople would be frozen to the spot, and the earthdragon banished back to Kendark, and Hoodwill would reign again in Feydom, and be free to destroy his own people once more, and my spell against the plague would be broken, and the drought would return, and death and famine with it, worse than ever. And Talisman's big brown eyes, and her love of living, breathing, running, being real. And the people of Feydom, living, breathing too. One little life. And all those other lives. Hurry, hurry!

Catchfire swerved through the open gates at a gallop, ducking her head to her horse's mane. She clattered down the cobbled street with a rattle like pebbles falling from a scree, and swept into the little square like a breaking wave, a pale grey swirl of skirts and riding-cloak. Her horse skidded to a halt, and stood there blowing and snorting through his nostrils. Well, mistress, I didn't do so badly, did I? You should be proud of me! Catchfire patted his neck.

And she gazed up in calm dismay at the window in the Mayor's tower. A little square window four floors above, with a conical pointed roof exactly the shape of a wizard's cap – and painted too

170

like a wizard's cap with stars and planets. Automatically, she took in the scene around her, Hoodwill's two spearmen on their horses, Mazewit standing in the shadow of the door, with a strange expression on his face, both frightened and self-satisfied. And her own two Kendark guards, frozen to the spot, gazing out blankly on the square, one of them with his hand up like the statue of an orator about to speak.

But the scene above her was what really appalled her. Hoodwill standing at the window, smiling as thinly as a snake, a naked dagger in his hand. Beside him, Talisman, tears in her eyes, choking with fright, her dark mane of hair clutched tight in the wizard's left hand, for he had drawn her head back and downwards against the window-sill, and her white neck was bared to the knife. He was about to cut her throat.

'You will not move,' chanted Catchfire. 'Your arms are pinioned to the air. You will drop your dagger . . .'

Hoodwill simply laughed. He released his grip slightly on Talisman's hair, so that she was able to straighten herself a little, gasp and take breath.

'Witch-girl,' he said, 'no magic can touch me. I seem to have lost my own' – and a shadow of regret passed momentarily over his face – 'but that has its advantages. As you see, I am unaffected by your spells.' And, in a show of triumph, he released Talisman still further, and bowed mockingly out of the window.

More clattering and ringing down the street behind them. In a shower of sparks, Catchfire's four companions, whom she had outpaced on the journey here, swung into the square, – Ewan, Tatterbeg, Bodefair, Pluckspur. Eyes still on Hoodwill the witch-girl acted quickly.

She gestured to the four men. 'The guards – disarm them.' And then, as Mazewit, lurking guiltily in the shadow of his doorway, raised his wizard's staff towards her, she pinned him with a glance. 'You will not move,' she was trying to say.

But, though her lips formed the words, no sound came from them. For Mazewit was uttering, too, the selfsame sentence. The apprentice wizard and the witch-girl struggled against each other for a moment, not a whisper coming from their mouths. Then Catchfire laughed – an odd sound, considering the circumstances.

'Take his staff,' she said to Pluckspur. 'And lead him away. I

may have no power over him, but neither has he over me
Deadlock. And where two equal forces meet, I think the one with
the sword has the upper hand.'

Strangely, from above their heads, Hoodwill too was laughing.
'You see,' he said, 'I have taught him well. Even the powers of
Kendark, it seems . . .'

'Hoodwill, do you not realise we wish Feydom well? Come
down, be sensible, talk to us, we'll work out an agreement. Don't
do anything rash.'

'You wish me', said Hoodwill poisonously, 'exactly what I wish
you. How can there be a pact between the dark and the light?'

Despite his words, a glimmer of hope kindled in Catchfire's
mind. If Hoodwill was willing to talk, and if he could be held for a
few minutes . . .

And she turned to Ewan, sitting his horse beside her, scowling
like a thundercloud. She whispered: 'Keep him talking, at all cost
keep him talking, take his mind off his dagger, don't threaten him,
detain him at the window.'

Mazewit, his magic held in perfect balance by Catchfire's own,
was led off down the street. And Catchfire, turning to follow him,
cried to Hoodwill (I only hope, she thought, he *will* be deceived)
'Be content! I have met my match! But think, oh think of the little
girl. Her life . . .'

For there was a way. What Hoodwill had told her on that last
evening before the battle . . . Yes, and there must be a fire in the
Mayor's parlour. For it was the first day of spring, the air was crisp
and cold, and there were still rowan twigs left in her pack-saddle.

Hoodwill's two guards were disarmed now, and standing glumly
by their horses. Tatterbeg and Bodefair watched them. Ewan
turned his attention towards the wizard in the tower.

'Don't try to get in,' he was saying. 'If any of you crosses the
threshold, the girl dies.'

'Mind you,' he added with satisfaction, 'she will die anyway.'

'But I don't understand,' said Ewan. 'How did you manage to
get in? I thought Catchfire had locked the door with a spell.'

Hoodwill laughed again. Ewan did not like the sound much. It
was as if the wizard were trying out an unfamiliar emotion, one
that he had long ago forgotten – so that the sound was angular,
ill-tuned, like a key scraping in a rusty door.

'So she did,' he said. 'But my apprentice neutralised it. Now you see, young man, it is true that even that would not have helped, provided that this young lady here' – and he shook Talisman by the hair with a sort of affectionate cruelty, so that she squealed and yelped – 'had not come down and let him in. But she was bored – weren't you, my dear? She wanted to see the battle! The young, these days! Their notions of excitement! And when Mazewit told her the fighting was over, she said: "Oh well, that's all right, because I was only told to keep the door locked till the end of the battle."

'And then *I* arrived.'

Well, there is still hope, thought Ewan. He seems willing enough to talk. And if, of course, there really is something Catchfire can do . . .

'I see,' he said flatteringly. 'That was really very clever of you both. But I beg you, your eminence, sheathe your dagger and come down and talk. For Talisman has done no wrong. Would you shed innocent blood? A nine-year-old girl with her whole life before her? And for what reason?'

'Are you as ignorant as you seem, young Ewan?' said Hoodwill unpleasantly, leaning out of the window. 'Or do you genuinely not know the truth about Talisman? This little girl – it seems she is so important that she must ride with you the length and breadth of Feydom. In time of war, imagine it! And I am not a fool: I know the words that are written in the Book. And among them you will find, how the sacrifice at Midriver was performed, that shut out the evil of Kendark, and who the victim was – *and her name.*'

'But you're not really trying to pretend', said Ewan, 'that this little girl is the same one who . . . Why, it's impossible. (Though the impossible, he knew, was true.)

'Well, my friend, that is tantamount to an admission, since opening the Gates is also by definition impossible. Now my guess is that this little wench' – and he pulled Talisman's hair again, so that she shrieked piteously – 'has been, shall we say, *restored* to us. Well, no matter. When I kill her, as I shall do in a minute or two, the Gates will close again. And Feydom will be safe once more.

'I had to wait, you see, till the battle was over. But now it is, and we are rid of Kennaught. Well, we shall be rid of Kendark too. I am not a traitor, you see, like Fetch. I am a true patriot.'

'But Kendark alone can save your country,' protested Ewan. 'Only by opening the Gates – as we have proved – can the rain be restored. If you perform this act, you condemn not merely Talisman to death, but along with her all the people of Feydom.'

'Nonsense. Even if what you say is true, evil must be held at bay. Let them die, so long as they stay untouched by darkness.'

'Your eminence,' said Catchfire's voice, softly. Somehow, unseen by the rest of them, she had returned while they were talking. 'You always said that the Gates were open! You always said . . .'

'And naturally, my young friends,' said Hoodwill with lofty contempt, 'I was right. It is obvious, isn't it? Our little sacrificial victim here must have been brought back to life, oh, at least two years ago. That explains everything, you see.'

'But she wasn't!' cried Ewan desperately. 'It is hardly a fortnight since . . .' Then he checked himself in dismay. Sun'sgift! What had he said?

Hoodwill, however, looked delighted at this confession. 'You see? You admit it yourself!'

'My dear young friends!' he added in unctuous tones, leaning still further over the windowsill, but taking care to keep a firm grip on poor Talisman's hair. 'Did you suppose . . .?'

But he never finished his sentence. His look of triumph changed to bewilderment. He let go both Talisman's hair and the dagger, which fell four storeys to the cobbles at their feet, and ricocheted away into the shadow of the doorway like a small metal animal scuttling for its burrow. He clutched at his throat with both hands. A strange alteration came over him.

He had been shining white from his wizard's cap to the hem of his robe, and his face had been its usual pallid grey. He had seemed almost luminous, as if lit from within by a magic lantern – for, in the morning sunlight, not a shadow, not a touch of shade was to be seen anywhere on his clothing. But now it was as if the inner whiteness that illuminated him had suddenly been cut off, and a blackness so dense that it seemed itself like a light was shining through him from within. It was as if he had been transparent – so that, now his shadow was restored to him at last, there was no brightness left within him: he was all night.

Ewan gazed, almost in consternation, at the dark figure staggering in the embrasure of the window above them. For

Hoodwill, turned all to darkness, looked the very image of the Necromancer whom he had defeated on the field of Midnight, it seemed so long ago. The two were as alike as identical twins.

And now death had overtaken them both. For the window-ledge at the wizard's knees was a mere two and a half feet high. Through the open casement Hoodwill pitched, turning with immense slowness in the air like a soot-grey blanket tossed from the summit of a tower, billowing and floating as it came. It struck the cobbles four floors below with the tiny splintering sound of a broken marionette. And lay still.

'Oh Talisman, Talisman,' said Catchfire, hugging the little girl who came running and weeping out of the tower door, 'it's all over, you're safe, no one can hurt you now!'

CHAPTER TWENTY-FIVE

Finale: Threshold

'But how did you manage it?' asked Caperstaff. 'If, as you say, Hoodwill had given up his shadow and had put himself outside the power either to rule or be ruled by magic . . .?'

It was a month later. All the companions of the quest were there, sitting in the keep at Threshold, where they had come to ensure that the armies of Kennaught had left the country. The selfsame keep that Catchfire had seen but six weeks ago, through Mazewit's crystal ball. The crops would be good this year, for sun and rain were falling in harmony, and the first seeds were already sprouting. Kennaught had agreed to sell them corn, and Feydom's year-long famine was over.

Caperstaff was asking his question over dinner, naturally. For, as he always said, 'Even the best of conversations is still better when there's food to eat and wine to drink.'

Catchfire turned to him, a mischievous light in her dark blue eyes. 'Well, I don't know whether I should answer you. I know a wizard who *loves* mystifying people.'

'Yes, but tell the truth now. You can't bear to keep it to yourself, can you? But wait, let me guess. Erebor . . . was Hoodwill's shadow. The shadow he had lost.'

'I think', said Catchfire ruefully, 'it must be rather difficult trying to mystify *you*. But yes, of course you're right. One thing that gave me the idea' (she turned to Ewan) 'was what Hoodwill told you himself all those months ago, about the Battle of Tearchart. You remember? He said that the Necromancer had multiplied his army eightfold by an illusion of shadows. And how when each was struck down the other seven vanished, including the real man whose phantoms they were.'

'Yes. For you cannot have a man without his shadow.'

'So when I saw him standing at the window threatening

Talisman, I ran to the fire in the Mayor's parlour. I cast rowan twigs upon it for the second time that day, and spoke to the dragon again through the eye of the ring. And she swam through solid rock to Midriver, as she does, being a creature of diamond and night – and swallowed Erebor.'

'And now we have sent to destroy the Necromancer's tomb. So Talisman will not be in danger again,' said the King fondly, patting her hand.

'But how did you know that Erebor was Hoodwill's shadow?' asked Caperstaff. 'It could have been simply a creature of the underworld.'

'Oh, Hoodwill told me that,' said Catchfire. 'On the night before the battle. He didn't realise that was what he was revealing, of course, Indeed, I think he did not know it himself – not consciously. But he was *furious* when . . . when I suggested that he might be responsible for Erebor. "I have no darkness in me," he shouted. "I am the Wizard of Light." And suddenly – I don't quite know how – I saw that Erebor must be his shadow. For it all fitted: the time when the monster first appeared, its usefulness in keeping the Gates closed for Hoodwill, its darkness and his whiteness . . .'

'But I don't understand', put in Ewan, 'how Hoodwill could have become so evil. He should have been so pure, so' (he made a face) 'so absolute.'

'There you are, you see, Ewan,' said Caperstaff, smiling. 'Even when you say that, you can't help feeling unhappy about it. For darkness is doubts and uncertainties. If you banish doubt, if you believe you are right every time and run no risk of erring, think of the damage you would do. Think of the damage Hoodwill did.'

'But why did he lose all his magic?'

'Darkness is also the depths of the mind,' said Catchfire; 'those parts of yourself that are not pure thought, pure intelligence, but your living, breathing human self; what you are rather than what you know. The heart and the passions – love, joy and (I'm afraid) fear and hatred too. The power of life that works in the hidden places of the mind. By casting that out, Hoodwill exorcised his own magic.

'And if you shut the magic out, what then? It takes its revenge, it turns you into a monster of darkness, but a monster who will assert through thick and thin that he is an angel of light.'

'But the darkness within the human mind – it is not all good.'

'By no means,' agreed Caperstaff. 'But that is like the image in Hoodwill's mirror. It was given its own independent life because Hoodwill refused to recognise it as an image of himself. He could not accept the darkness within him, so he cast it out. The image stepped from the glass and walked away, a separate reality – a reality that was now out of its master's control.

'But recognise the power of life in yourself, recognise its potency for good and for evil too, and – well, there is no other way to master it.'

'Ah,' said Catchfire, nodding. 'And that must be the hidden meaning of the words carved on the entrance to the Necromancer's tomb. *Kina léceti Neicos, kladhyâ wertos. Aïnec Calos wiktu.* "Here lies darkness, imprisoned by a sword. May Hell never open." But it also means: "Here lies darkness protected by a sword. May Hell never weaken." '

She mused for a moment. 'It may be that a man has evil motives in casting out his own darkness. For then he ensures he does not know it, and therefore cannot master it.'

'Darkness and light,' said the wizard. 'There is a need of the one for the other. The unknown powers of the mind are a deadly danger unless the light of understanding is shed upon them. And, if it rejects the unknown, the pure intelligence is a vanity, static, rigid, cruel in its certainties.'

In the distant west, far out over the sea of Eventide, the sun was setting, painting the soft shoals of cloud a fiery crimson. And in the great hall of Threshold the rafters too were sinking into darkness, as if the ceiling were dissolving and melting, opening slowly up onto dark infinities of sky above the castle turrets. The glitter of torchlight and firelight was brighter now, mingling on the walls with the moving shadows of the men and women who sat around the table, an arabesque of flame and shadow blending together on the stone, the dancing fire in the crystal. Through the expanding lake of evening, ripples run inwards to the stone's heart, the kernel of life and light. Catchfire's eyes flash as she laughs and tosses her black hair. The star Cera opens like a flower in the indigo sky.

'This talk of dark and light', said King Dermot, sighing, 'is all a little beyond me. I shall just have to take your word for it.'

'I do wish you sometimes wouldn't, father,' said Catchfire with a touch of impatience. 'Take our word for it, I mean.'

'But what about our little Talisman?' went on the King, turning to the girl on his left. He had specially pleaded for her to be allowed to stay up late, this night of all nights. The end of war, the dawn of peace. 'She's just like you at the same age,' he whispered to Catchfire. 'Just as wilful.'

'You spoil her, father,' said Catchfire. 'As you used to spoil me. Fortunately,' she added, 'I was *also* brought up by peasants in Kendark.' But she smiled gently at her father.

'Have you had enough excitement now?' the King asked Talisman.

'Well, quite enough *nasty* excitement,' said Talisman carefully. Then her eyes brightened. 'But I do wish I'd seen the other dragon.'

'We shall introduce you,' said Ewan, 'when you're old enough.'

'Grown-ups always say that,' sighed Talisman.

'Well,' said Catchfire, 'we haven't thanked Earthquake yet. Not properly. You could come along. Provided you keep your promises this time.'

'And Mazewit?' asked Ewan. 'Where do you suppose he's gone?'

'Yes, a pity he escaped from prison,' said Tatterbeg. 'He deserved to have someone put a sword through him. I'm sorry I didn't do it at the time.'

'He is as dangerous as the old wizard in his way,' agreed Catchfire. 'Hoodwill thought he was always right. Mazewit doesn't care if he's right or wrong. He just does what he's told.'

'I agree,' said Ewan. 'But it's difficult holding a wizard in prison.'

'A slippery individual,' said Caperstaff. 'So slim it wouldn't take much of a spell to let him wriggle through the bars. Now if he were only a little more well-covered!' And he rubbed his own comfortable paunch affectionately.

'Well, I'm very pleased at the way things have turned out,' said the King. 'Very pleased with my son-in-law to be' – he nodded approvingly at Ewan – 'though I must admit you young people frighten me a little. Still, that's hardly my business now since, as you know, I am abdicating. It's not that I'm bad at ruling,' he admitted, 'it's just that I've never really done any. A peaceful life, that's what I'm looking forward to from now on.

179

'But you know, I'm still not quite happy about this business of the Crown. Now I know', he said, holding up his hand as they all tried to speak at once, 'it was a very great exploit finding it. The ancient Crown of Unity, symbol of the Two Kingdoms, by which my ancestors used to rule. And by which you will rule again, young Ewan, reuniting Feydom and Kendark. Oh yes, I know all that. But . . .'

'But what?'

'Oh well, my ancestors, you know . . . King Niall, my great-great-grandfather, found it far too much of a handful. The Crown wasn't lost or stolen, you see, there wasn't a thief or a crooked chancellor. The Necromancer had nothing to do with it, either. It was deliberately hidden. Put safely out of the way.'

'Hidden?' said Ewan and Catchfire in chorus, gazing at Dermot in amazement.

'Well, yes,' said the King, lookng slightly uncomfortable. 'I suppose even royal families have skeletons in their cupboards. The Crown was the skeleton in ours. You see, there is a curse attached to it.'

'A curse?' said Caperstaff, frowning.

'Did I say a curse? I'm sorry, I meant of course a blessing. But it's the sort of blessing a king can well do without. You cannot rule by that Crown except in peace and kindness, justice and mercy. And that is very hard for a monarch these days. I daresay in the time of the old fairy-tales it was different. In any case, that was why Niall, er . . . disposed of it. It seems they did talk of melting it down, but they were afraid of the power it contained, so they thought it was better to keep that power safely locked away inside it, and bury the Crown somewhere. Where it couldn't be found. At Midnight.' He looked round at the circle of surprised faces gazing at him. 'Oh, yes, the secret was passed down from father to son, kept carefully within the family. My father told me on his death-bed. I was only six, but one does not forget such things.' Then, a little anxiously: 'I'm sorry if I've offended anyone's feelings.'

'No offence taken, father,' said Catchfire. 'But I really don't think you need worry. Ewan will be able to manage the Crown, I'm sure. After all, he is the destined champion.' And she appealed to Caperstaff: 'Isn't he? You said, all those months ago at Witshift Castle . . .'

'What I said,' replied Caperstaff, 'was, as I remember it, rather ambiguous. I said he *might* be – but that he had to believe in himself, not his destiny.'

'Well surely,' said Catchfire, 'it's all proved now, isn't it? Ewan has defeated the Necromancer, and Hoodwill his pale counterpart; and the Two Kingdoms are united once more after a hundred years of fear and hatred. Surely he is the Champion!'

But Ewan broke in before the wizard could speak. Pressing Catchfire's hand affectionately but firmly, he said: 'Caperstaff, if you answer that question at all, do it with one of your riddles. We have seen what evil followed from Hoodwill's thinking he was infallible. I should prefer not to make the same mistake.'

The wizard burst out laughing. 'Ewan, didn't I always tell you, you're the lad for me!'

'Good, I'm glad you approve. And I shall make no easy promises, but only this hard one, that I shall try to rule with the Crown. There shall be no more bloodshed if I can help it. For we have just fought a bloody battle, and I know how much pain can come from ruling.'

Knifeskin scowled at this, but it was hard to tell through his warpaint whether it was from dissent or agreement. '*Drus avallons surons vuti, se vo aï stati.* The tree grows bitter apples, but at least it still stands. For there are times when one has to fight, or the people die.'

'Besides,' he added with pride, 'we have reason to congratulate ourselves. The Frore has never fought better. In fifteen minutes we cut the traitor's cavalry to pieces. A little longer,' he said regretfully, 'and I'd have lopped Fetch's head from his body with my own hands.'

'The Frore is a peerless helper,' said Ewan warmly, 'and the King thanks you from the bottom of his heart. You are one of the sources of our strength. And without strength there will be no peace.'

'Yes, and your oakmonsters are another,' said the King. 'That's one of the things that perturbs me. Are you sure you have them locked away safely?'

'I have taken Caperstaff's advice,' replied Ewan. 'I have given them Treetop Forest for a domain. Two thousand square miles of woods and mountains. Under the peace of the Crown, they will not come forth again unless we need them.'

181

'We shall drink to that,' says Caperstaff, raising his glass aloft so that the torches in the banqueting hall kindle together in its depth like a celebratory bonfire seen in a wizard's crystal. A curving ruby goblet in which – look close! – all the companions of the quest are reflected: Tatterbeg and Slashbuckle clad in their tough leather armour; Knifeskin fierce in his warpaint; Dermot nervously fingering his beard; Talisman demure in her pale green dress; and, by some strange trick of reflected light, two images of Catchfire, slender, doubled and identical. Ewan, mirrored in the glass, smiles at them both, and she at him; and they silently toast each other. A red crystal holds them all, as the sun sinks far to the west over Eventide, itself kindling into a bright red sky-jewel.

For the red of life is that of time departing. The rays of that far-off age are slowed and lengthened as they swim through space towards us, like a message from a distant planet. The curve of the earth comes up, turning its back on the sun, tilting towards forgetfulness and night. The glass tilts too, at the wizard's lips. They are almost gone.

'And shall we go to thank the dragon *soon*?' asks Talisman.

THE END

APPENDIX

A Note on the Pronunciation of the Old Tongue

The men of Hemdark would no doubt be flattered if the reader could pronounce their language more smoothly than Ewan could. The Old Tongue has been spelt as it sounds – except for the following conventions:

c – to be pronounced as a guttural German or Scottish *ch*, as in *buch* or *loch*.

dh – is the English *th* in *this* or *that*. (*th* of course is the English *th* in *theatre* or *thought*).

The majority of the spells recorded in this book are not, however, in Gwaséna, the Old Tongue, but in Gwaestúsa, the Future Tongue – which we, in these even more future times, call Latin. For the wizards of that ancient period had rightly calculated that no language would be more likely to produce surprises than a language which had not yet been invented.